PRAISE FOR J. CARSON BLACK

THE SURVIVORS CLUB

"An utterly engrossing thriller. *The Survivors Club* grips us from the very start and simply doesn't let go. The novel seamlessly achieves that rarity in crime fiction: making our palms sweat while bringing the characters and their stories straight into our hearts. Bravo!"

—Jeffery Deaver, *New York Times* bestselling author of *The Kill Room*

"Welcome to *The Survivors Club*—where cheating death just once may not be enough. J. Carson Black's latest thriller takes you into a whirlpool of conspiracy, blackmail, and betrayal, where no one can be sure who is the hunter and who is the prey—a game of blood whose outcome may leave no survivors."

—Michael Prescott, author of *Cold Around the Heart*

"J. Carson Black's *The Survivors Club* is a twisted, diabolical cat-and-mouse game that will keep you riveted."

—CJ Lyons, *New York Times* bestselling author of *Hollow Bones*

"Black serves up a breezy thriller with a killer premise: What if people who cheated death once weren't so lucky the second time around? By the time the plot snakes through twist after twist, you'll be asking yourself . . . do you feel lucky?"

—Brian Freeman, bestselling author of *Spilled Blood*

"J. Carson Black delivers desert heat with her latest cool thriller, *The Survivors Club*. Detective Tess McCrae shows us again why she's the southwest's top cop."

—Alan Jacobson, national bestselling author of *No Way Out*

THE SHOP

"*The Shop* is a hair-raising thriller from start to finish. With a complex plot and finely drawn characters, J. Carson Black draws the reader into a world where nothing is as it seems. This book is both spooky and convincing, just what a thriller should be."

—T. Jefferson Parker, *New York Times* bestselling author of *The Jaguar*

"I'm a big fan of J. Carson Black and *The Shop* is a truly original nonstop locomotive ride of a thriller. You won't even think of putting this book down."

—John Lescroart, *New York Times* bestselling author of *The Hunter*

"Fresh and imaginative, J. Carson Black's *The Shop* is a riveting read and a compelling tale of character. From FBI agents to local cops, from heroes to villains, *The Shop* is an exciting, sweeping thriller that will linger in your mind for a long time."

—Gayle Lynds, *New York Times* bestselling author of *The Book of Spies*

"Infused with an original voice and packed with compelling characters, J. Carson Black's *The Shop* is a thriller to pay attention to."

—David Morrell, *New York Times* bestselling author of
The Brotherhood of the Rose

ALSO BY J. CARSON BLACK

The Survivors Club
Icon ·
The Shop
Darkness on the Edge of Town
Dark Side of the Moon
The Laura Cardinal Novels (Omnibus)
The Devil's Hour
Cry Wolf
Roadside Attraction

Writing as Margaret Falk
Dark Horse
Darkscope
The Desert Waits
Deadly Desert (Omnibus)

Writing as Annie McKnight
The Tombstone Rose
Superstitions

Short Stories
The Bluelight Special
Pony Rides

HARD RETURN

J. CARSON BLACK

THOMAS & MERCER

Published by Thomas & Mercer, Seattle

www.apub.com

Amazon, the Amazon logo, and Thomas & Mercer are trademarks of Amazon.com, Inc., or its affiliates.

ISBN-13: 9781477825136
ISBN-10: 1477825134

Cover design by *theBookDesigners*

Library of Congress Control Number: 2014937366

Printed in the United States of America

To John Peters, my MVP, whose remarkable knowledge, expertise, wit, and intelligence were invaluable assets in the writing of this book

- and -

To my dear friend and mentor, Maynard Allington, a fine man, a beautiful writer, and a stalwart champion. You are in my heart.

HARD
RETURN

- In Memoriam -

Four dead.

Every day, no matter how busy he was—and he was up to his ears in busy right now—he made himself look at the crime scene photos.

After that first year, it had gotten so that he could look at them without emotion. A cop friend of his had cadged the photos for him. They had been friends since Baghdad. Different branches of the military, different areas of expertise, yet somehow they had forged a friendship in that godforsaken hellhole.

What were the odds?

The youngest of the three victims was a towhead. Even in death his hair stuck up like a dandelion—the part that wasn't drenched in blood, anyway.

He was a good kid. He'd been underqualified for the job, that was true, but it wasn't his fault. Someone should have made that call for him.

He went back through the photos, all six of them. The floor, the open door to the bedroom, the legs and feet and shoes on the other body, intruding into the frame.

The blood.

A nicked carotid artery. A broken neck.

Not one or the other, but both.

There were three dead men in the house.

The fourth had died separately, days later.

If he'd died at all . . .

CHAPTER 1

Barbara Carey didn't know what to make of her best employee.

Joe Till had been here at the farm for nearly six months. He was good with horses. *Very* good with horses. The kind of guy you could trust to do what you asked. You could go away and leave them in his care and they would be fine. Not just fine, but better than fine.

She'd been looking for a foreman but took Joe Till on as hired help. He had no references, but she could tell he knew his way around a horse. She had tested him by handing over the lead rope to the colt she had been taking back to the barn. The colt was high-strung and had a tendency to bear in on people, from leaning on them to running them over—a very bad habit. The man handled him like a pro. He was strong and authoritative without being angry. The colt backed down and followed Till to the barn and walked right in. Not exactly horse whisperer stuff, but he was definitely experienced.

And he was decent looking in a rugged kind of way. Her long-dead father's favorite movie was *Shane*, and this man reminded her of the film's title character. He had an air of mystery about him, as if he'd lived a tough life. There was a small scar above his upper lip. Could have happened with horses but she didn't think so. He seemed levelheaded, although he gave the impression he would fight back if someone tried to crowd him.

Regarding the foreman position she'd put in the newspaper and on the Internet, there had been no takers—she wasn't offering a lot of money—and so eventually Joe Till ended up filling a foreman's shoes. Barbara still ran the ad in the paper on and off, but wasn't really looking anymore. Joe Till wasn't just good with the two-year-olds, he had an eye for them. He knew what they were going to do before they did it. He knew them cold, every single one of them, as if he had read their most secret diaries. He understood their potential or lack thereof.

Somewhere along the line he had clocked hours, days, weeks, months, and years to be able to handle horses this way.

Somewhere.

She found herself relying on his advice more and more. What do you think of this colt? What do you think about this race for the filly's first start? Do you think this boy will ever make a racehorse, or should we cull him?

Saying "we."

If she'd just met him, say at Hollywood Park or Santa Anita, she would have thought he was an assistant trainer to one of the Big Guys.

So . . . how'd *she* get so lucky?

Joe was no spring chicken. Barbara guessed he was in his mid- to late forties, and a beat-up-looking mid- to late forties at that. Good looking, although she wasn't really sure about this, because if she tried to picture his face right now, she wouldn't be able to.

He was the kind of guy who would never stand out in a crowd, except for his height. He was tall. He wore the uniform of the men who worked around horses: knit polo shirt, jeans, a ball cap with the farm's name on it, and tennis shoes. Gum boots when it was muddy.

He drove an old, beat-up Dodge Ram.

Joe Till didn't seem to have any bad habits. He didn't drink. He didn't smoke. He didn't act lascivious with her or the women she worked with. He liked the room she gave him just fine, washed the dishes after she cooked up dinner, used his own hot plate when she wasn't in the mood to cook. That first day, Barb was surprised he had only one big duffle, which went with the fact he was former military. Couldn't miss that. Her two brothers were former military.

He was the kind of guy you'd see at the racetrack or on a breeding farm or at a training center all the time.

A horseman with a forgettable face.

Except his face had been transformed to handsome somewhere along the line.

Maybe around the time she'd first slept with him.

- — -

Barbara lay in the crook of Joe Till's arm. The birds had just started up, mourning doves mostly, and the golden Santa Ysabel light stole across the bright green pastures and into her room.

Their room.

She felt as if she were lying in the arms of a giant bear. She'd been on her own for a century, it seemed, but here with Joe, Barbara felt something she hadn't felt for so long.

She felt feminine.

His breathing rose and fell as if he were asleep.

But she knew he wasn't asleep. She knew he was awake and alert.

There was something preternatural about the way he could lie still, appear to be asleep, but never was. He'd told her he "slept with one eye open" and she believed him. Both her brothers were like that. There was a wariness to them both, as if they were always expecting someone to shoot at them from over the next hill.

Her younger brother Ben had suffered, though—nightmares, getting fired from jobs, drinking and drugs. Lots of problems. But her other brother was fine.

Don't overthink. Joe Till's the best man you ever met.

She moved in his arms and he stirred.

"I have a surprise for you," she said.

"Oh?" His smile looked lazy, but it wasn't. She didn't know how to think of it other than that. He trailed a finger along the hollow of her neck and she shivered with pleasure.

She had her own gift to bestow. "How would you like to go to Santa Anita?" She rushed the next words. "I need someone I can trust, and I can't go. Cousin Ginny's wedding. So I thought you could . . ."

He straightened his right arm, looked down at her, and smiled. "No thanks."

For a moment she wondered if her jaw had cracked loose from her face and fallen to the pillow. "But this is a big deal."

He said nothing.

"It could lead to, I mean someday, not right away, you could . . . work your way up to trainer."

She was surprised by the words as they tumbled out of her mouth, but she'd been thinking it.

"Honestly," she added, "I know it's a surprise. But I mean it. I'm not just saying it."

He said nothing.

"I've already talked to Peter. It's all set. I want you to take six of our two-year-olds to Santa Anita."

Midnight Auto, Pussycat Doll, Mexican Lucky, Chillax, Nowhere Man, and A Whiskey Girl.

"It's all worked out. I arranged for you to get your license. I want to make you assistant trainer."

He said nothing.

This was not going the way she thought it would. "You can come down on your days off. Ginny and Rod will be back soon and they can take over the everyday work on the farm and I can stay weekends . . ."

She became aware of his stillness. Then he said, "Barbara, I'm not going to Santa Anita."

She saw his lips move. Heard the words. Thought: This is crazy! What is wrong with you? Here's your chance! This could make you. This could make you be someone I could fall in love with.

Did she say it out loud?

No.

But he was looking at her as if he'd heard her say it. As if he'd read her mind.

The lining of her mouth suddenly felt thick. She swallowed. "I'm not, I didn't mean . . ."

He smiled. "That's okay. I'm not offended."

He continued to caress her jaw.

She shouldn't have been so pushy. Intimating that he was somehow inadequate because he was a drifter. Even though he *was* a drifter. "What I meant to say was—"

"Shhhhhhh," he said.

His finger trailing along her jaw and down into the hollow of her throat.

And suddenly, she was scared.

He was former military. Sometimes they came back broken. Most times, in her experience. His body was hard—*honed*—almost as if he was a weapon kept sharp.

Silly.

But his hyperawareness. She had to admit, sometimes that spooked her.

Abruptly, she felt as if she were walking down a dark road at night all alone, and headlights appeared in the distance. The sight of the headlights—the thought of who might be on that road coming her way—caused a tiny stab of fear. The kind you were embarrassed by and you said to yourself, *Don't be silly.*

That was what it felt like.

He gently traced the hollow of her throat. "It's okay," he said.

"Okay?" Her own voice faint in her ears.

"Okay."

Abruptly, she *did* feel silly. In fact, she felt ridiculous.

He was Joe, *her* Joe.

She said, "If you don't want to go, that's fine, too. But—"

He pressed a finger to her lips. "Thanks," he said, "but no thanks."

"Can you at least tell me why?"

"Because I don't want to. Isn't that a good enough reason?"

But it's Santa Anita.

He seemed to read her thoughts. "I like it here just fine."

Then he kissed her on the lips, and before she knew it, they were making love.

The dark lonely road, the headlights in the distance, were forgotten.

CHAPTER 2

It took the man Barbara Carey knew as Joe Till an average of one hour and forty-five minutes to drive from the horse farm north of Santa Ysabel to Gordon C. Tuttle High School on Forrest Avenue.

That included swapping vehicles.

He drove to his rented town house and parked the Dodge Ram in the closed two-car garage, swapping it out for a Ford Econoline. The town house was on a quiet street where everyone seemed to either work days or stay inside their townhomes—he'd never seen another soul here.

He kept another van at another town house on another street just like this one, only that town house was in Lake View Terrace.

He drove the six city blocks to the high school.

The school he was going to was located in a recently incorporated area east of LA called Torrent Valley. He made the trip five days a week.

Like most teenagers, seventeen-year-old Kristal Landry was a creature of habit. Her last class let out at three p.m. She walked out to her car parked by the chain-link fence facing the football field. She always parked in the same spot or one or two spots on either side, not far from a massive California pepper tree.

If he could trace her movements, so could someone else.

He watched through binoculars through a vertical metal flap at the back of his van as Kristal walked out to her car.

He knew how much the 2011 Toyota Yaris cost new. He would have chosen another car—larger and heavier—but making choices for Kristal was no longer his job. He wasn't crazy about the color, either—"Yellow Jolt"—but young girls were attracted to bright colors. Yellow and red were accident colors. They also attracted attention. A pretty girl in a cute yellow car could be a draw for some kinds of people. But he had to leave it to Kristal and her mom.

He wasn't crazy about Kristal's boyfriend, either, the kid who was walking her to the car. He watched as they kissed. She gently pushed her hand down and against the kid's crotch.

A slow burn started in his throat and flushed his face.

If she lived in his house, if *he* lived in his house, he would have had a serious talk with her. A very serious talk.

But Cyril Landry was on the outside. He could do nothing about his daughter's behavior.

He couldn't expose her to those who would still be looking. He doubted anyone was, but that was not a guarantee. He couldn't be there to do his duty as a father because he would be putting her and his wife in danger, along with his brothers and sister. So Kristal would just have to figure it out. He would have forbidden her to have sex with that boy, Luke Brodsky, and she would have had no choice but to obey. But now he could only watch over her and hope she figured out that they needed to use birth control. Abstinence was preferable, but he'd prefer she use birth control rather than end up with a kid, which would tie her to Luke for a long time.

It was a helpless feeling to watch her through binocs and not be able to warn Kristal about all the things she would have to deal with. A kid without a father to protect her, at the most vulnerable time in her life—all those raging hormones. Trying to pick a college, and who knew what else? Her grades had never been good, and he'd found out that in middle school she had been bullied and she had been mortified when he'd rectified it by going to the bully's parents.

His wife didn't speak to him for a week.

That was the way it had always been, two against one, but he didn't mind it so much. He knew they loved him. Cindi once said that he "exasperated" them both. That was the word she used. But she also understood that he would die for them. Left unsaid was the fact that he would kill for them, but Cindi knew that, too. They both knew he had stood watch over his family like the sentry on the ramparts.

But now his wife didn't know if he was alive or dead.

The DOD told Cindi he was dead, so that was what she probably believed.

The two kids were getting hot and heavy, in broad daylight out by the car. The boy was leaning into Kristal, holding her against the Yaris. Their crotches almost rubbing. Tangled together.

Three in the afternoon.

Other kids walking to their cars.

So many kids, funneling into the parking lot.

He looked away.

- — -

Barbara Carey looked at her watch. She'd seen Joe Till drive his old truck off the property at exactly noon, as he did five days a week.

When she hired him, he'd told her he needed time off between noon and five p.m. on weekdays. He told her he would be back before evening feed. In exchange for this, he worked weekends. On weekends, he was available twenty-four seven, and could be there every day of the week *except* between noon and five p.m.

There wasn't much to do with racehorses in the middle of the day. It was their siesta time and hers, so the strange arrangement worked out fine. She suspected he had another job to make ends meet. She knew as well as anyone that work on a horse farm didn't pay a living wage.

He didn't share that part of his private life with her, so this was purely conjecture on her part.

The other job was probably a condition of his probation. If he *was* on probation. That was the case with her brother Ben. *They* decided where you worked and when. She didn't ask. You had a good worker in the racing business, you don't ask too many questions.

Barbara knew she was falling for Joe Till. She'd lived a long time, through two marriages, one ending in young widowhood and the other in divorce. She was no fool. She had cautioned herself not to fall for him. Reminded herself she didn't know him very well.

Very well? Hardly at all. Just that he was a good horseman. Okay, a *spectacular* horseman. And a good lover. A *spectacular* lover.

He was a good friend, too, as far as that went.

She trusted him for the most part, so she wouldn't rock the boat. She didn't *want* to rock the boat.

Barbara stuck to her guns on that all the way up until five o'clock in the afternoon, when the news filtered in.

CHAPTER 3

Three p.m.: thirty or more high school kids were strung out along the asphalt apron of the parking lot, ambling along, some in groups, some by themselves, talking, joking, grandstanding. Shoulders slouched, some of them sullen, some lonely, many of them thumbing their cell phones. Beeping to unlock their cars. Pretty girls. Handsome boys. The sunlight lying flat on the parking lot, shadows lengthening, smog burned off, deep blue sky, palm trees, bright green lawn.

Friday. Week over. Everyone happy to go home.

His daughter and her boyfriend making out against the yellow Yaris, oblivious.

Then:

Hard loud claps, rapid fire—

M-16.

Kids in a group hitting the ground like dominoes, others stopping, turning, twisting, trying to run. Some wandering aimlessly, in shock.

Crawling.

Screaming.

A slender dark figure advancing through the lot, shooting at anything that moved. Reports in rapid succession—*bangbangbangbangbang.*

Landry saw his daughter duck down behind the engine block of the car—good. Her boyfriend crouched above her, covering her with his body, head, and arms. The shooter in black, body armor head to toe, shooting methodically, a gunslinger walking down the street. Casings raining behind him.

Detached.

Nonchalant.

Landry retrieved his rifle from the storage compartment of the Econoline, twisted the can on the barrel, loaded five subsonic rounds. One in the chamber. No time for the bipod.

The shooter dumping ammo, waving his rifle back and forth, creating a swath. Mowing down anything in his path. Now he was past Kristal's car. If he turned back . . . Kids were running, screaming. Falling, drenched in blood. A blond girl crouched over her friend's body—sheltering her. The shooter aimed—casually but in control—and the top of her head vaporized. She collapsed in a heap on top of her friend's body. A boy running for cover was hit between the shoulder blades. He skated crazily for a moment in the blood of the two girls, before he fell.

The man with the rifle moved forward. Calm and methodical, picking his shots.

This is not your average school shooter.

Kristal and Luke by the car. Luke frantically pushing Kristal under, trying to scuttle in behind, still covering her with his body—great kid.

Another terrifying burst.

Landry dragged a sandbag to the vertical flap in the van's right back door. Sandbag in place, rifle on top: prone position, push the flap aside.

The way he was parked, the loophole didn't true up with the target. *This won't work.*

Contingencies, none of them good. He could bash out the taillight with the butt of his rifle, but a van with a broken taillight would be noticeable. He looked around. The sound of gunfire, so far, had kept people inside. Anyone driving by might see the barrel but he'd have to take that chance. *Open the back doors.* Risky, but doable. He pushed open the right side first, not too far, then shoved on the right. There was a gap of about a foot and a half, enough so he could train the rifle and follow.

No time to worry if someone saw the barrel protruding from the van.

He had one good shot. After that, there might be an infinitesimal alteration in the rifle's accuracy. *If* the barrel heated up too much. Betsy had a tendency to run hot, but otherwise, she was perfect. Nineteen times out of twenty, her performance was precise to the nth degree. But Landry knew he couldn't take any chances.

The first shot had to be good. It would be. The shooter was no more than eighty-five feet away. Landry had made kill shots at a mile—and more.

It was his choice, how to take down the shooter, with less than a second to make it. Even with body armor, one shot to the outside torso would drop him. It wouldn't kill him, but it would stop him. It would put him right down. A live shooter would help the investigation, and give Landry answers.

A shot to the head would make *sure* he was dead.

His *daughter.*

It would be the head shot.

He peered through the scope—

And saw the blood lighting on Luke's back like a half dozen locusts.

The boy's body went still.

Someone yelled. The shooter turned his head. His back to Kristal, who was now all the way under the car. The bad guy's back to Landry, finger on the trigger, and he started shooting again, neck bent slightly forward. He wore a bulletproof vest, and a helmet, but he'd left the sweet spot open: where the base of the skull met the vertebrae.

Acquire the target.

Breathe.

Slow squeeze on the trigger.

The shooter went down, dead before he hit the ground, his oblongata pulverized by a bullet moving at eight hundred feet per second. The vertebrae popped, shards of bone disintegrating in an instant. There wasn't even a blurt from the assault rifle.

Like turning off a light switch.

Blood spread out from under him, shiny, dark, and black. Like crude oil.

The satisfaction of taking the shooter out was brief and followed by a tsunami of pain.

So many of them down.

Sirens. Landry pulled the doors shut and peered through the flap. People were coming out of the building, a little late. Like the Munchkins in Oz after the witch died. A rent-a-cop. School officials. The loudspeaker blaring. Dead and wounded.

The cops will be here in less than a minute.

His daughter was crying. Slippery with the blood of her boyfriend. Screaming for help, strangling on her tears.

She was alive, but the boy, Luke, was dead.

That was how it always happened: the kid just gone.

Luke had been a good boy after all.

Landry wanted to hold her. Tell her he was alive and that he had watched over her as a good father should. He wanted to but he knew it would only bring danger to her and her mother.

He needed to go.

His van was parked across the street from the school in the side parking lot of an auto repair shop and nose-in to the back of a Chinese food place, so neither would be able to claim it. The

Econoline was just one junker among many waiting for repair in the California sun.

Landry heard sirens, and two cop cars shot by on the street between his van and the school. People were already gathering in a knot near the automotive shop.

He rummaged through the toolbox, found the rat-tail file, twisted the silencer off Betsy, and dropped the file into the barrel. He placed the rifle loose in the compartment of the Econoline. He wanted it to rattle around a little.

A few stops and starts—and a turn or two—would suffice; the rat-tail would scratch new marks inside the barrel. If the police stopped him—if they confiscated the rifle and ran her through ballistics—they would have nothing to match it to.

He was about to drive out onto the side street, his usual entrance and egress, when he heard the shriek of brakes and a car bounce up onto the curb behind him, smashing into a light post. The car behind it stopped dead in the road, blocking both lanes. The driver tried to start the car but the engine flooded.

He heard the whoop of another cop car and saw two patrol units stopping dead behind the disabled car. His usual exit was blocked.

The only way out was covered by cameras surrounding the school. He knew the location of every security cam. If he turned left, there was no way to avoid them.

The area was already saturated with law enforcement; they would have already set up a perimeter.

Twenty-seven years in the life told him to turn into the teeth of the storm. So he turned left.

CHAPTER 4

Landry had done his homework on his daughter's school.

Gordon C. Tuttle High School was relatively new—only fourteen years old. In that time, the population in this area had boomed, and the administrative buildings of the school had been expanded beyond its original boundaries. He had the blueprints and so he knew that Security was housed in an annex across the street.

Landry drove the half block down to the school's maintenance yard and parked in the lot with the other personnel vehicles.

He reached into the back for the jumpsuit and ball cap he always carried with him, as well as a pair of wire-rimmed eyeglasses and a lanyard with a generic card bearing the name "John Anderson." *Instant janitor.* He changed his footwear. One was a typical work boot. The other was an orthopedic boot, the kind a person would wear after surgery.

He rummaged around in his toolbox for a cordless drill (he had two) and broke the drill down until it exposed the electric armature. He pulled the magnets from the armature and used a hammer to bust them into a powder. He poured the resulting magnetic dust into a rag, folded the rag carefully, and put it in his coverall pocket.

Doing all this kept him from thinking about Kristal's terror and

Luke's death. Landry didn't know how he could have reacted any faster, but if he'd been able to, Luke might still be alive.

Could've, would've, should've. There was no point in going down that road. Stay in the moment, formulate a plan. Check it twice, and hold on to your sanity.

Landry closed up the van and entered the building. He glanced around for the security room. There was a knot of people—some of them police—outside the administrative offices. He could hear the crackle of their radios.

Listening carefully, he learned that the parking lot where the shooting had happened—the crime scene—had been secured. There were cops, SWAT, ambulances, investigators, FBI. All of them on scene. The parents were to gather in the auditorium on campus, where they could meet their sons and daughters—

The ones who were alive, anyway.

He wondered if Cindi was there yet. If she had met up with their daughter.

Walking gingerly on the orthopedic shoe, he headed down the hallway to the office. Law enforcement didn't give him a first glance.

The place was chaos. A glass partition divided the general space from the offices in back. Knots of people talked in hushed voices. There was a large police presence—they were already interviewing people. One woman was at her desk. He caught her eye and mouthed "Electronic center?"

She looked at him, but he could tell her mind was elsewhere. "I'm afraid—"

"I was sent by the FBI to make sure the electronic center is working . . . It's important." He paused for a moment to let that sink in. But she didn't seem to be comprehending much. He added, "Can you direct me?"

"What?" Still confused. Distracted. Devastated. Still in shock.

"The electronic center. It would be a room, probably in Security. Can you direct me?"

She nodded, finally comprehending. "It's that way!" She motioned to the north. "Around the corner. The first door on the right."

"Okay. Thanks."

As he walked past, she asked, "Are you with the FBI?"

"My company is the subcontractor."

"Oh." She turned away, back to a knot of people who had drifted into the picture.

He limped his way around the corner and found the room. He could have found it on his own, but he wanted to fit in to the chaos, be a working part of it, interchangeable with other pieces—one of the crowd. That way no one would think of him as unusual.

The hall was overflowing with people. He nodded and pointed to his toolbox, pushing his way through the crowd to the hallway leading to the electronics room. When he turned the corner he was surprised to see the hall was empty. The cops had not made it here yet. But they would, soon. He used a credit card to open the door, closed and locked it behind him. He had three minutes to do what he needed to do.

First things first: use a pair of locking pliers to clamp the door dampener above his head. This would prevent anyone, key or no key, from opening the door.

Outside he could hear babble, movement. An individual voice. They were on their way. He located the security-camera box and realized pretty quickly that all he'd have to do was pull a few memory sticks and drop them into the toolbox. Done, he stood the recorder unit on its side, took the rag containing the magnetic dust from the pocket of his jumpsuit, and tipped the filings down inside the recorder. He gave it a couple of blasts from a can of compressed air so the dust would circulate throughout the unit. The mag dust would guarantee there would be no further surveillance.

There was a cupboardful of supplies above. He found the memory sticks and inserted blanks in place of the ones he'd taken.

It took him ten seconds to close the toolbox and look over the room and wipe the area down.

Done, he picked up his toolbox and went to the door. He listened for noise and heard babbling.

Landry opened the door and walked out into the hallway. There were a lot more people now. A lot more babble. He saw the FBI. He saw the police. There were numerous grave-faced officials and probably some politicians. Some of them were on the way up the hall, walking and talking with one another. A radio crackled and they all stopped, a knot of concerned men still in shock.

Landry assumed a concerned expression. He was a harried worker with a toolbox, still limping with his orthopedic boot, shocked to stunned silence by the carnage that had happened at a school.

He was almost to the T in the hallway when a man called out. "Hey!"

Landry knew the man was calling to him.

Shit.

He turned around.

A man in a dark suit walked toward him. He looked like FBI—all business.

Landry waited. His entrails turning to ice.

"What kind of shoe is that?" The FBI agent pointed to his orthopedic boot.

Landry put on his clueless look. "It's orthopedic. I have a tear in my Achilles tendon and it hurt like hell 'til I got this."

"Yeah, I know. My wife just had surgery, and hers doesn't fit too well. How does it feel?"

"Good. No complaints. Only thing I worry about is the buckles are plastic, but so far so good."

"What brand is it?"

Landry rummaged through his brain. Aware that another FBI agent had detached from a group and was walking their way. What started out friendly could go south in an instant, but Landry knew the kind of boot he wore. "It's an Össur Air Equalizer."

The agent gave him a curt nod. "Thanks."

Landry limped on down the hallway.

The FBI agent called out, "Leave your name at the desk if you haven't already. Everyone has to check in."

"Will do."

He turned the corner and walked through the crowd, finally working his way outside. Half-expecting the van to be gone, or for a dozen cops and agents to be crawling all over it.

But the van was untouched, one in a crowd of vehicles. Sweet relief.

The cars in the lot all had green stickers in their windshields— parking permits for the employees. He looked around and saw no one on his side of the lot. Used his lock picks to open one of the cars and took the permit and hung it on the rearview mirror of his van.

He threw his gear inside. Cracked the windows on both sides, but not enough so they were noticeable. Propped the sunshade up, making sure the permit showed in the windshield. Crawled back into the body of the van and stretched out. He inserted the memory sticks into his laptop and ran through them, replaying his exit from the auto shop parking lot. The feed was fuzzy and indistinct. A portion of his van turned onto the main drag—all he could see of the driver was a shadow overlaid by a reflection of street.

He replayed it several times. The car behind had come up on

him quickly, blocking his muddy license plate. *Nothing to see here.* It was a moot point, since he had possession of the memory sticks.

He went backward from there, replaying the shooting scene. But it was fuzzy and indistinct, just shapes fleeing and no sign of the shooter himself.

He shut down the laptop, pulled the cap low over his eyes, and lay down. He'd wait until the end of the day when everyone drove out at once.

Someone with the police or FBI might figure it out. They might stop each car as they drove out, but he doubted it. Even if they did, they would probably just ask his name and he would give them one of the names he'd seen on the nameplates in the office. Jim Overton. Or Larry Schweikert.

He doubted it would come to that.

Most likely the police—if they were in the parking lot at all— would wave them all through, his van along with all the other cars and trucks.

This was known in the profession as protective coloration.

- — -

It was all over cable and the Internet. Barbara had the TV on in the tack room and when she heard about the shooting, her first thought was Joe Till.

Crazy.

But she had a feeling. There had always been a streak of voodoo in her family—mostly in the form of a well-developed sixth sense. She had friends in Lake View Terrace, which was right next to Torrent Valley. She stayed with them when she went to Santa Anita. Barbara did the math in her head: he could make it to Lake View Terrace and back in that time.

She didn't know why she thought that this was where Joe had gone.

No idea why.

But the feeling solidified as the hours went by and he didn't return by the usual time.

They didn't show his likeness on television, so there was no way she could tell it was him. But by then, she knew he would not be coming back.

CHAPTER 5

Landry left the van—wiped down and stripped of everything important—in the long-term parking lot at LAX, and caught an evening flight to Vegas. Before that, he had disassembled the H&K .308 sniper rifle he'd named Betsy and shipped her to a PO box in Vegas he kept under another name.

Betsy was the third in a line of Betsys. His father waged war in Korea with his Betsy, and his grandfather waged war in World War II with his. Landry didn't see any reason to change names. He had many years with her. He knew her as well as he knew himself, and he refused to spend time and energy zeroing a new rifle that might not be anywhere near as good. This was nonnegotiable: Betsy went where he went. And right now, he was going to find sanctuary.

A wise E-7 in Iraq once told him: "If you want to get lost, get lost in a crowd." And plain sight was the last place anybody looked.

There was no more anonymous place than Vegas. Just try to stand out.

On the way to LAX he'd stopped at a CVS and bought a zippered toiletry case, a Los Angeles T-shirt with an image of a sun sporting dark glasses, a ball cap, a nylon carry-on duffle, spray-on tan, black hair color, some dark shades, a bestselling thriller novel he planned to read on the plane, and a small bag of cotton balls. Next door was a filling station. In the men's room he dyed his hair, sprayed on the tan, and changed into the loose-hanging shirt. He stuffed his gums with cotton balls on each side to make his cheeks look fatter. It wasn't much of a difference, physically, but it would change the way people saw him—if they saw him at all. And the way people watching the cameras would see him. He looked like just another dull tourist heading for Vegas. He carried his laptop on the plane but didn't crack it.

The flight was uneventful.

At McCarran International Airport, Landry rented a midsized sedan under the name Jake Sylvan. The car was silver and nondescript—a typical tourist rental. Not too flashy, not too plain. Comfortable, but not too expensive. He stopped at Costco and bought more tourist clothes: another couple of cheap T-shirts, a ball cap, basketball shorts, two packs of underwear, and a soft-sided suitcase. One garment actually appealed to him: a Hawaiian shirt with a tarpon print, ultramarine and pale gray.

From there he went to Java Wars, an Internet café he liked on Sahara Avenue. From his laptop computer he accessed the Wells Fargo bank account already set up under Jake Sylvan's name and transferred more money to the account. He drove to the Strip and picked out one of the big hotel-casinos, Xanadu, for his stay.

It was going on nine thirty at night. Las Vegas was just getting started. He didn't get a room right away. The cotton balls tucked into his mouth would help fool the facial recognition cameras. (They weren't as good as advertised, but why take a chance?) Landry melted into the crowd and played the slots, watching the check-in counter and hoping for a rush. He sat on a stool and pulled the one-armed bandit, the clanging bells filling his ears. Cigarette smoke made his eyes smart. He didn't approve of places that let people smoke, but this was Las Vegas and smoking was ubiquitous. It went with the buckets of quarters and the buses full of elderly women in pantsuits and old men with cigarette packs in the breast pockets of their knit shirts, with the constant harmonic ringing in his ears and the clank and spill of quarters into the coin trays when someone hit the jackpot. He'd have to spend a lot more time here to succumb to secondhand smoke, so it was just an annoyance. Once he got a nonsmoking room he would change clothes, and that would take care of the problem. A former Navy SEAL, he knew there were several levels of bad beyond annoyance. Unbearable, for instance. His comfort meter had made it to the red line many times when he was in Iraq. So breathing secondhand smoke and the constant din of the slots was really nothing, when you looked at it as part of a continuum.

He played the slots for a while, melting into the crowd. Xanadu wasn't that old, but already it was showing what age it had. The smell of cigarette smoke had embedded into the carpet and the walls, and there was a dankness underneath that he'd noticed in casinos—a night-worn smell. He had been raised Catholic but it didn't take. He'd had enough inculcation to remember those formative years, and he thought the casino smelled like sin—if sin had a smell. Venial sin, for sure. It was a minor, sad stink.

Landry had chosen Xanadu because it appealed to an older crowd. In the last few years, Las Vegas had been turned into a playground for twentysomethings. Landry wanted a place where he could fit in. College kids seemed to give Xanadu a wide berth, leaving it to the jaded gamblers and senior citizens.

Still, Xanadu went big. It had been built during the days Las Vegas tried to attract families instead of reprobates. One wall was all waterfall, with fake rock, colored lights, what looked like real moss, and lifelike caged tigers and real actors—natives with spears. It smelled fishy, though, and the men in the loincloths looked like they didn't know what to do with their spears. The woman on the trapeze was a marvel of female construction, but all she did was swing back and forth in her leopard swimsuit.

Landry knew he fit in. The trick was in the eyes. He always focused on the slot machine—never wavering. He wore the wire-rimmed glasses. In addition, he'd attached a fake ponytail he liked to carry with him, which along with the Hawaiian shirt and the wire-rims made him look like a hippie professor on a junket.

There were cameras everywhere. But the best protective coloring here was the sheer number of people packed like sardines into the hotel-casino.

He saw a crowd of tourists coming in. It looked like they had been on a bus all day. He fell into line with them.

That was when he spotted the call girl.

She was good looking for a prostitute. She was also older than a lot of the prostitutes around here, possibly late twenties. Leggy. Sure of herself.

He liked that. Everyone had something they could do well, and she gave off the vibe that she was quite likely a spectacular prostitute.

Yes, she dressed like a hooker, but she was a stylish hooker. To be fair, his daughter Kristal didn't dress all that differently.

For a moment, the slide show came up: Kristal frantically trying to squeeze under her cute little car, Luke shielding her with his body.

That kid, Luke—he was a warrior. The one and only time in his life, probably, but he'd died brave.

The prostitute smiled at him. The image of Kristal spattered with her boyfriend's blood dissolved. He had things to do.

He smiled. "You busy?" he asked.

"Honey, I'm always busy."

"Does that mean you're too busy for me?"

"No way, hon. I love big strong men."

Her delivery was perfect. Believable. He almost found *himself* believing it, she was that good.

It was important to him that she was a pro. He motioned her over to stand by him. "Don't be a stranger."

She came up to the line and stood with him. He asked her if she had kids and she said two. He told her he had a daughter. He asked her if she liked the life and she said it paid the bills. That was pretty much the extent of the conversation. She shifted from one high-heeled foot to another and her eyes roved the crowd, already picking out the next john. When he checked in, he made sure to look embarrassed. Tried for the family dog who pissed on the carpet and didn't think it was such a big infraction, but felt he should at least look chastened. He had a dog like that once when he was a kid. Frodo wasn't supposed to be on the furniture, but many times, when Landry got up in the night, he heard a thump and a jingle. The dog jumping off the couch, even though no one could see him in the dark.

Frodo always gave away the farm.

So in this story, Landry was the dog. He felt guilty, but he was going to do it anyway.

No embarrassment on *her* part, though. He could hear her snap her gum. He thought she was putting on a show, but why call her on it?

The young man at the desk was trying not to be harried. It was very busy. This suited Landry, and the prostitute, who went by the name Laurella (had to be a made-up name), who hung on his arm and kept brushing his chest with her long hair.

It was funny. Both of them had hair extensions.

- — -

The room was over-the-top—Landry counted three phones, two fountains, a writing table, a suite of high-backed brocade chairs, and tapestries fit for the queen of England—everything done in burgundy and gold. The king-sized bed had the crispest, whitest sheets he'd ever seen, with rich-looking coverlets and bolsters as big around as punching bags. One of the fountains was an element of feng shui in the room—a waterfall over polished stones spilling over a narrow lip into another pool filled with lily pads. The bathroom fixtures were all gold plated—at least they looked that way. A rich mahogany cabinet held a wide-screen TV. The carpet was the color of tree bark with a repeating crown design. If he looked at it for too long, his vision blurred. The air-conditioning was turned up high but the room still smelled a bit stale, despite the grandeur.

The hooker was standing there, like a stork, trying to pull the strap on one of her shoes.

"That's okay," he said.

"Oh, you want me to wear them. I getcha."

"Go ahead and leave your clothes on."

She looked confused.

"How much?" he asked.

"Two hundred."

He reached into his wallet and pulled out two hundreds and a fifty.

She watched as the money crossed her palm. "Hey . . ." She drifted off. She didn't want to spoil anything.

"Do you know how the term 'tip' originated?"

She just stared at him. He believed her expression would be described as "bemused."

"It means, 'to insure promptness.'"

"Oh. That's nice." She sat down on the bed and started picking at the strap of her shoe again. He noticed that she made herself look as sexy as possible. Shoving her butt backward and her chest forward, reaching down languorously to work the buckle, flipping her hair a little as she did so.

She sensed him staring at her.

"Prompt is the way we're going to go," he said.

She must have realized it was a different stare than she was used to. She stiffened, like a deer suddenly smelling something dangerous. "What?"

"You can go."

She stared at him. Her mouth slightly open. "What? Look, I can do all sorts of stuff that'll make you go insane, I guarantee you'll love—"

"That's okay. I'm not feeling amorous right now. Since I got you up here and took you out of commission, it's only fair I pay you."

She stared at the money still grasped in one hand. "Two hundred and fifty dollars," she said. "Don't you at least want a blowjob?"

He shrugged. Smiled. "Not in the mood, sorry."

"Look, why don't you just lay down on the bed and we'll see what happens."

"*Lie* down on the bed."

"Okay, now we're cookin'."

"No, I mean it's *lie* down on the bed, not *lay* down on the bed."

"Huh?"

He didn't feel like explaining it to her. He wanted to be alone. "Is there a back way out of here?"

"Sure. There are stairs that way." She motioned to the wall opposite the way they had come.

"Tell you what. You take the money and go out the back way, okay?"

She just stared at him. Finally, she said, "You don't want to? Really?"

"My wife just died. I'm not in the mood."

"But—"

"I thought I was, but I can't do it yet. You understand?"

"Oh, you poor thing." She shuttled the money to her purse, but her expression, at least, was sad. She hesitated. "You sure?"

"I'm here with some friends. Friends of my dead wife. I wouldn't want them to see you. So if you could go down the other way and not mention this . . ."

"I gotcha."

"Thanks."

She practically ran to the door and slipped out.

If anyone bothered to look, the cameras would show a tourist soliciting a hooker. The cameras would show the hooker going up to his room.

He'd kept her here long enough for a quickie.

He sat down on the bed for a moment, feeling every bit of his forty-eight years.

Then he turned on the television.

- — -

Landry switched among the "news" channels. All of them had a different slant, but they all vamped like vaudeville performers, because even now, eight hours after the shooting, they had nothing real to go on.

He decided to switch between MSNBC and Fox News, because CNN was beginning to sound like Henny Penny covering the falling sky.

The remaining two cable channels' nonstop coverage featured repetitive footage of the high school grounds and people milling in the auditorium where the lucky parents met with their kids, and an interview with a school security guard who had "engaged" the shooter.

Landry thought he saw Cindi and Kristal in the background, but he couldn't be sure. Every time that segment came on he strained his eyes, and every time it was too fast and too dark and too hard to tell if it really *was* them.

A reporter interviewed the new hero, a security guard named Brendan Hillhouse. He told the reporters he heard shots and ran outside. His eyes were bright with excitement, and he spoke in little bursts. The reporter shoved a mic in his face and asked him if he had "taken down" the shooter.

"I think so," he said between huffing breaths. "You don't really know what you're capable of until something like this happens."

Maybe he believed it. Even though he had come from the auditorium exit, the shooter facing him, and he was out of range. He must be the best shot on the planet if he could get a bullet to ring around the shooter and hit the back of his head. But the cable channels were getting no new information, so for a while Brendan Hillhouse was a hero.

No name on the shooter.

No mention of the single subsonic round that killed him.

Of course not. The FBI would hold that piece of information back. Knowledge was power, and knowledge that other people didn't have was *more* power.

A lot was made about his body armor and helmet. He fit right in with the last few (cowardly) mass shooters, and this seemed to please the cable-channel talking heads to no end. It allowed them to be their own experts.

They had official experts, too. Plenty of them. Some were good (although the information they had was sketchy and they couldn't reveal much due to the ongoing nature of the investigation), and others were just spouting hot air. There was endless speculation, punctuated by more photos of the parking lot now that it was night, traffic cones, cops in fluorescent green vests, flares, and crime scene tape. Very dramatic. Finally, the sheriff of Los Angeles County held a press conference. He appeared grave and used plenty of words but no specifics.

The coverage continued on in an endless loop, interviews on the street with bystanders and teachers and the school principal and parents whose kids were still alive, and solemn dirge music taking them into commercial breaks.

Landry lay on the bed, still in his shorts and shirt, bathed in the blue light of the television, and that was how he fell asleep.

The next morning was the same—no progress at all.

He went down to the coffee shop for a cheap breakfast. He knew where the cameras were likely to be and avoided them. He wore his new tarpon shirt, the ponytail, the wire-rimmed glasses. They didn't call it a coffee shop these days, although that was what it was. It was called the Amazon Room. The food was good, though. The link sausages were especially good, and he ordered an extra helping.

By midafternoon there were names. Luke Brodsky was one of eight dead: six boys and two girls. Landry divided his time between the television and the Internet. The aggregate site *The Huffington Post* seemed to have the latest. But the latest was just more of the same—except for the names of the kids who were killed.

Nothing on the gunman, except for speculation.

He was referred to as a "school shooter," and the news channel hosts, with nothing better to do, started jumping to conclusions. They talked to psychiatrists to fill up time. The shooter's age went from twenty-two to eighteen to "unknown." By now the authorities would know exactly how old he was and who he was and probably what his parents did for a living and where he went wrong as a child.

But there was nothing. No age, no description, no name, no reason for his disaffection, no trauma from his childhood, no failed grades in school, no bullying, no abandonment by his parents, no Mensa IQ, no girlfriend who spurned him—nothing. The talking heads didn't cite statistics, but to Landry's ears they were thinking of this guy as a typical school shooter. A kid, fifteen to twenty-two, maybe. But even then, they tiptoed up to the edge and didn't say it outright.

A full fifteen hours later, the killer was still a cipher.

When Landry was a kid he read a lot. His life had been nomadic—his family had moved from racetrack to racetrack, from race meet to race meet, and when not doing his chores, he spent a lot of time in the fifth-wheel trailer watching TV and reading. One summer he read every Sherlock Holmes story he could get his hands on.

One of them was called "Silver Blaze." He'd liked it because there were horses and dogs in it, and because he liked Sherlock Holmes and wanted to grow up to be like him. In the story, the clue wasn't something that happened. It was something that *didn't* happen: *the dog that didn't bark in the nighttime.*

Watching the news, Landry reflected that this shooting was becoming a lot like a dog that didn't bark in the nighttime.

The kids who had been killed had been identified. The kids who had been wounded, too. There was even an animated re-creation of the shooting. How the shooter proceeded through the parking lot, whom he shot. Lots of trajectories.

The instant hero, Brendan Hillhouse, had been dropped from the story.

Some of the talking heads began to speculate about the shooter. He was dead, right? But they didn't go beyond saying the investigation was continuing and they were certain the shooter would soon be identified.

Except he wasn't.

They covered it well, but Landry knew the experts were confused. You could see it on their faces, in the hesitation in their voices: they were playing for time. Landry could see the thought bubbles over their heads: They had the killer, right? He was lying on a slab in the morgue. Why couldn't the authorities give him a *name*?

It was obvious to Landry that the talking heads on television had never run into this before. There had always been an answer, even if it was slow in coming. Yet this time, there was nothing. No name. No description. No stats. No update on that part of the investigation at all.

Other stories—an aviation mishap in Brazil, a terrorist act in Mumbai, a disgraced congressman resigning from office—started to take over.

Landry knew what that meant.

Somebody had shut them down.

CHAPTER 6

Landry kept the "Do Not Disturb" sign on his door. He ordered room service for breakfast, lunch, and dinner, and stayed inside the room with the TV turned to one of the news channels, reading about the shooting on the Internet, and compiling his list of the dead and wounded.

In most of these shootings, he knew, there was no rhyme or reason as to who was shot and who escaped injury. Generally, the shooter just wanted to shoot as many people as he could. *Who* was shot depended on a number of factors. The victims closest to the shooter were the easiest targets. If someone tried to run, that might catch his attention and he would shoot them. Or maybe he'd seek out the ones who tried to hide. The point was to kill as many people as possible. As to how the shooter accomplished his goal: no telling what was in his mind. No predicting what he would do.

Mostly, though, they picked a place and just shot at what was in front of them.

From what Landry himself had observed, the guy decided to walk through the parking lot spraying kids with bullets.

Eight high school kids died in the shooting. Their names had just now been released. There was a secondary list somewhere—the eleven who were wounded—but that list had not been disclosed and might never be.

All but one of the wounded had been released from the hospital as of today. The last boy was in critical condition; it was possible he wouldn't make it. In which case Landry would have to adjust his list to ten.

Landry got off the chair and went to the window. He looked down at the Strip below. The sun on the pavement, the cars, the tourists, the palm trees, the endless line of high-rises. Suddenly, his lunch threatened to come up.

He was bombarded with images of his daughter. The moment he first saw her as a baby, blue eyes staring up at him from that puny, solemn face. Riding the trike they bought her for her third birthday. The poster she'd painted in first grade. All the way up to the teenager who worshipped celebrities like Brienne Cross, the teenager who was sullen and embarrassed to be seen with her parents and yet still looked to them for security and sometimes validation. She had snippy friends who dressed like whores and boyfriends who ran the gamut from clueless to lecherous, and of course she had her iPhone.

Landry had observed that half the time Kristal and Luke walked out to their cars, they were going at it not with each other, but on their phones.

It was in the fall that she hooked up with Luke. The boy who might or might not have already slept with her but who had definitely saved her life.

And Landry had killed the man who'd killed Luke.

It had felt good at the time, but now he wished he hadn't.

It had been a split-second decision. He'd chosen the head shot—and that was on him. If he'd shot center mass, he would have gotten the same result: the guy would have gone down. The bullet would have stopped him instantly. Even with the body armor, the impact would have dropped him.

No telling when the shooter would be able to get up again, but Landry guessed it wouldn't have been in time to evade the cops. They would have got him. They would have been able to interrogate him and get answers.

But Landry had chosen to kill him instead. He'd done it because while the cops probably would be there within two to three minutes, it wasn't a done deal.

If they had been delayed, the guy would have started shooting again. And the person closest to him, the person right in the line of fire, had been Kristal.

CHAPTER 7

Barbara Carey walked along the side of the two-lane highway, the night air cool on her bare arms and face. The road stretched out before her toward the horizon, black against the indigo night sky.

A halo of light flared briefly on the horizon and disappeared.

A car's headlights.

She was not far from the farm and had no idea why she was walking along the highway, which traversed the low hills near Santa Ysabel.

Another flare, and her heart throttled up like a racing engine. The light was closer, and this time she saw two pinpoints. Headlights.

She looked around. No place to hide. Moonlight spotlighted her. There were pastures but few trees, and the outbuildings of the nearest ranch were at least a mile away.

The car topped another hill, the headlights pinning her in place—

And she awoke with a gasp.

Her heart thumping hard.

She turned on the light. Looked at the bed she had up until yesterday shared with Joe Till.

She'd watched the news yesterday evening and well into the night.

A massacre at Gordon C. Tuttle High—nineteen kids shot.

She *knew* it was Joe Till.

He'd never given her any indication of violence up until yesterday. Yesterday morning, when he'd refused to go to Santa Anita, when he ran his finger along her jaw, he'd frightened her. That was when she got the image of the headlights in the dark. An image so strong, she *knew* she was in danger.

She'd known there was something off about him. Something *wrong*.

His strange schedule. Five hours in the middle of the day, every weekday. She'd suspected he was on probation, or worse, parole.

There was that one time—she was so ashamed!—that one time she'd followed him. She had stayed well behind. He'd taken the freeway north, and she'd followed him, until she thought better of it and finally ditched—her other employee had called to say one of the mares had colicked. And so she'd turned back. But by the time she did, she was almost to LA.

Now she sat up in her empty bed. Half past eight! She'd overslept. She could hear the horses nickering for their breakfast. It was Eddie's day off. And Joe Till was gone.

She'd had the dream twice now. The lonely road, the headlights coming.

That will teach you to read In Cold Blood. She seriously needed to stop reading books like that. And cut out the scary movies, too.

But she worked with horses. She understood that there was more to the world than just logic. There was instinct. She had saved herself several times from getting trampled or bitten or thrown or kicked, because she respected that sixth sense.

And now she'd experienced that feeling of doom, the feeling that something evil was on the road. It manifested itself that way, in her dreams. Someone in a car, someone coming for her. To kidnap her? To rape and murder her?

A friend of hers in middle school had disappeared one day. She'd been walking three short blocks back to her house from a Circle K. They found her body in a field months later. Barb would never forget that. How evil could just come up on you like that.

She knew that Joe Till went to LA every weekday. She knew whatever it was he did, he kept it secret.

As attracted as she was to him, as much as she'd hoped he was *the one*, now the thought of him returning terrified her.

Barbara had always been intuitive. She'd always *known* things. And right now she knew that Joe Till had lied to her. She'd mapped it out, how long it took him to go and to come back. Five days a week. Such a strange schedule. It had worked on her, the idea that he needed that large section of time in the middle of every day. She'd worried it like a dog with a bone. Why five days a week?

He wouldn't say.

She had started to fall for him. But something—a sixth sense— had warned her.

Like yesterday morning—was it only yesterday? When he'd run his fingers along her jaw.

For one terrifying moment, she'd pictured him choking the life out of her.

She got out of bed.

She should tell someone. Maybe it was ridiculous, but she felt the need to tell someone. What if he *had* been involved in the shooting? And she said nothing! The downside was this, though: who'd believe her? Her brother Ben. He'd been in the armed forces. She knew as sure as the sun rose and set, Joe Till had been in the armed forces, too.

She texted Ben.

He didn't answer.

She called her other brother, although that was more for moral support than anything else. But Justin didn't answer, and neither did his wife, Marcella.

Kind of a relief. Maybe she was blowing this all out of proportion.

Joe Till was a good horseman. She knew he must have worked with racehorses, because he knew so much. He didn't talk about what he knew, but she could tell. So on an impulse she called Charlie Baines, who was the guy who manned the horsemen's gate at Santa Anita.

"How you doing?" he asked, his usual jovial self.

"Great. I'm sending up some horses in a few days, just wanted to give you a heads-up."

Her heart beating fast.

"We'll be looking for them. You need more stalls? Because we can't—"

"No, no. Just the ones we already have." She swallowed. "Everything's good." She never was a good liar. "I'm thinking of sending Joe Till."

Silence. Then, "Who?"

"Joe Till? You don't know him?"

Her mouth was so *dry*!

"Don't believe I've had the pleasure."

"Oh." The air blew out of her sails and suddenly she wanted to get off the phone. "Okay."

"You know the rules. He's gonna have to apply for a license."

She nodded, although he couldn't see her. "I know. Well, I guess we'll cross that bridge when we come to it." She hung up.

Joe Till had never been to Santa Anita. He never claimed he had. But she'd been sure that he was avoiding Santa Anita for some reason. Then it came to her:

Fingerprints.

He would be licensed if he worked at any racetrack in the state. Any racetrack in the country. He would have been fingerprinted.

So maybe he was scared of being found out. Afraid of his criminal past, if there was one.

He *must* have a criminal history. That's how he came to work on her farm for less than minimum wage.

She turned on the television—wall-to-wall coverage of the school shooting.

They were showing pictures of the kids who were killed. Describing them. Who they were, what they were interested in, the kind of people they were growing up to be.

Like Danielle Perez, a cheerleader. But not just a cheerleader. She planned to be a doctor. She was such a pretty girl. She had a mole above her lip, like a beauty mark.

She had a dog named Tippy.

Barbara couldn't believe Joe Till would shoot all those kids. Why would he?

But then she thought of him lying next to her in bed.

His fingers trailing over her throat.

The strength in those fingers, the idea suddenly coming to her that he could snap her neck in a moment. Why would she think that? Why would that even occur to her?

It should *never* have occurred to her.

This was not just her imagination.

The way he had run his fingers along her breastbone. The way she tried to picture his face now and couldn't. Couldn't get a grip on what he looked like.

She looked up the mileage between here and Torrent Valley, California.

Expected to be wrong about it.

But the mileage only muddied the waters. An hour and fifty minutes up, an hour and fifty minutes back. And some time in between.

Maybe that was time enough to shoot up the school. Maybe he went there every day because he had an obsession—he *planned* to kill those kids. That's what killers did. They planned their crimes, blocked it out the way they wanted it to go. Fantasized.

Although he didn't seem like a fantasizer. He was more of a nuts-and-bolts person—straightforward.

But what did her mother always say? Still waters run deep. Till was gone for around five hours every day of the week. Five days a week. Schools were only open on weekdays. Maybe he watched the high school students leaving school. Why would he do that if he weren't planning something?

And yesterday, the day those children were shot?

He didn't come home.

He was gone. As her brother Justin, who had been an MP in the military and was now a cop in civilian life, would say, "He's in the wind."

Only he wasn't in the wind.

She knew in her heart he was in a cold-storage locker at the medical examiner's office.

Barbara thought about something else: the one time she wanted her groom Mario to take a picture of them together, Joe had said no.

He didn't say any of the things that most people would say: "I hate the way I look" or "I just don't like to have my picture taken." He said flat out: "Don't take a picture of me."

He was serious when he said it.

What she'd done next was willful. She'd wanted to share him with her friends. For one thing, she thought that finally she'd met a real man. A man who was gentle, smart, considerate, but still male. She had always been the kind who had gone for boys, really, the kind who seemed to want a boss or a mother figure to tell them what to do. But Joe Till was his own person. He appreciated her, he made her feel good about herself, but he didn't look to her for his own validation. He didn't need her . . . *permission*, for anything. Their relationship (she'd thought) was healthy. Adult. No one was the mommy and no one was the daddy. Respectful.

So she sneaked a picture of him to send to her girlfriend in Hawaii. To show that she had finally found a good man.

Okay, admit it. A damn good-*looking* man.

He was bringing in the broodmares one by one for evening feed and bed-down. It was a glorious day, the sun almost below the wooded hills, slanting golden light and throwing dark shadows across the field. There was a grackle in the tree, its harsh repetitive call making a piercing noise. She took a picture of the grackle with her phone. Joe Till led the mare along the path and under the giant cottonwood tree. She reached for some grass and he let her. He rested his hand on her withers and looked back toward the mountain, which was bathed in light. He was still for a moment, just looking, the lead shank loose in his hand. Never taking his eyes from the mountain, he reached over to brush a burr from the mare's mane. His face was not completely turned away: she caught his profile. On an impulse, she snapped a shot from her phone—

—and sent it to her friend in Hawaii in an instant.

The grackle was loud as a pneumatic drill. Joe Till didn't hear her snap the picture.

Barbara had been glad the grackle drowned out the sound.

She knew the rule.

At the moment she'd hit "Send," she felt something. It was like the quiet shutting of a door.

Now Barbara looked for the picture. She'd hidden it so well that at first she couldn't find it. But finally she worked her way through her photos and found the image.

His face was in profile, but he was recognizable.

Barb stared at the television set. Was she sure that the shooter was him? She couldn't be. But she had always gone by her instincts, and this time was no different. *Do I send it to the police? Just how do I do this? Will they think I'm a crank?*

Should *I do this?*

If she sent a photo of Joe Till, standing there with the shank in one hand and the other brushing away a burr from the mare's mane, what were they going to think? Assuming she could find the right person in the right law-enforcement facility to send it to.

What else do I have to say to back it up? That he drives out five days a week, and is gone for five hours? That I followed him on the freeway once? That I woke up one morning and he stroked my throat and for a moment I just knew *he could kill me?*

That he didn't want to go to Santa Anita?

She stared at the photo. The sun dappled his face through the branches. He looked calm. Handsome. His smile was for the horse. He was good looking, but . . . generic. It was almost as if his face were a slick surface. Her eyes slid right off, no matter how much she tried to concentrate on him.

But what would she *say?*

Truth was, she wouldn't say anything.

They would discount her completely. She wasn't about to make a fool of herself. So many people would be calling in with tips. A lot of them hoping to be mentioned on TV or maybe for the chance the FBI would come talk to them and they'd have something to tell their friends. That wasn't her. She didn't need that kind of attention. She wasn't a publicity seeker.

But the feeling persisted.

There was something wrong with Joe Till.

She was sure he was somehow involved in the shooting.

Those poor kids.

The only thing she could think to do was call her brother. Justin had met Joe once, when she'd had everyone over to dinner. She would ask him what he would do. Whom he would contact.

She hoped Justin would take it out of her hands, that he would feel the way she did.

She already knew he didn't like Joe Till.

CHAPTER 8

The new Las Vegas City Hall was big, sprawling, and beautiful—a modern marvel. Imposing, as big city halls should be. Phalanxes of windows reflected the clear blue of the desert sky. City Hall was sleek and shiny—there was nothing Rat Pack about it. This was the new Vegas, rising from the ashes of the older, romantic, seedier Vegas. The Las Vegas City Hall looked intimidating, as it should.

Landry parked his rental sedan on the street west of the parking lot. His hair was now dishwater blond and cut short. The glasses he wore changed with the light—they turned darker in full sun. He wore jeans, tennis shoes, and an orange knit polo shirt he'd picked up at a secondhand store blocks away from the Strip. The knit shirt had a logo: Datatec Cable. This had been an amazing turn of fortune. The shirt gave him both legitimacy and anonymity.

He sat in his car and consulted his to-do list.

First on his list was research. He had looked up articles in the *Los Angeles Times* and learned the name of the detective in charge of the investigation—Detective Sergeant Joseph Ruckman. Landry Googled Joseph Ruckmans in Los Angeles, and on the third try he got the right one. Detective Joseph Ruckman belonged to several police organizations and a classic-car group—muscle cars specifically. Landry found a pic of Joseph Ruckman at a car meet with his arm around a woman who was probably his wife. Short gray hair, beet-red face, aviator shades, a belly pushing hard at the open-necked bowling shirt he wore. Faded jeans, tennis shoes, and a diver's watch completed the look.

Old school.

Landry judged Detective Sergeant Joseph Ruckman's age to be between fifty and fifty-five. He was clearly reliving his youth in the form of a bright green 1972 Dodge Challenger with black racing stripes. Landry was old enough to have served his twenty on a police force somewhere, so that would give him something in common with Ruckman. Landry would sound like a cop on the brink of retirement.

He'd chosen the lunch hour to make his walk-through of City Hall. Inside the cool and spacious new building, Landry walked around in his Datatec Cable uniform, carrying a phone-repair diagnostic kit he'd found on eBay. It didn't take him long to get a feel of the place. It was an easy place to be anonymous—to be just another cog in an elegant wheel. At this time of day, the building felt empty. The first floor held a radio station, KCLV, which took up quite a bit of space and was an entity unto itself. He thought this floor would be a good place to start.

He tried a few doors. Most of them were locked. He opened one and a woman looked up from her desk. He apologized and said he was looking for the Human Resources office. She told him Human Resources was on the fourth floor. From the size of the room and the number of doors to the hallway, he now had a feeling for the configuration of this part of the building.

At noon on the dot, doors opened and people headed out for lunch. Pretty soon the workers slowed to a trickle. He waited until the hallway was empty before looking for an unlocked office. Some offices were open to the public, like the radio station. He avoided these, because he wanted a room to himself. He tried a door down the hallway and again encountered a woman, this one just grabbing her purse. He told her he was with Datatec Cable and needed to test a landline in the building—had she noticed any static? She said she didn't know.

"I'll take a look," he said. "Hopefully it's nothing major and I'll be gone in a few."

"Doesn't matter," she said. "I'm off to lunch. Make yourself at home."

He grinned. "Thank you, ma'am. What about the door?"

"It's self-locking. Just make sure you close it on your way out."

"Sure thing."

She left and he sat down at the desk and lifted the receiver.

He dialed nine and the number for the Torrent Valley PD. When the operator answered, he identified himself as a homicide detective and asked to speak to Detective Sergeant Joseph Ruckman in the Homicide Division. "It's about the Gordon C. Tuttle High School shooting."

"Your name again?"

"Detective Jim Branch, Homicide, Kalispell, Montana."

Ruckman answered on the first ring. "Detective Ruckman."

"Detective Ruckman, my name is Jim Branch, and I'm a detective with the Zephyr Police Department in Montana, a stone's throw from Kalispell. I know you're busy, but I may have something similar to your shooting—"

"We are busy here."

"Thing is, we had a case that was similar."

Silence. Then, "Where did you say you are?"

"Where am I now? I'm in Vegas, visiting my son. He's with LVMPD Homicide. I'm calling about what happened in Montana two and a half years ago. There are strong similarities. When I heard about your shooting, I felt I had to call."

"What kind of case?"

"Mass shooting at a community college in the valley. Only three casualties—"

"Only three," Ruckman said. "Used to be that was a lot. So how does this fit with my case?"

"You sure got that right about the casualty number," Landry said. "These days it doesn't even count unless it's six or seven. Maybe you heard about it? Deer Valley Community College? Could have been identical, except the guy we're looking for—*still* looking for—got away clean."

A pause on the other end. Ruckman was absorbing this. "So you think this could be the same guy? What are the odds of that?"

"We have some evidence left at the scene, and the crime scene photos. I could send them to you."

"What kind of evidence?"

"Bullets. Also tire-print casts and photos. Bullets are .223 Remingtons."

"Yes, I'd like to see them. The FBI would be interested, too."

"Oh, you mean Bigfoot? They sure as hell bigfooted us."

"Tell me about it. This has been one massive clusterfuck. Crawling with agents. It's like the Keystone Cops."

"Speaking of which, I'd like to talk to the special agent in charge. You have his number?"

"Yeah, but you want to talk to the special agent who's working it—the SAC's not gonna take your call. The SA's name's Andrew Keller." It took him a moment to find, and then he rattled it off.

"Bet he's the kind doesn't want to get his shoes dusty."

"I can tell you've been there."

"You know it. The guy I'm talking about, the shooter? He wasn't a kid. He was older than that. I'm thinking—"

"Former military?"

"Yeah. Considering you have him on a slab, I wanted to see if maybe there was a connection. Our guy was obviously a pro."

"*This* guy was *definitely* a pro."

"Mine got away," Landry said, "but he ran a red light and wrecked a car, put the driver of the other vehicle in the hospital for six weeks."

"He did?"

"Must've lived a charmed life. He was able to drive away . . . and then he disappeared. Unbelievable. We think he must have had friends—a place he went to ground. Those mountains up there . . . Impossible to search, especially after the first snow. The only thing we had was a witness."

"Oh?"

"Not the shooting," Landry said. "The other driver was able to describe the car. Late model GMC Sierra. Never found it, though. It was just gone. The other driver's car was totaled. Get this: a 1963 Chevy Nova, cherry."

"Really?"

"It was cherry until this guy hit it. Now it's spare parts. Damn, it hurts my soul just to talk about it."

"No kidding." Then Ruckman said, "I have a 1972 Dodge Challenger. Three-hundred-forty-cubic-inch engine, four on the floor—"

"Oh, man. That's sweet. I had a '74 Charger when I was a kid. Wish I had it now."

"I'll bet you do."

A pause as they both cherished their respective cars. Then Landry said, "I thought I should tell you about my guy, just in case they're the same. I just have this feeling . . . You know the kind. My spidey sense. You say your guy was a pro? Why, because of the body armor? That doesn't mean anything these days."

"Yeah, but this guy was older." Ruckman lowered his voice. "Early thirties."

"You kidding me? That doesn't fit the profile."

"Nope. And he was in prime physical condition."

"I just can't wonder if it's not the same guy. I used to be in the service—navy—and this looked like a professional job from the get-go. I couldn't figure it out, why anyone would shoot up a community college. You got a driver's license at least?"

"Nope."

"*What?*"

"You heard me," Ruckman said. "Nothing. No DL, AFIS has no fingerprints on him, no criminal record, no credit cards, nothing. It's like he was a ghost."

Landry decided to push it up a notch. "So who put him down? I saw that security guard on the TV. Don't tell me *he* put him down."

Silence.

Had he gone too far?

Then Ruckman said, "It was one of our guys."

"One of your guys?"

"Yeah. It was luck. One of our guys, he's on SWAT, was driving by."

Liar. And not a particularly convincing one, either. "Figured it had to be something good," Landry said. "You get anything at all from the body? Tats, stuff like that?"

Silence.

"Was he in the military?"

Silence. Losing him? But Landry could almost feel it crackling through the air. Like minds. Two cops, smart cops, who'd seen a lot of the world. Both of them ready to retire. Two cops who'd seen a lot.

The brotherhood.

Landry decided to push it. "He was in the military, wasn't he?"

And then the dam broke.

"You know what I think?" Ruckman said. "He was elite. In fact, I know he was elite."

Landry whistled. "Special Forces?"

"I can't say. And do *not* say a word to anyone—we're not releasing that. This is between you and me, okay? We're still trying to figure out who he is. So you'll send me what you have on your investigation?" He rattled off his e-mail address.

Landry said, "Will do. But I gotta ask. How did anyone get the drop on this guy? He sounds like a pro."

A pause. Then, "Beats me."

"And you can't find out who he is? Dental charts?"

"None."

"Fingerprints?"

"No fingerprints on file."

Now Ruckman was acting cagey.

Landry said, "Tell you what, if he *is* my guy, I'm glad he's dead."

"It's possible you'll never know." The man's voice was suddenly weary. "This guy, you ask me, is off the grid. Maybe former Navy SEAL or Delta Force or something like that, and either he snapped or someone hired him to shoot those kids."

"Hired? Seriously?"

"It's a theory. Too bad whoever took him out killed him instantly."

"The SWAT guy."

"Yeah. The SWAT guy." Just a tiny hesitation in Ruckman's voice when he said it. Landry was right. Ruckman was not a good liar.

Landry regretted he'd taken the shooter out. Too late now.

Ruckman added, "Now he's just a John Doe. We might *never* know. I think he's a ghost. But send me what you got, okay? You show me yours, I'll show you mine."

"Will do."

Landry disconnected. He looked at his watch. He had about twenty minutes left before the woman came back. Ten minutes by his reckoning, because he always cut his window of opportunity in half. As far as he was concerned, that was standard operating procedure.

He had seventy-two hours at the most before Ruckman realized he'd been scammed—if he ever realized it at all. Landry had to move quickly to talk to the FBI special agent, Andrew Keller. If Ruckman discovered Landry wasn't who he said he was, he would tell the SA, so it was now or never.

First, though, he had to know who Keller was. He needed to learn everything he could about the man's interests and passions.

He Googled Andrew Keller and found some interesting things right off the bat. Keller was a member in good standing with the NRA and aligned himself with the conservative right. This was a perfect way in. Landry had pulled the politics lever on countless occasions—with people on both ends of the political spectrum—and achieved excellent results. It was easy to assimilate the lingo and talking points of the target's political faction, inserting key words and phrases into the conversation and conveying the potent message that they were brothers under the skin.

Landry himself was apolitical. He thought all politicians were just out for what they could get, and would say anything to anybody to keep feeding off the public trough. But politics was an important tool if used correctly. For the conservatives Landry used words like "tyranny," "oppression," and "the nanny state"; for liberals he used "troglodyte," "fairness," and "war on women."

But this time Landry discarded the political angle. He didn't want to go for the obvious. FBI agents, in general, weren't dumb, and it was possible that Keller himself might have perfected the same ploy. It was too risky; the SA would know a put-up job when he saw one. So Landry looked for something less volatile and more specific. With Ruckman, it was muscle cars.

With Keller, it was fishing.

Strangely enough, considering how covert and elite the FBI considered itself, Keller had a Facebook page.

Facebook was the easiest way for any stranger to figure out what made a person tick. Landry was surprised that a special agent would have a profile page, but then he guessed FBI agents were like anybody else. Looking at Andrew Keller's timeline photo said it all. While he wasn't shy about right-wing causes, his real love lay in hunting and fishing.

Fly-fishing, mostly. Landry appreciated that in the man, since he was a fly-fisherman himself.

Landry searched Google for Montana resorts and found several near Kalispell that ran packing trips for hunters and fishermen. One in particular stood out—a family concern, catering to sportsmen since 1926. Landry modeled his own imaginary family business, High Mountain Outdoor Adventures, on the Kalispell outfit. He swiped a few generic Google images he could send to his new buddy Andrew: a scenic lake mirroring pine and fir, a pine log mansion, packing guides on horses wending their way through hip-deep meadows, and a fisherman up to the waist of his wader boots in a swirling river.

Using the landline, Landry punched in Keller's extension. He reached a recording saying Keller was out of the office. That was fine with him. The special agent would see the City Hall number come up on the ID as "Municipal"—one of three ways a caller ID came out of a police station. Landry left Keller a message, saying he'd talked to Detective Ruckman at Torrent Valley. That he'd worked a similar case in his own jurisdiction in Montana, and would like to compare notes. He added that he would be out of the office—he was on vacation at the moment—so Keller should try his cell.

Landry wasn't worried about Keller getting back to him. Desperation was a strong motivator, and Landry sensed there was plenty of desperation with a puzzling case like this one. A school shooter shot and killed by an anonymous sniper? He'd call back just out of curiosity.

Landry left the City Hall office and walked down the hallway and out the doors into the desert sunshine. Back in his car he cranked up the AC and drove back to the hotel parking garage. As he reached the elevator, his phone chimed.

Keller.

His voice gruff, Keller introduced himself and said, "I hear you have some information on a similar shooting."

No hello, no how're you doing. Some FBI agents were like that. Maybe they watched *Dragnet* reruns too many times as little kids.

One of the greatest tools available to man was the ability to mirror the person he was speaking with. People love their own mirror images. They loved to talk to themselves, or reasonable facsimiles of themselves. So Landry spoke in the same kind of shorthand. He launched into a dry description of the shooter at the community college, his escape from the school, the crash, and how he vanished into the mountains. He said it concisely and neutrally—no hail-fellow-well-met. Copspeak.

"Interesting. Is your theory that we are dealing with the same subject?"

"At first glance, it looks like the same deal, which is why I am calling."

"I'm calling *you*."

Anal-retentive. He could work with that. "Do you think there may be a connection?" Landry asked.

"Doubtful." But he didn't hang up.

"It sure is a puzzler, which is why I called you. Do you have a make and model on the vehicle he left behind?"

"I'm afraid I can't share that information. You understand. Ongoing investigation."

"I understand. The man we were seeking—still *are* seeking—I was hoping we were seeing something similar. We believe our guy stayed with his vehicle, and found a way to hide it."

"Our man didn't have a chance to do that."

"Because he was shot and killed."

"Yes."

"This sounds a lot like the guy we're looking for. Did his car have Montana plates?"

"No, the vehicle did not have Montana plates."

Talking to this guy was like trying to pull a sliver out of your finger. "I'm thinking that the shooter in Zephyr favored a particular kind of vehicle. A big SUV with four-wheel drive. The kind a wealthy rancher would drive." Feeling like he was playing Twenty Questions.

"Do you have any photos of your shooter?" the SA asked. "From the school cameras?"

"Unfortunately, the school was new, and they hadn't gotten around to putting cameras in yet."

"Oh. Too bad."

Landry said, "A witness saw him, though."

"What did he look like?"

"Describe your guy and I'll tell you."

Silence on the other end.

Crickets . . .

Landry started mentally counting down from one hundred. Ninety-nine, ninety-eight, ninety-seven.

Landry hit eighty-three when the SA spoke up. "Might as well tell you—a description will be in the news tomorrow. Caucasian male, five foot nine inches in height, one ninety in weight. Brown and blue."

"Was he fit?"

"Yes."

"What kind of car?"

Silence again. Then, "Two thousand eleven Chevy Tahoe, dark green, four-wheel drive. Wiped clean. Stolen."

"Stolen? From where?"

"San Diego. Three days before the shooting. Now, your turn. Did anyone get a good look at your man?"

"The driver of the car he ran into," Landry said. "He described him as medium size, medium build, brown hair. The man wore dark glasses so he couldn't see his eyes. Dressed in black, bulky around the torso, so the driver thought he might be wearing a bulletproof vest. He wasn't sure about age. Somewhere between twenty and forty."

Silence once more. Then, grudgingly, "Sounds like ours."

"What about his teeth?"

"We're still running that down."

"Any distinguishing marks?"

"Couple of moles."

Moles. Thank you for sharing.

"And a bullet wound in his calf. Old. So you're in Zephyr, Montana? Never heard of it."

"You been to Kalispell?"

"I wish."

Bingo.

"You know Montana?" Landry asked.

"No. But I know enough to want to go there—it's a fly-fishing paradise."

"You got that right—Montana's God's country. My brother has a lodge up here just west of Zephyr."

"Oh?"

Landry sensed a sudden spring in the SA's step. "High Mountain Outdoor Adventures."

Keller said, "Where's Zephyr?"

"Oh, it's just a little wide spot in the road . . ." He consulted the map. "Off Highway 93. Not that far from Kalispell as the crow flies. Hard to believe we'd get a guy shooting up a school out here. But I guess nobody's safe."

"Ain't that the truth."

Loosening up.

Keller said, "Your brother's lodge?"

"That's right, and let me tell you, it's like heaven up here." Landry Googled "Kalispell and mountain ranges." "When I retire I'm gonna join my bro and lead packing trips up into the . . ." He had a choice of two: Swan or Salish mountain ranges. Pick one: ". . . Swan Mountains. We're kind of a cross between a guest ranch and a hunting lodge. Hang on, I'll send you some pics."

"The fishing's good?"

"Are you kidding? It's Montana. Hey, if you can help me find out if this is the same guy, shoot, I'm sure Dan will give you a free trip. All you'd have to do is get here."

"No kidding?"

Thrill to the sight of an FBI agent transforming into a hopeful little boy in the space of twenty seconds.

"Hey," Landry said. "I'm a man of my word. This shooting has been giving me fits. My sister-in-law has a daughter who goes to that college. She saw her best friend get shot. *Still* has nightmares. So you better believe it, anything you can do to clear this up. I just want to know, you understand?"

"Yeah, I hear you."

Landry heard typing on a keyboard. "What kind of trout you have up there? Rainbows, of course—"

"Oh, we have rainbows all right. And westslope cutthroats. You have to see them to believe 'em."

"Oh, *man.*"

"Say," Landry said. "Your guy—the shooter—he wasn't Muslim, was he?"

Gilding the lily?

"Nah. But he was a lowlife just the same. Tell you what—if there's a break in the case, I'll be in touch. These two cases really could be related."

He hesitated. Landry thought he wanted to say more, but he'd stopped himself. So Landry filled the void. "All's I can say, bro, this is God's country up here. What's your e-mail addy? I'll send you the pics."

The agent rattled off his address.

"All right," Landry said. "We're good. Anything you can do on your end."

"Better believe it. Westslope cutthroat trout. Never caught one of those. Never even *seen* one of those. I always wanted to go to Montana, but, you know . . . an FBI agent's salary . . ."

"I hear you. You won't believe how nice it is up here. Dan knows what he's doing—he's the *man*. He'll set you up, don't you worry. Knows the backcountry like nobody else. We've been in the business since 1926."

He was enjoying this too much. Time to get off.

"I'll be in touch," Keller said.

I'm sure you will.

CHAPTER 9

Jolie Burke awoke to the clamoring voices of the coyotes out on the *bajada*. She lay in bed thinking that Tejar, New Mexico, was one hard little nut of a town.

Maybe that impression came from the prison looming over the cotton field across the road. Or the old trucks and older people, leather faces shut up tight. *Don't you tread on me!*

Jolie loved the land Tejar was on. She knew so much of it by heart—the dry air, the desert, the aching sky. Jolie herself was born western, and yet the people in Tejar didn't see her that way.

But Tejar wasn't like Hatch, New Mexico, where she'd spent the early part of her childhood. In Hatch there were shady cottonwoods and a timelessness that moved along with the Rio Grande. Big Mexican families, roadside vegetable stands, the smell of roasted chilies in the black iron barrel outside the grocery mart.

Hatch was cheerful.

In Tejar, nearly everyone was combat ready and anxious to get started. Jolie never had to go farther than the front step of the post office or the sit-down counter at the diner to see it brewing. Discontent rode a hair trigger and there were many times when her fingers itched to close around the grip of her SIG Sauer, just to make herself feel better.

Time to get going. Jolie Burke started the coffee, showered, and dressed in her deputy's uniform. Strapped on her duty belt as she walked to the refrigerator, her mind already on the job.

Sometimes, late at night when the wind blew off the *bajada*, Jolie imagined she could hear the shouts of marital discord, the screams of terrified children, the last gasp of an illegal dying in the New Mexican desert. All these voices mingled together, entreating her to intervene.

The belief that she could ride in like the cavalry and take every hill had been ingrained deeply inside her. But now she knew that the idea of one person saving the world was a fantasy.

Now she knew you just had to keep on going, making what small differences you could, and do the job assigned you. Her dad had a saying that he'd learned at his mother's knee—it came from a hymn.

"Brighten the corner where you are."

Jolie took it to heart.

Jolie ate her usual breakfast of wheat toast and an egg, scrambled, with hot sauce made from Hatch chilies.

Her uniform pressed, her boots shined, her service weapon cleaned, Jolie stepped off the low porch of the renovated bunkhouse she rented from the sheriff's cousin. The one good thing about the ramshackle place was the enormous cottonwood tree that spread its shade over the yard—she'd rented this place specifically because of the cottonwood tree. Because it reminded her of Hatch.

The morning was already hot. The heat lay on her hair, even though it was coiled into a neat bun, and slanted down past the rim of her dark glasses and into her eyes.

She drove the three blocks to the sheriff's office, got the daily briefing from overnight (petty crimes, one domestic, and ongoing surveillance on a suspected meth house) and got rolling.

Tejar was a town of twelve thousand people. The main employer was the private prison that had gone up two years ago. It had attracted one new development on the outskirts of town, but in Jolie's opinion, the development, Shade Tree Village, was headed for failure. Tejar was a place where the recession had hit hard. Only the toughest and meanest were able to hang on—and they didn't like to share.

Which led to a lot of adventures.

Sometimes Jolie wondered what was wrong with her that she'd choose such an antisocial kind of town. A town that came from nowhere and was only going to go downhill from there.

The truth was, Jolie only came here because Tejar was in New Mexico and there was a job opening.

Sometimes she wondered who she was. She'd turned down three solid-if-not-spectacular offers: from the BATF, the US Treasury Department—specifically the Secret Service—and the FDLE.

All she'd wanted to do after Florida was go back to her roots. After the whirlwind of a high-profile trial and over-the-top television, Internet, and print coverage, Jolie only wanted to go home.

She wanted quiet.

She wanted anonymity—and she had it.

Boy, did she have it.

She drove to the outskirts of town, looking for trouble. From where she was, the town was in a shallow bowl of land, and it looked like a circuit board that had been cracked in a few places, mostly by the dry riverbed that ran through town. Then she drove the plat of six streets downtown—the north–south streets four lanes, the east–west streets two lanes. Half the shops on the main drag closed up. Plenty of cars, though.

She drove past Safe Harbor National Bank on the corner of McCarron and Juniper. The bank opened at ten, and it was just past seven thirty now. A couple of cars were in the parking lot. Jolie drove by, squinting against the sun. A woman in a blue suit walked briskly to the side entrance, went inside, and closed the solid door behind her. Jolie made the turn and drove past the front. She could see the lights on beyond the bank of windows near the ATM machine.

She drove to the next street, made a U-turn, and drove back up the main drag, cruising past storefronts in Old Town and then farther out, past the IHOP, followed by an Olive Garden, a car wash, and another bank-slash–credit union—this one for the employees of the prison. She turned left and then left again on the street paralleling the first one. Second Street wasn't as busy as the main street would be in another half hour when people commuted to their jobs. She passed a tire store, a Foot Locker, a Staples, and an older diner, Bart's—right out of the sixties with mosaic rock facing on the wall by the front doors, and one long window where you could see the people in the booths and the globe lamps hanging down from long rods from the ceiling. They had good omelets there, and just thinking about it made her hungry.

Jolie spotted some kid peering into the locked doors of the Sports Authority, so she slowed down and cruised by him and he looked at her furtively, and went back to walking. Shoulders slouched, hands in his pockets. He looked suspicious, but it could be due to the fact that he was young and the young always had something going on inside their heads. He wore the uniform: sweatshirt and hoodie, low-riding pants, boxers peeking demurely over the waistband—but that was really all she could see that pegged him as possible trouble, except for his darting eyes. She decided to round the block again. Oftentimes just the sight of a sheriff's car kept them on the straight and narrow.

As she turned left on the street one block down, she saw a car speed past on the main drag—right through the light.

Something—she didn't know what—kept her from using lights and the siren. As she reached the intersection, another car flashed past, this time with the light—a newer model, small car. Two cars speeding? One after the other?

She accelerated to the intersection. The first one was blue, a new SUV of some kind—

There was a loud collision—metal on metal, and glass.

And the manic whooping of an alarm.

Unbearably loud.

Jolie made the corner, left tire bumping over the curb, and heard through her open window the dying-animal howl of an engine, then screeching tires. Ahead of her on the left she saw the blue SUV perpendicular to the street, blocking one lane, its nose crumpled against the building, mashed up against the Safe Harbor National Bank.

An accident?

Then the SUV's tires chirped and it shot backward, stopping in the middle of the street. A car had pulled up perpendicular to it—and at first Jolie thought it was because the SUV was blocking the lane. The car was stopped dead in the middle of the street: a small late-model silver car.

The blue SUV's engine roared. Even inside her own car she imagined she could hear the clunk of the differential as the SUV lurched into drive. With a rhino scream the SUV lunged forward and collided with the building and the ATM it was attached to.

Jolie called it in, as she hit the gas.

A car came out of a side street, middle of nowhere, and suddenly she corrected, almost overcorrected, and spun to the left and up onto the curb, the front fender barely missing the building next to the bank.

ATM. *Bank*.

Two men, bulky in black clothing, hoods on their heads, armed to the teeth, jumped out of the SUV and ran into the open building. It was a smash-and-grab—a smash-and-grab wedded to a bank robbery. There would be cars from the sheriff's and PD momentarily, but for now, she was alone. The other car Jolie had first pegged as stalled in the outside lane—the silver car—looked like an abandoned toy. But it wasn't abandoned—the engine was running. The silver car that had run the light—looked like a Mazda CX-5 model. The alarm bell yammered. Jolie saw one of the men barge out through the rubble and the glass, dragging a heavy bag in each hand. She reached back and grabbed her long gun from the bracket that held it fast. She had her service weapon, but these days, you almost always needed a long gun. You were naked without it. Cops these days were outgunned, anyway.

Jolie's weapon of choice was a twelve-gauge shotgun—one of the most powerful and effective firearms ever made. With a twelve-gauge, you didn't need to be a marksman. All she needed to do was get close. One three-inch twelve-gauge Magnum double-aught buck putting out twenty-one nine-millimeter-sized lead balls would be devastating.

Jolie was qualified as an expert with the shotgun.

A guy holding two big bags of money bulled his way out of the hole in the wall like a linebacker, dragging the bags along the sidewalk. Another figure dressed in black was bashing the ATM with a sledgehammer and trying to pull it from its moorings.

The man dragging the two bags dropped them to the pavement and opened fire. Jolie took cover behind the engine block of her car. Even as she shot, she was formulating her explanation during the officer-involved-shooting hearing. She hit him square in the chest and he staggered back, bent forward, caught his breath, and put his hand on the trigger.

He was wearing body armor.

Shoot for the head.

He walked in her direction, spraying bullets. Jolie realized this was very likely going to be her last day. But she also knew she didn't have to be perfect—not with a twelve-gauge shotgun. *Head-shot-head-shot-head-shot.* She took her time and squeezed off another shot.

It caught him under the chin of his balaclava. He seemed to take a little skip, almost a pirouette, kind of whimsical, chin tipping up, and with a blurt of automatic fire from his AK-47, he collapsed to the sidewalk—dead.

At least she thought he was dead.

Somebody was in the silver Mazda, the getaway car. He was nervous—she could see him change gears and angle out past a car parked along the curb, and the car almost died. Jolie shouted, "Police! Freeze! Get out of the car and *do it now!*"

Abruptly, the car slewed in an arc in reverse, coming straight at her and on a direct trajectory with a man running across the street. She held her ground and shot through the back window.

The car skewed sideways, missing the man by inches, then abruptly stopped accelerating and drifted.

Pretty sure she hit him. She'd killed two people in a matter of seconds.

She pictured her explanation during the officer-involved-shooting hearing—her mind running on two tracks.

How many more were there?

Three more people poured out of the hole in the side of the bank like insects. Two were well dressed and panicked; the other had an automatic weapon and he was using it. The shooter held one of the hostages by the arm and used her as a shield. He tripped on the curb and the woman stumbled, too, sitting down hard. The shooter managed to keep his feet but now he had no shield. He aimed at Jolie.

Jolie had a good shot and she took it.

Twelve-gauge shotgun.

The guy collapsed in a heap.

Were there more inside the bank? Was someone holed up in there with a hostage?

She heard sirens, the big roaring engines of police cars—pedal to the metal. Brakes screaming, car doors flinging open. Shouting, "Police!"

But it turned out there was no one to shout to. All three of the robbers were dead.

Jolie's first thought was: *Now I'm in trouble.*

CHAPTER 10

Luke Brodsky, 17: Luke was a free spirit who marched to his own drummer. His favorite song was Daft Punk's "Get Lucky." He was good at math, loved his little brother Chad and his girlfriend Kristal, but his passion was skateboarding. Some of his stunts defied gravity. Earlier this year, he placed in the Central Valley AM JAM in Riverbank (16–17 years of age) and planned to go on to the second leg of the competition. Luke was a hero who pushed Kristal under her car and covered her with his body. —"In Memoriam," Special Section, the *Los Angeles Times*

Landry sat at the desk by the window in his Las Vegas hotel room and looked up from his computer at the blue sky. Cars honked and he heard a bus slowing and stopping. One car's thudding bass cut through the thin glass to reside in his gut. Eight dead. Six boys and two girls:

Hunter Tomey

Mike Morales

Noah Cochran

Danielle Perez

James Schaffer

Devin Patel

Taylor Brennan
Luke Brodsky

- — -

Luke Brodsky.

A good kid.

For now, Landry set aside the eleven wounded. He could always add them back in later, if need be. But he didn't think he would.

The shooter was a pro. Landry had read between the lines. No ID. No credit cards. Apparently no fingerprint matches. A Chevy Tahoe that had been wiped down. The SA didn't say, but Landry guessed the Tahoe was stolen. Or it could be that they had that information but were not releasing it. The shooter was in his late twenties, older than your average angry young male, and apparently in excellent condition. His teeth matched no dental charts. He had no Social, he had no driver's license, he had no credit cards.

Unless the SA had been lying. But Landry doubted that. Why would he?

Even before their meeting of the minds over Montana and fishing, Keller's first instinct would be to lessen the intrigue, not expand on it. His instinct would be to pretend the shooter was an average guy who'd "just snapped."

The "just snapped" theory was all over cable television. It was one of the few things they could say, because they had no real information. The TV pundits and cable hosts and experts had plenty of time to fill and very little to fill it with, except the shock, the horror, the stories of the dead and wounded. These Landry listened to, recorded, and made notations on. He wrote down every piece of information on the kids, including Kristal.

Cindi had managed to keep Kristal from being interviewed; all the cameras got of their townhome in Torrent Valley was the entryway—tan stucco alcove, wooden door, the potted palm that always looked half-dead, and the concrete driveway. They were free to film that all they wanted, but a Navy SEAL's wife knew better than to respond. She knew how to keep her silence, knew how not to *engage*.

His wife had always been a good soldier.

School was closed for the week at least. Cleanup of the parking lot was already under way. Landry had seen that parking lot probably twenty times on the cable channel shows and the nightly news. The blood-blotched asphalt, books and backpacks and other detritus lying on the ground, crime scene tape. The elm tree near the football field was festooned with streamers for "The Eight." At its base was a shrine to the victims—teddy bears and candles and balloons. Just like every other massacre. Everything went the way it was expected to go. No surprises.

Except for the coverage.

Still, nothing on the shooter.

They couldn't identify him. In addition to that, the FBI wanted to keep the fact that he was a pro to themselves. Landry understood that. Why tip your hand?

But it didn't help him. All he had were the names of the kids. He knew that the shooter was a cipher and a pro, and he knew where to look for him. Where to look for his kind. But he had plenty of questions.

Someone hired the shooter to kill students at random for some reason—just another school shooting. Which didn't make sense. The people who shot up theaters and gatherings and schools wanted attention. They wanted the hands-on experience of killing people, because generally they were disturbed, angry individuals. They wouldn't want someone else to do it for them.

So why hire it done?

To make it look like a massacre. To target one kid?

One of the eight. *One among many.*

Landry saw it like this. The school shooter would come in, make sure of his target, and shoot additional victims as cover. Because he was good—a trained, hired gun—he would have an escape plan. By the time the police arrived he would be gone. Problem solved.

But he didn't figure on Landry. He didn't figure on another professional across the street, across four lanes of traffic. He didn't figure that that professional would have a sniper rifle and was an expert marksman. He didn't figure that his life would be over even before he hit the ground.

Landry ran the tape of the shooting back through his mind.

When did he first notice the man? Did he see him first? Or hear him first?

He closed his eyes. Shut out the muted traffic noise coming through the window. Sent himself back to the parking lot.

He had been in countless firefights. Time always slowed. He saw it now, as if he were watching a television show. A threat here, a potential threat there. The moment the shooting started, he had clicked into combat mode.

He replayed the scene. Kristal and Luke walking to the car. Luke's arm around her shoulder, the two of them bumping hips as they moved. She was thumbing her phone. He was speaking into her ear as if he were telling her a secret. They stopped by the driver's side of the car and made out. She reached down for his crotch . . .

The other kids were walking out, too, at various rates of speed. Some peeling off to go to their cars. Some stopping to talk. Landry had zeroed in on Kristal and her boyfriend. He had concentrated on them. He didn't like the intimate way they moved against each other.

The background was filled with other kids. They were superfluous to him. But now he had to focus on them. He rummaged through his memory.

One kid had called out to another. No—he'd whistled. Loud and harsh. Boys and girls walked down the patch of asphalt, breaking up to go to their cars. A car backed up and stopped as a knot of kids funneled past, then completed the arc backward. Changed gears, turned the wheels, and drove out. Music blaring; loud woofer thumps.

The car was cruising to the exit when Landry first heard the sound of automatic gunfire, coming in bursts. It sounded like Iraq. Like Afghanistan.

A kid slumped to the asphalt. Bullets ripping through him, kicking up the asphalt.

The man in black walking through, coming from the direction of the entrance-slash-exit to the parking lot. He may have walked in through the gap where the kids could reach the sidewalk, or the open gate where the cars went through. Landry could see him in his mind's eye, sauntering down between the two rows of cars, waving his rifle back and forth, aiming sometimes and other times just mowing them down indiscriminately. Bursts of automatic fire.

Landry missed seeing it all. He estimated it had taken him a minute and ten seconds to assemble the rifle, and twenty seconds to assess the situation with the flap in the van door, push open one of the doors, and acquire the target.

He did see Luke pushing Kristal under the car.

But before that . . .

A memory.

The shooter had been aiming at a kid near the row of cars opposite Kristal's car. Stepping toward that kid. Definitely aiming. Which could mean nothing, or it could mean everything. He'd shot the kid. Then he'd come back in the direction of Luke and Kristal.

Hitting Luke.

The next second, he turned slightly away, still shooting, and Landry put him down.

So Landry had possible targets.

The first kid, and the other kid near the car opposite Kristal's car. And Luke.

Three kids. It could be the shooter had intentionally gone after three kids. It was possible that Luke was one of them.

Another thought shouldered its way into his skull.

Maybe the shooter wasn't aiming at Luke.

Maybe Luke was just in the way.

It could be he was aiming at Kristal.

Landry punched in a number he almost never used. It was a secure number he'd set up two months ago, replacing five other numbers he'd used over the span of three years. He waited for the beep and left a message. The message was simple. "Hey, bro, how you doing? Give me a call when you get the chance."

Ten minutes later his brother Gary called back. Landry said, "Speak."

"It was you, right?"

"I'm throwing this phone as soon as we're done," Landry said. "You know the drill. Speak."

"This was because of you. Am I right? Were you the one who killed him?"

"Progress report?"

"What do you expect? They're shattered. Don't tell me this is just a coincidence."

"There's a fifty-fifty possibility that it was a coincidence."

"But you were there, right? You should have acted faster."

Landry said nothing. In truth he did blame himself. His motto was "Be prepared," but he'd cut the wrong corner this time. He should have lined the van up to make sure the trajectory was right—just in case—but he'd eyeballed it instead. The flap in the van was too narrow to account for error. If he'd taken the time to do it right, if he had set a pen down on the pavement and lined it up with the pepper tree where Kristal usually parked, if he had marked the trajectory and lined the van up with the chalk line on the pavement, he wouldn't have had to take the extra fifteen seconds to decide on Plan B, to open the back doors of the van and move the sandbags to set up.

Gary said, "You do know about Cindi?"

"*What* about Cindi?"

"Her fiancé."

"*Fiancé?*"

"Yeah, fiancé. Todd Barclay. He's a comptroller for a finance company."

That was a blow to the gut. "The guy she was seeing? I thought that was more of a friendship."

Landry had seen Barclay once, from a distance. Balding, skinny with a paunch. White as a grub. Madras shorts and a limp T-shirt, boat shoes. If it was the eighties he'd be called a yuppie. They hadn't seemed to be anything special to each other. He'd thought that maybe the guy lived in the neighborhood, or maybe had a kid Kristal's age. He couldn't imagine a weakling like that would interest Cindi. But now it was clear he hadn't read between the lines. It was hard to get a good read on a situation, looking through high-powered binocs.

Cindi was the love of his life. His best friend—and for a man like him, that was a big deal. In the back of his mind he had planned for their reunion. He had always planned on reuniting with his family.

"It's *been* almost three years," Landry's brother said.

Your fault. That was what Gary was saying. But Landry knew that Cindi wouldn't take a soft-looking comptroller over the husband she had lived with for eighteen years. They loved each other; there was no doubt about that. She just hadn't been given the choice—yet. "What about the boy, Luke?"

"Kristal is all torn up—why wouldn't she be? The body hasn't been released yet, so they can't even plan the funeral."

Landry said, "That kid's a hero."

"A lot of comfort *that* is."

Gary, his little brother, the one who always looked up to him, the only person on earth Landry trusted with his whereabouts—the only person who knew of his existence—was judging him. Landry almost said something, but his other motto was "Never apologize, never explain." Their mother had drummed that into them at an early age.

Gary said, "Who is that guy? Is this because of you? Because—"

"It has nothing to do with me."

"You're sure?"

Landry wasn't, so he changed the subject. "I want you to hire a bodyguard. You have the money."

"How do I—"

"Not any guard. I'll give you a list of names." He rattled off three, and made sure that Gary was taking it down. "Tell whichever one you talk to he has to take the job. In my memory."

"In your memory," Gary repeated. He sounded like he was eating an unpalatable vegetable.

"Make sure you do it now."

"I'm on it."

Landry checked his watch. He had been on too long. "I have to go. Call you later."

He disconnected.

CHAPTER 11

Hunter Tomey, 17: Hunter was a star on the field, a wide receiver for the Tuttle Tigers. He received a football scholarship at UCLA, where he was accepted into the premed program. Hunter leaves behind a brother, James, 14, and a sister, Tanya, 13. Hunter was an honor student and Student Body President. His girlfriend, Alexis Borowic, says, "He was always considerate of people. It didn't matter who you were, a football player or a freshman. He made me a better person just being around him. —"In Memoriam," Special Section, the *Los Angeles Times*

Landry checked out of the Xanadu, turned the Mercury Marquis in at the rental car company, and walked five blocks to a used car lot where he bought a 2012 Ford Explorer with tinted windows, using another one of his names, Perry Groves. The Ford Explorer was a popular product—there were millions of them on the road. The vehicle was dark gray, a common color. On the way out of Vegas, he picked up his parcel from the post office—his sniper rifle, Betsy. He was on the road out of Vegas by three p.m.

He stopped to eat dinner at a HomeTown Buffet in Victorville. Victorville was not far from Apple Valley, the home of Roy Rogers. Landry was a little young for Roy Rogers, but he'd seen a few reruns of the television show on their small TV in their trailer at the racetrack.

He knew that Roy had his beloved palomino, Trigger, stuffed and mounted. Landry tried to picture what that would be like, but couldn't. It seemed ghoulish to him. If Roy loved Trigger so much that he wanted to keep a stuffed version of him around, what about his wife, Dale? Would he do the same to her?

It was a moot point. Dale outlived Roy. But the thought was macabre enough that it kept him occupied. Had he ever loved someone enough that he couldn't bear to be parted from them even after death? Was there anyone he'd want to have stuffed so he could touch them or just look at them?

Dead was dead. You couldn't bring a person back, no matter how much you wanted to.

He asked the waitress at the HomeTown Buffet about the Roy Rogers Museum.

"It's closed. They packed it up—lock, stock, and barrel."

"Where'd they move it to?"

She brushed a lock of blond hair from her sweating brow. "I have no idea. They probably put everything in trunks and left 'em in a storage shed somewhere."

She didn't seem too put out by the fact.

An elderly man at the next table said, "They auctioned the whole shebang off. Everything. Even Trigger."

"They did?"

"Yup. Made a mint, too."

Landry was surprised at the sadness he felt. Roy Rogers was part of Americana. But now Americana wasn't quaint and striving and earnest. It was all over the map. It was just a string of disconnected places held together by freeways and overpriced diners like the HomeTown Buffet. America was both amorphous and disjointed at the same time. But then, things weren't so great even back then. Landry recalled reading somewhere that unbeknownst to Roy Rogers, an assistant to the taxidermist who mounted Trigger parceled out the famous stallion's meat to local restaurants.

Landry realized he had been feeling melancholy most of the day. It was tied to the massacre at Gordon C. Tuttle High, but it was more than that. He felt alone.

Actually, he felt lonely.

Landry was never lonely. He had what was called an introverted personality. That did not mean he was shy, because he wasn't. He just needed a lot of downtime from people. A little bit of people went a long way, even if he enjoyed their company. Even if he liked them, he often needed to get away and recharge his batteries. There were times in his life when he was part of a team—in fact that had been his entire career as a Navy SEAL—but left to his own devices, he preferred to be by himself.

The only exceptions to this rule were Cindi and Kristal. Cindi and Kristal were family, and their proximity didn't take energy away *from* him. Their presence added to his feeling of well-being. All three of them were independent by nature, so their relationship worked like a well-oiled machine. They each had their own rituals, private jokes, annoyances—a whole history of being together in every conceivable circumstance.

Family.

He loved them and they had loved him . . .

But was that true now? Did love fade as time went by?

Did love fade if you thought your loved one was dead?

He got back into the Explorer and drove back onto the freeway. As his headlights pierced the dusk and the night closed around him, Landry felt something stutter in his heart. He found himself asking the eternal question people ask themselves in the quiet and the dark of their loneliness. *How the* hell *did I* get *here?*

The answer was clear, now that he was looking straight at it.

He had turned his back on the people who meant the most to him.

His wife was engaged to be married to some pale bald guy who worked for a finance company. His daughter barely avoided being shot to death. Her boyfriend was shot dead before her eyes.

Luke had *tried* to save her. He had sacrificed his life for her.

Luke, not Landry. Landry himself had been too late. He made it a rule never to second-guess an action—it was a zero-sum game in his line of work—but this time . . .

He couldn't help but think: If he'd been able to act a hair faster, would Luke still be alive?

Driving through the moonscape of the desert in the dark, the headlights like pinpoints that grew and grew and then flashed by in the other lanes, Landry felt he might as well be on the moon.

Because he was all alone.

- — -

The traffic picked up heading into LA—a stream of red and white. Like blood cells teeming through an artery. Every car a self-contained pod, rushing in the same direction.

It wasn't as if Cindi didn't know that Landry could disappear. They had talked about it in the abstract: "I may have to go off the grid. When it's safe, I'll come back." But they both knew that if he went off the grid, it would be impossible to come back. Cindi had friends whose husbands were SEALs. They knew it was unlikely their husbands would just disappear, but they also knew that the men they loved were trained to do one thing better than any other thing.

And that skill set would be hard to translate to civilian life.

A lot of men he knew had suffered, once their usefulness came into question. A guy you could depend on in a firefight was suddenly trying to sell shoes in a strip mall sporting-goods store—if he could get the job. Or a fast food place.

His superior officer called it "repurposing," but it didn't make it any better.

Landry had taken the easiest route. He'd worked for Whitbread Associates during the Iraq War, and he stayed on with them afterward.

He was paid well and he'd socked a retirement away. Two retirements. He did well in the stock market. Money seemed to come to him.

But he didn't quit. He didn't enjoy retirement, because he *couldn't* enjoy retirement. He was skilled. He was one of the best at what he did. And Whitbread worked for the United States government, so Landry could even tell himself he was still working for his country.

Until Florida.

He skirted LA and took an off-ramp into Fullerton. He had a friend, a former Navy SEAL, who lived there. Dan was out of town most of the year, but Landry and Dan had an agreement. Landry kept a mono vault in the backyard of his condo in Lake View Terrace for Dan, and Dan did the same for him in Fullerton. It was just another option they both had.

The neighborhood was quiet. Landry parked under a tree along the sidewalk and climbed the wall. The house was dark, but there were security lights everywhere. A dog barked three houses down. Landry waited, expecting to hear a door open or close or someone rebuking the dog, but the dog just kept barking halfheartedly, and finally stopped. Landry headed for the back terrace. Standing at the edge of the terrace was a large Mexican Talavera flowerpot.

He hauled the pot sideways. Instead of the brick that covered the rest of the terrace, the place where the flowerpot had been was a round patch of dirt. Landry brushed away the dirt and unscrewed the polyurethane lid, setting it to the side, and aimed his flashlight down into the vault. There was the packet, wrapped in oilskin: a passport and a driver's license under the name Jeffery Peterman.

Landry was out in five and back on the freeway in nine.

He went south to I-8, and found a hotel just off the freeway in El Cajon, east of San Diego. He checked in using Jeffery Peterman's driver's license.

Thinking about the kids.

Inside the room, Landry fired up the laptop and searched for articles on the shooting. Right at the top on Google was a new story from the *Los Angeles Times*, perfect for his purposes. Profiles of the kids who were shot and killed, one paragraph each.

He lay against the headboard fully clothed, propped up against the pillows, and read the story.

Luke first.

Luke was seventeen. The photo they had of him was a selfie. To his right Landry saw a bare shoulder and a swatch of longish dark blond hair that might have belonged to his daughter. Luke's expression was goofy. With his free hand he flashed some kind of gang sign. Your average high school kid, not old enough or smart enough to look into his future.

And in Luke's case, there was no point.

He wore a long-sleeved shirt with the word "Quiksilver" on the front. His black hair on the long side. Landry knew from looking up his clothing, his skateboard, and his attitude that he was a "skater," and this wasn't just a style but a *lifestyle*. The memorial named Luke's favorite music—Daft Punk, some musical group Landry had never heard of. They wrote a song called "Get Lucky."

This was not so different from Landry's day. Kids were kids. They identified with a group and dressed that way. It was protective coloring. They tried to fit in with their tribe.

If he saw a kid like that on the street, he wouldn't give him a second look, but Landry was possessive of his daughter. He had disliked Luke from the beginning, even though they'd never met face-to-face. It was enough that he knew Luke had either had sex with his daughter or was about to. The thought of that alone had simmered and threatened to boil over if he ever came face-to-face with the kid.

But instead, Landry had remained on the sidelines, helpless. It was hard for him to reconcile this with who he was. He knew it was for the safety of his wife and daughter, but it still rankled. But now Landry felt some pride that his daughter had chosen right. The boy had turned out to be a hero.

Now the kid was dead and Landry pictured his mother folding the Quiksilver shirt and putting it away.

Landry scanned down the photos of the dead and read their stories. Nothing popped out. They were typical high school kids. Maybe one of them had a father or mother who was an FBI agent. Maybe one of them was involved in the occult. But from the short bios, he couldn't read between the lines. Most of them he could identify now by their clothing—which group they belonged to. Landry needed to pare down the number.

He had to start somewhere. He'd already picked out two besides Luke and Kristal. His choices were purely based on instinct and on the memory of what he'd seen. The first kid who was killed, and the boy opposite Kristal's car.

The first boy could have been shot just to let the shooter get his head into the game.

So Landry homed in on the boy across the parking lot from Luke and Kristal:

Hunter Tomey.

Hunter was a nice-looking kid. Blond hair and blue eyes. Startling eyes. He could have been a model, like you'd see in a catalog. All-American kid, uncomplicated smile. Not preppy, exactly—preppy was an old word—but clean-cut.

So, two ways to go. Hunter Tomey, and Landry's own enemies. He read the bio again.

The kid sounded like he was comfortably middle class. Typical American family fare, down to the football team, college, the girlfriend. He could have been living in the 1990s, the 1980s, the 1970s, or even earlier. Which in itself was unusual in 2014. But the school catered to upper-middle-class and even wealthy residents, so he fit in. Handsome and blond—a standout, but not that much of a standout. White bread. Maybe he'd gotten into a scrape or two, but as he was a juvenile it would be hard to find out if he did. So Landry took him at face value for now.

The shooting seemed random, but it was not. It was clear the shooter wasn't a disaffected youth, but a hired killer. He was good at his job. If Landry hadn't been there, he might have killed twenty or even thirty more.

But Landry knew this about the military, and he knew this about cops. You take out the biggest threat first. In this case you would take out your target first. You'd make sure you'd get the one you're after before adding window dressing.

This was truer of cops than the military. Landry's uncle was a cop. Cops looked for trouble, and their plan was to cut that trouble off at the knees before it got out of control. You could say cops were proactive. They had the upper hand and they wanted to keep it that way, so they always saw trouble and ran to meet it, to shut it down so that they were in charge and out of danger.

The cops' motto was "To protect and serve." First and foremost, though, protect and serve your*self.*

This man couldn't be ignorant of tactics.

Tactically, if possible, the shooter would kill the kid he was hired to kill early on. Maybe in the first three or four, maybe the first seven, but it was doubtful he'd go beyond that. Time had a way of moving forward, dynamics changed, the window of opportunity slammed shut, and you didn't want to come away empty-handed.

This was borne out in the man's actions. He had gone into the lot and walked one way along the rows of cars, then turned and walked back.

Another memory: *the shooter only went halfway through the parking lot before turning around.*

Which meant his target was closer to the exit gate than to the school building when the shooter started. He aimed at the kids who came out first and were making their way through the parking lot—and his target was in the vanguard of that group.

His target had been one of the first of the kids to come outside.

Landry had drawn a diagram of the parking lot, including his own position across the street. He had drawn it from a diagram put out by the *Los Angeles Times* that was everywhere on the Internet.

Landry's trued up pretty well with their diagram. There were black circles where each of the kids had fallen—the dead and the injured.

Tomey was the only other student who, to Landry, appeared exceptional—except for Kristal and Luke.

Kristal was the obvious choice, because of who her dad was.

As much as he would look at the other victims, Landry had a feeling that the shooter had been aiming for Kristal and Luke. And the only reason he would do that would be to draw Landry out.

Then his cell rang. It was Special Agent Andrew Keller.

CHAPTER 12

Taylor Brennan, 17: Taylor wanted to be a singer. Her friends and family said that was all she thought about. She had big ambitions, and even made it to *America's Got Talent*. Her idols were Ke$ha, Ciara, and Beyoncé. She loved her cat, Timmy. She was fun to be around, and was the life of every party. —"In Memoriam," Special Section, the *Los Angeles Times*

Landry was surprised by Keller's call. He would have thought that by now the FBI agent would have copped to the fact that Landry was a fake.

Must be busy over there.

"Jim Branch, Zephyr PD," Landry said.

"Jim—Special Agent Andrew Keller."

"Andrew. Hello."

"I need to ask you something."

"Shoot."

There was a slight hesitation. Then: "Look, I'm taking a risk with you and I hope it's justified."

Landry waited.

"This can't go any further."

"I understand, sir."

A pause. "Was there anything about your guy that was unusual?"

"Unusual?"

Silence. Keller was conflicted about talking to him. Landry's guess was that Keller was on to something, and thought his new friend at Podunk PD in Montana might just have some corroborating evidence.

Think fast. What could it be? Something to do with the body, was his best guess.

"Anything unusual at all?" Keller said.

"Well, yeah." There were only so many things it could be, so Landry made an educated guess. "There was. We found traces of wax on the steering wheel. Is that what you're talking about?"

Silence.

Bingo.

Professionals removed their fingerprints a certain way. They spread laminated latex over a soft gelatin pad, wrapped the pad around their fingers down to halfway, and let the mixture warm under an ultraviolet lamp for approximately sixty seconds. The wax coating would eliminate fingerprints.

Landry decided to give him a nudge. "Latex? That was my thinking."

"Your guy—you think he was just some backwoods asshole with a grievance?"

"No, I don't."

"So there were traces of latex on the steering wheel?"

"Roger that."

"You sound like you were in the military."

"I was."

"Elite?"

"What kind of question is that?" Landry said.

"Elite. I thought so."

Landry waited.

"You ever hear of a company named Sabrecor?"

"Sabrecor?"

Landry wished the guy would stop playing coy. He decided to rise to the bait. "I've heard of them. Works with the military, or is it the government? Top-secret stuff, right? You think they have something to do with this?"

"We think there might be a connection. One of their products."

"One of their products?" That would mean an institution of some sort. A company specializing in special ops, or another type of institution—for instance, a government.

Keller said, "Another thing. Whoever shot the shooter placed the shot perfectly."

"I thought the shooter was killed by a security guard."

"That was what we put out to the press, yeah."

Landry said nothing. He'd hunted at many a waterhole, and he knew not to spook the target.

Then Keller said, "Thing I want to know is, why would someone shoot the shooter?"

Landry pretended to think about it. He decided it was time to state the obvious, since that was where Keller was headed. "Maybe that was the plan all along? Hire somebody to shoot up the school and then shoot the shooter? If it was me, I would be worried the first guy would get caught."

"Yeah. What I was thinking. Dead men tell no tales."

Landry said nothing.

The silence stretched. Then: "I was just thinking out loud," Keller said. "You *sure* that was wax on that steering wheel?"

"Yeah. I'll go look for the pics, although I can't guarantee—"

"Okay. Look. Not a—"

"—word. I know."

"Where were you?"

"Iraq. Afghanistan." He rattled off a battalion he didn't belong to.

"Might've run into you. Well, you take care now, and tell your brother I'll be coming out there soon."

"Come in June. The cutties will be rising by then."

"You know it!" Keller disconnected.

Landry removed the SIM card from his burner phone and stomped it to pieces. He dumped the *LA Times* into his duffle and hit the road back in the direction of San Diego—putting as much distance between himself and the phone as possible. He guessed Agent Keller had triangulated the call.

A minute later, he saw a cop car, lights off, moving fast in the opposite lane. In his rearview he watched the car take the El Centro exit.

Inconclusive. But better safe than sorry.

He drove back the way he'd come, landed in Mission Bay, and found a backwater motel from the fifties. He suspected that the clerk looked the other way, and often, judging from the cars parked out front. It was a place where no one would ask questions.

It was stultifying in the room, so he grabbed his laptop and went out onto the walkway outside his door. It was now almost three in the morning and no one was around. Down at the end of the walkway, the ice machine ruminated. He looked out at the sliver of bay he could see from here. The smell of seaweed and fish was stronger. He sat down on the resin chair beside the door. The wind was picking up. A paper cup scuttled through the parking lot and the dwarf palm fronds heaved in the sea-scented air. Landry found the "In Memoriam" page and stared at it in the yellow of the porch light. The neon sign sizzled nearby, making him think of a busy hive of bees.

His brain felt like that.

He had several pieces of information. Some pieces would be superfluous, and he'd have to toss them out: triage.

According to Special Agent Andrew Keller (if he was telling the truth) the FBI was operating on the theory that the first shooter had been taken out by a second shooter, and that the second shooter had been hired just for that purpose. Which meant that Special Agent Keller believed that this shooting had bigger implications. The SA had been on a fishing expedition, and he had tipped his hand.

By now Landry was fairly certain that Keller would have done a background check on "Detective Jim Branch" and would have discovered there was no such person. In fact, he would have found out that there was no Deer Valley Community College, no Zephyr, Montana, and no brother with a hunting lodge.

Landry was likely now Keller's chief suspect as the man who took out the shooter.

And yet Keller had given him information—the existence of Sabrecor. In the hope that Landry would say something stupid?

What was he trying to find out? What did he think Landry knew?

What was the bigger picture?

Had Keller used a story about the cooked fingerprints as bait? Or was there a shred of truth to it?

There still was the possibility that the special agent *wasn't* on to him, in which case Landry could learn a lot more . . . No. He couldn't take a chance.

Landry had enough to go on. If in fact Keller was telling the truth, he'd learned something important about the shooter. If the shooter had indeed cooked his prints, he was a serious operative, and in this way Landry could narrow his search.

Sabrecor International. The mention of Sabrecor was intriguing. Landry had heard stories about them, but they were only stories. Sabrecor International was a deep dark secret. They worked with the United States government. They worked for other governments, too.

Even mentioning Sabrecor to a civilian was taking a chance. Was Keller trying to get something out of him?

Landry thought so. The only thing he didn't know was why. But he had to start somewhere, so he would start with the idea that this killer had indeed been hired to shoot up the school—which led him back to the students killed.

The most obvious secondary target was Landry himself. If someone suspected he was alive, they might try to draw him out. The only thing that would make him break cover was a threat to his daughter or his wife.

He removed another burner from his duffle and put in a call to Gary.

Gary responded within the hour. "What's going on?"

"You need to get Cindi and Kristal to a safe place."

"Why? Did something happen?"

"This is not a game," Landry said. "If you don't get them to go now, their deaths could be on your head. You saw what happened at the school."

"You gave up your right to call the shots, bro. I—"

"If someone's after me, if someone knows I'm alive, what are they going to do? Use your brains. How will they try to find me?"

A pause on the other end of the line.

"Bingo."

"So you think . . . ?"

"They were trying to get to me? Yes. I'm looking at the other kids. I'm going to eliminate all of them to make sure, but—"

"It's you."

Landry heard the accusation in his brother's voice. "I want to get them out of here fast. Any ideas?"

"I don't . . ." Gary was silent for a moment. "It could work."

"What?"

"Jim's training for Robby Marin now."

Landry knew whom his older brother was training for. "So?"

"Then you probably know Monica's Selfie won the Santa Anita Derby."

Landry saw where Gary was going with this. "He's going to the Derby."

"Well, yeah. The horse came out of it okay. Not sure he can get a mile and a quarter but—"

"Focus, Gary. This is important. He's taking the horse to the Kentucky Derby."

"Uh-huh. Man, he's loaded for bear this year. Has three with enough to get in the gate, and one on the bubble. So what if he asked Cindi and Kristal to go?"

"They *have* to go."

"Whoa, bud. They don't have to do anything. I'm betting Kristal won't wanna go anywhere."

"She's going to miss a chance to go to the Kentucky Derby?"

"Her boyfriend was shot to death trying to save her life. Might just be she's not up to having a good time."

"It will take her mind off her troubles." Even as he said it, he realized he'd said the wrong thing. And truth was, he didn't really believe that. Kristal was in love—at least what passed for love in a teenager's eyes. And considering what Luke had done to save her life, it was plain to Landry that she'd loved the right kid after all.

Gary's voice broke his thoughts in half. "What the hell's the *matter* with you?"

"What's the matter with *me*? I'm trying to save their lives. If the man who ordered that school shot up is after me, then he's not going to stop until he draws me out. He has one lever, and he'll use it if he can. You know that."

Silence on the other end.

"You get my point," Landry said.

"Sure I do, but I don't know if I can get them to go. It's a free country."

"Tell them they need a change of scenery."

"It's not like it's you telling Cindi. Those days are over."

"I know my wife. Her first thought is that someone's trying to get to me through her."

"She thinks you're dead, bro."

"Yeah. But—"

"Look, I'll do what I can."

"No," Landry said. "You'll *do* it. I don't care what it takes, you get them out of there, and you do it fast enough they don't talk about it."

Landry could almost hear his brother think. "I'm gonna need money. Airfare and a place to put them up."

"I'll reimburse you."

Left unsaid between them: Landry had infused Gary's farm with money several times in the last three years. It was because he loved his brother, and because he didn't need much money living the way he did, but it was also a way to make sure Gary kept his silence.

Landry believed in redundancy. He never left something to chance, even loyalty. Even though he knew his brother would never betray him. It might be the only thing he knew for sure. He could trust Gary with his life. He *did* trust Gary with his life.

"I don't feel good about this," Gary said.

"About what?"

"All of it. Letting them think you're dead—"

"Stop."

"It's just—"

"No."

"Okay, okay. I'll get them to go somehow."

"Shouldn't be too hard. Kristal used to love being on the back-stretch."

"When she was a little girl. She's all grown up, almost . . . Ah, man, poor kid."

"Someone may be after them."

"You don't know that for sure."

"I know enough not to take a chance. You know that, Gary. You have to get them to go."

"If they're that good—whoever they are—they could easily find them in Kentucky."

"If they know."

"Okay, okay. I'll see if we can make it a surprise." He added, "She'll want to go."

Todd the comptroller. Landry tasted iron in his mouth and his throat was suddenly full. *It's your fault*, he told himself. *You're not there. You gave up your right to your wife.* But he said, "You sure she's sleeping with him?"

"What do *you* think?"

"You're a sarcastic SOB."

"And you're nuts if you think after three years Cindi and Kristal aren't gonna move on. They're alive. And as far as they know, you're dead."

"I know that."

"Maybe you should think about keeping it that way." Gary cleared his throat. "It's not the same, bro. It will never be the same. It's been three years and they've moved on. They had to get over you and now they *are* over you. You can't un-ring a bell like that . . ."

"I'm not going to—"

"I know you. You're gonna try. I'm just telling you it's not going to work."

"Listen—"

"What are you going to tell them? That the guy was trying to draw you out so he shot up the school?"

"You don't know that for sure. Neither do I."

"You don't think Kristal will blame you for Luke?"

That got through. Yes, that was exactly what his daughter would do. And she would be right. He said nothing, because there was nothing to say.

Gary sighed. "I'll do what I can. I'll figure out a way, but you can bet Cindi will want Todd to go with her."

"Nothing I can do about that," Landry said.

"Nothing you can do about anything," Gary said.

CHAPTER 13

Devin Patel, 18: Devin always had a smile for everyone he met. He transferred to Gordon C. Tuttle this semester from El Cajon. —"In Memoriam," Special Section, the *Los Angeles Times*

Landry lay awake in the lumpy motel room bed with the thin sheets that had been laundered a million times. The light from the sign threw a patch of yellow on the bed. He couldn't sleep. His mind was brimming with theories and rat mazes and dead ends.

He admitted to himself that he had been looking for another reason for the school shooting. He did not want it to be on his head. He didn't want to be the cause of all those kids dying. But the odds were in favor of someone trying to draw him out. He had reviewed that possibility, going back through all his years as a Navy SEAL, all his years in Afghanistan and Iraq, all his years working for Whitbread Associates—first in the Green Zone at the beginning of the war, and later here at home.

Whitbread Associates was one of dozens—now hundreds— of private military contractors that had sprung up after Vietnam. They had gone on to spread like wildfire after the United States and its allies invaded Iraq and Afghanistan. The job at Whitbread had been lucrative for Landry in the extreme. He had been wise with his money and hidden it in many places, including an offshore tax haven. Landry had always known that there might come a day when he would have to pull the plug, when he would have to disappear. Over the years, though, he'd become complacent. What had at first seemed like a temporary solution to his loneliness almost twenty years ago had turned out to be a true relationship—he became a husband and then a father. There was a whole other world he lived in when he was not deployed, when he was not working. Landry had always been a compartmentalizer, and it had stood him in good stead. He concentrated on what was in front of him, and in many ways, there were two Landrys. There was the happily married man who loved his wife and daughter and would kill to protect them, and there was the other Landry, who did his job without question. When he worked, he put his emotions away. As a Navy SEAL, he didn't debate policy; he carried it out. There would always be pros and cons, but that wasn't his job to sort out. His former employer, Mike Cardamone, liked to say that Landry was "mission centric." Mike Cardamone also said that Landry was the purest of the pure, in that he was apolitical—he would kill anybody, no questions asked, as part of his job. Mike called him "Switzerland."

Neutral.

Turned out that Mike Cardamone didn't know Landry as well as he'd thought he did. He didn't understand that the loner had a wife and a kid, and he wasn't like Switzerland at all.

Landry thought back to the island in Florida, the place where, for all intents and purposes, he had died and gone to heaven. He went over who had been there at the end. The attorney general of the United States and his daughter and her daughter and her daughter's best friend. And the sheriff's detective, Jolie Burke.

Everyone else was dead.

The AG was in prison, which didn't mean anything. He could still call the shots from prison if he wanted to, but Landry doubted that the attorney general would be interested. If it wasn't centered around him and his needs, he wouldn't care. And Landry was positive the AG thought he was dead—that all of them thought he was dead.

Scratch that—all of them thought he was dead except for the sheriff's detective, Jolie Burke.

It was possible she might have seen him at the Washington National Airport months later, after the trial.

A moment of indulgence—disguising himself and attending the trial the day the verdict came in. He'd flown out afterward. It was bad timing that she had been at the airport the same day he was there. They had passed like ships in the night—or more like airline passengers in the day—and he was not convinced she'd recognized him. Although she did stop for a moment—like someone walking out to the car and suddenly remembering they'd forgotten their car keys.

Landry couldn't remember any other time he would have left himself bare like that, but he had, and he thought he knew why.

She'd trusted him.

There was something about trust that got to Landry. Misplaced trust can lead to disaster, and so Landry didn't depend on very many people at all. He could name those he trusted on one hand. His wife, his daughter, his brother Gary.

And Jolie Burke, the cop.

He looked at Devin Patel's memorial again. "Devin Patel, 18: Devin always had a smile for everyone he met. He transferred to Gordon C. Tuttle this semester from El Cajon."

Every kid had something they liked to do. Two were skateboarders. Several loved music. Some performed music. Some liked math, or cars, or had pets, or had fallen in love. But Devin Patel's memorial wasn't just short; it was skimpy. The kid had been here almost a whole semester. Did they have that little on him? He was eighteen. And all the memorial said was that he smiled at people and had transferred from a school in El Cajon this semester. Why was the Patel kid's memorial so short? There wasn't one specific trait or interest or attachment. By nature, the Patel boy's memorial was different from every other memorial. Even the sentence "Devin always had a smile for everyone he met" sounded canned, as if someone took pity on the kid and thought they'd throw him a bone.

Landry looked at his diagram again. Devin Patel wasn't the first kid shot. He wasn't the kid whose car was across from Kristal's car. He was three cars beyond Kristal's car, in closer to the school. He was at the far end of the shooter's outside radius. He was either the last or the second-to-last kid killed before the shooter turned back, and shot Luke.

Luke was the last, not the first. Which didn't true up with the way Landry had been looking at it. If Kristal and Luke were the targets, why did he shoot at them last?

Except he didn't. Kristal's little yellow car had been hit on the passenger's side, too. Did the shooter come around the car *because* they were on the driver's side? In which case Devin Patel was probably collateral damage.

All he had was the Patel kid's face and shoulders and the two simple sentences, but the boy's face told him a lot. The kid looked unhappy. He was somewhat overweight. His complexion was white and pasty. His eyes were half circles, like two lemon slices lined up next to each other, curved at the bottom and straight lines on the top. Cartoon eyes. It wasn't going too far in the imagination to see the kid's lip quivering. He looked both cowed and resentful—but more resentful than cowed. Like the world owed him something and it hadn't delivered.

Landry knew he might be completely wrong about the kid. It was just a school picture, and for some kids—like this overweight boy—posing for the picture could have been torture.

He wished he could ask Kristal about him, but that was impossible. And she might not even have known him at all. He decided to start with the simplest way to find someone. He typed the boy's name into the Google search box—

—and found nothing on Devin Patel, except for the articles on the mass shooting. Landry assumed that there had been one or two major articles on the shooting and then many shorter pieces, probably disseminated by the Associated Press. All mirror images of what had been written in the paper—a list of names.

There was more on what the politicians said, what the cops said (not much), what the gun-control people said, and what the NRA said. But nothing else on the victims themselves. Aside from the memorials, the kids who died got no press at all—individually. Maybe because there had been so many shootings of late that it didn't make that much of an impact.

If he wanted to know anything more about Devin Patel, he'd have to talk to someone who knew him. He wasn't ready to do that just now. Mainly because there was the other theory, and that theory was a lot more obvious.

Someone knew he was alive.

There was Gary, his brother. And there was Jolie Burke—*possibly* Jolie Burke. She could have glanced at him at the airport and for a moment had a fleeting sense of having seen him somewhere. He could have reminded her of the man who had taken them hostage on the island off Cape San Blas, the man who had then fought beside her against the men who invaded the island.

He found another hotel. This one was downtown and very nice. He made it a practice of staying on the move, to remain anonymous. In a high-rise hotel he would be just another cog in the wheel, as he had been in Vegas.

And if need be, he could always drive to Torrent Valley and check on his wife and daughter.

He was pretty sure Gary could talk them into going to Louisville. Gary was a great talker. He could talk anybody into anything. Landry had seen him sell some pretty poor-looking horses in his day to people who weren't just happy to buy them, but thrilled. Gary turned almost everything into a story.

The hotel provided a complimentary *USA Today*. Landry went through it, looking first for anything on the shooting, but there was nothing. It was as if it had never happened. The news cycles were getting shorter and shorter, especially when it came to public shootings. They had become the norm. There was almost a "here we go again" quality to the reporting. The news channels had their big story, so they ran with it—probably good for two or three days—before something else flitted across their ADHD brains.

But one article stood out to him.

"Female New Mexico Cop Thwarts Bank Robbery, Three Dead."

Landry'd always had somewhat of a sixth sense. He knew when something was going to happen, especially if it was a danger to him. He knew when ordnance was about to explode in Iraq, he knew when someone had him in the crosshairs in Afghanistan, he knew when someone was gunning for him.

Even before he saw the name, he knew it was her.

He closed his eyes for a moment. Then started reading the article.

Jolie Burke.

Maybe it was because he knew she had the ability to do it. That she had taken on many killers on the island in Florida. Maybe because she'd told him she grew up in New Mexico. But it sounded like her.

He read through quickly. This was just a small piece in *USA Today*, but he imagined it would become bigger. It had only happened yesterday. He turned the news on and there she was, being interviewed.

She looked good, like he remembered her. She had the cop sunglasses on; her hair was pulled up tight in a bun. She wore a deputy uniform. The sun beat down on her—it was New Mexico, after all—and she gave the sense she was squinting behind her shades. The female reporter had thrust a mic in her face. Behind them was the bank and a crashed car. Pieces of the car all over the road—a smashed bumper, broken glass.

"Can you tell us how it unfolded?" the female reporter asked.

"Quickly," Jolie said.

"But can you—"

"Can I what?" She had a poker face.

Somebody came over, also wearing a tan-colored sheriff's uniform, and nodded to her. She said, "Excuse me, I have to go."

She turned and was escorted away.

Landry waited.

She was gone, off the screen. But there would be a press conference by the sheriff. He just had to wait for it. He turned the sound down.

Jolie Burke, in another firefight. What were the odds? Even for a sheriff's deputy, that was a little odd. It used to be that some police officers never shot their weapons in ten, twenty, thirty years. Those days were gone. There were a lot more shootings now. Times changed. But for Jolie to be in a firefight in Florida and three years later in another serious firefight probably beat those odds.

He read the article.

An audacious robbery, to say the least. Two cars had been used in the robbery, both of them stolen: a blue 2014 Acura MDX and a silver Mazda CX-5. The blue SUV was used to smash into the glass door of the bank next to the ATM. The silver car was the getaway car. There were three robbers. Two of them were brothers. The ringleader was the older brother, Joseph Terrazas. His brother, Arturo Terrazas, was with him in the first car that crashed into the bank.

They had an arsenal of weapons, including an AR-15 and two nine-millimeter handguns with two magazines each. The driver, Monty Chessen, had a shotgun and a semiautomatic pistol. They also had forced the bank manager to open the vault at gunpoint. One of the bank employees was wounded, but it wasn't too serious—she would live. But they were terrorized. The three robbers were confronted by Doña Ana County sheriff's deputy Jolie Burke.

She dispatched all three of them in the gun battle that ensued.

"Damn fine shooting," an unidentified Tejar police officer said.

Damn fine shooting.

The statistics were piss-poor for cops hitting their targets in a stressful situation. It was not like aiming at a target on a shooting range. Mostly, they missed. They hit their target less than one-third of the time. Other statistics he'd read made it even worse than that: less than 10 percent of the time. That she could hit all three—kill shots no less—was remarkable.

More amazing than that: What were the odds that three years after Florida, she would be in the headlines again?

Until today, he hadn't thought of Jolie Burke in years but now she was there, front and center.

Landry knew her. He had fought beside her. When you depend on someone in a battle situation, you get to know them in short order. There's no mating dance. He felt he knew her as well as anybody, and Jolie Burke was not the type to seek headlines.

He imagined she would have been offered a whole string of elite positions after Florida. But there she was, in a one-horse town in New Mexico.

Some people just found trouble. The fact that she worked in law enforcement enhanced that probability.

He felt a sudden urge to see her. For one thing, she had a skill he did not have: she was a cop. Not just a cop—she had been a homicide detective back in Florida.

He needed to see her for another reason: If someone killed Luke to draw him out, Landry had an enemy who knew he was alive. And if that person had learned it—directly or indirectly—from Jolie Burke, he needed to know.

Landry was nothing if not thorough.

CHAPTER 14

Noah Cochran, 18: Noah was in drama and band. You would always see him at school parties, and he was a popular kid who recently came out to his school. Noah was one of seven children. He moved here his sophomore year from Lancaster, Pennsylvania. He loved movies and TV shows like *Breaking Bad* and *Justified*, and wanted to be a writer—his stories always had dark themes. He recently uploaded his first story, "The Murder," onto Amazon.com. His horror and fantasy stories were popular with his schoolmates. —"In Memoriam," Special Section, the *Los Angeles Times*

Landry took the red-eye to El Paso. He rented a four-wheel-drive SUV (one of the most common on the road in a common color—gray) and drove the sixty-three miles to Tejar. Jolie Burke's house was on the outskirts of town, near the river.

At this time of year, the river wasn't much of a river at all—it was a dry riverbed.

The daytime temperature in Tejar yesterday had reached eighty-five degrees, but the morning air was chilly. Clear days and dry conditions led to a cooldown at night. The air lacked moisture, which would have retained the day's heat. It was downright chilly when he reached the outskirts of Tejar, and still dark.

Lights off, Landry followed the graded dirt road to Jolie's house. He parked a mile back, in a patch of mesquites off the road, and walked in. He went the long way around, staying away from the road.

There were cottonwoods along the riverbed, and Landry set up to watch the house and the road.

Everything was still in the gray predawn. Jolie's house dark.

He heard an engine idling slowly along in the not-too-far distance. Faint at first but coming his way. The engine cut off.

He worked his way toward the sound.

A car door opened, slow and stealthy, just a little creak. Then there was the sound of the car door coming to—no click, just a touch of metal to metal.

When the door opened, a dim light flickered on and off briefly in the trees across the riverbed. The dome light of the car.

This told him something right off the bat. Whoever was driving the car was an amateur. He hadn't even bothered to make sure the dome light stayed off.

Landry waited.

Thinking: What were the odds?

Actually, the odds were pretty good. If someone planned to retaliate, if they were nearby, they would strike as soon as possible and capitalize on surprising their victim.

He looked over at the house. Still dark. The cottonwood tree dwarfed the house, which was little more than a miner's shack. Across the front was a low bunkhouse porch. No steps, just a drop-off of about four inches to the dirt, like you saw in the westerns.

A tiny breeze sprang up, dry, and the cottonwood tree's leaves stirred, restive, and then the breeze gave up and everything was still again.

He heard the click of a boot on rock as the owner of the car walked up the road. His movements furtive and quiet, but not furtive and quiet enough.

Landry followed him.

The man was dressed in black from head to toe. He wore combat-style boots, probably knockoffs. Everything about him was sloppy. But Landry could feel the anger coming off him, radiating like the heat from the sun behind the mountain.

Landry had read in one of the accounts of the robbery that there was a brother. On the run, a fugitive, the brains of the gang that smashed into the bank. He was one of three brothers. Two of them were dead. It didn't take a super-sleuth to think that this might be the third Terrazas brother, Carlos, looking for revenge. Stupidly looking for revenge.

Foolish, yes, but Landry knew that even foolish killers were dangerous. In fact, in most instances, they were more dangerous, because you never knew what they were going to do.

Landry worked his way through the desert, keeping his eye on Terrazas's progress along the road. He wasn't exactly an armored tank division, but his boots clicked often enough on gravel and rocks to make him easy to track by sound, along with his breathing.

Foolish.

Landry knew where he was going. Jolie Burke's house was around the bend. He took a shortcut and set up behind the wooden gate of a fallen-down tack shed on the property. At this time of day it was just another dark cutout in the grayness. He waited.

The boot crunching stopped.

Carlos had decided to get stealthy. He melted into the mesquite and creosote alongside the road, but Landry still saw him pushing his way through the whiplike branches of the creosote bushes. Landry tracked his progress, wishing he'd pick it up.

As Carlos came to the edge of the clearing, he decided it was time to lurk. He crouched behind the propane tank, under the restive cottonwood tree. Waiting to ambush her when she came out to go to work?

Landry took advantage of the darkness. He was close, and he moved closer.

Carlos lay down on his stomach behind the propane tank, rifle at the ready. He reached around for something, fumbled, and realized he needed to stand up to reach it. His torso was twisted slightly to the left, propped up by one hand, his other hand reaching for something in his pocket.

That was when Landry got him.

It was quick. He stepped up behind him, pressed down on Carlos' neck, and at the same time grabbed an ear. He held fast to the other side of his head, pulling backward but with a sharp twist at the same time—one good jerk. Snap. The man sagged. Dead instantly, his neck broken. The thing in his pocket had fallen out onto the dirt. It was a Twix bar.

Landry gently laid him out on the ground, pocketed the Twix bar, and considered his options.

Landry had a cat once. The cat hunted. It always brought Landry its kill as a gift. It would lay the mangled corpse at Landry's feet.

Landry looked at the dark house and the tall cottonwood tree, black against the navy sky. He didn't think Jolie Burke would like the gift. The guy was big—six foot four and two sixty at least. Dead weight. Normally, Landry would leave him where he was, but again, this was not the kind of gift Jolie would like. So he would drag him into the brush and cover him up, and when Jolie left for her shift, he would take it somewhere else.

As he bent down to drag the corpse, he heard the unmistakable rack of an automatic weapon.

"Drop it."

From the sound of the woman's voice, she meant business.

Still straddling the body, Landry dropped the dead man's arms and held his own hands high. "Jolie?"

"I've got the drop on you, so don't move."

"Let me at least straighten up. It's uncomfortable with my ass in the air."

"I always did like your ass. In fact, it was your ass I recognized—that's what kept me from shooting you."

Landry grinned but kept his hands high. "Glad to hear it, since I spent my life covering it. About time it paid me back."

"So's this a friend of yours?"

"No. And I'm thinking he's no friend of yours, either. Let's talk."

- — -

The sky had lightened to gray. In the distance, the mountains were dark blue cutouts against the pale sky. The sun getting ready to spill over. First, a faint peach glow, and eventually stove-burner red.

They sat on the porch drinking coffee.

It was good coffee. Some kind of hazelnut blend.

Landry was still embarrassed, but he didn't draw attention to it. Instead, he said, "I hope there's not another brother."

"Nope," Jolie said. "That's the last."

He didn't have to ask. Jolie had known there was another brother, known that he was a hothead, and known he would be coming for her. But the question was, "Why didn't you let the police handle it?"

Jolie held her coffee mug in her hands, not by the handle. As if she was trying to warm her fingers. Which was ridiculous, because despite the last cool breath of dawn, the sun was hitting them both in the eye. "They don't like me."

"They don't like you?"

"No. They think I'm a grandstander."

Landry looked around: at the broken-down ranch building

111

across the clearing, the propane tank, the sagging porch that was only one half step up from the dirt. "Because of Florida?"

She nodded. She looked neat, even at this time of the morning. Her hair wasn't in a bun like it had been on television, but it was certainly sleek. "They think I attract trouble."

Landry thought of the daring robbery, and the shot-up street— three bad guys lying in the middle of town bleeding out. "They have a point," he said.

"What was I supposed to do? Let them get away?"

Landry sipped his coffee and didn't answer. He liked the hazelnut. She'd put some cream into it for him.

A coyote yipped, followed by his friends—a high-pitched, manic yammer. The brother, Carlos Terrazas, was under a blue tarp, stowed in the old tack shed while they decided what to do with him.

Landry said, "Why did you come here?"

Jolie shrugged. "It's home."

"Tejar?"

"No. New Mexico. The job was here. We've got to figure out what we're going to do. I wish you hadn't snapped his neck."

Landry regretted that, too.

"No way that's going to look like self-defense."

"We'll have to get rid of him."

"How?"

"We'll figure it out."

"Well for God's sake we have to get it taken care of before the flies start showing up. Or rigor sets in. Jesus!"

Landry realized this was far worse than a breach of etiquette. His thoughtless actions had put her in a bind. She had been more than capable of dispatching Carlos herself, and now he'd made it worse. "So what were you planning to do?"

"Shoot him in the face."

"What if he got you first?"

Shrug.

"For what it's worth, I don't think he would have got you first."

Jolie stared at the mountain opposite. "Me neither."

Landry said, "I could bury him."

"Here?"

"Somewhere in those foothills."

"Better get to it, then."

Landry said, "What time is it?"

"Half past six."

"I have a better idea," he said.

— — —

They removed Terrazas's big boots, wrapped him in a tarp, and loaded him into the back of the rental SUV.

"You don't want to take his clothes off?" Jolie asked.

"No, just in case I get stopped. A naked guy in the back would draw attention."

"No kidding. This way it looks like he's sleeping."

"Crashed out in the back. You have a newspaper? We can put it over his head like he's dozing off."

Jolie produced a newspaper and handed it to him. "You sure you don't want me to go along?"

"If it's just me I'll look like one employee doing his job."

"Right again."

Landry grinned and did his best Arnold impression. "I'll be back."

He drove by the crematory he'd seen on his way into town. Nobody was there. The rear parking lot was empty of cars except for two company pickup vans. The parking area was bordered on one side by a narrow gravel alley. There were businesses on the other side, their roofs hardly visible above the tall stucco wall they all shared. He chose the pickup van farther from the alley, a white Ford Econoline, which was parked nose-in to the back of the building. The place was dark. No one around. Landry jimmied the van's lock with a door tool Jolie had the sense to own. He admired the fact that, like him, her motto was "Be prepared." She'd used it a few times in the course of her career as a homicide detective.

He rummaged around in the van and found a body bag and a box of toe tags, then pulled the gurney out of the van and drew it around to the back of his rental SUV. There, he spread the bag flat out on the gurney and moved Terrazas onto it. Not easy—Terrazas was very heavy. Landry scrawled a name on the toe tag in illegible cursive and hooked it on Terrazas's big toe, then split open the corpse's cheap black tee with a pocketknife and tore it down the middle. He pulled off Terrazas's black jeans and underwear and tore the remaining material out from under him, leaving him naked as a jaybird. All that was left to do now was remove the knockoff Rolex. He left the man's rings, which were unremarkable. He didn't want to cut his fingers off—talk about obvious. Finally, he zipped up the body bag and rolled it up to the back of the van.

With any luck they would just wheel him inside the crematory and load him in the oven.

The gurney's wheels collapsed as he shoved the gurney and its contents inside. As he was shutting the van's doors, he heard tires on gravel. His back was to the alley, so he went about his business, looking like a guy who had been called out to a death early in the morning and had a long day ahead of him.

The car stopped, the engine still running. Landry saw it out of the corner of his eye—a black-and-white cop car. He ignored it, making a big deal of checking the straps over the body bag.

The cop called out, "That from the scene on Seventh Street?"

Landry glanced back, just a quick "hello" smile, and said, "Don't know." He kept his face turned away and worked the strap on the gurney.

The car engine changed. It was the sound of the air-conditioner fan. Then the cop shifted into park. "Hey. You in there."

Landry almost froze, but didn't. He moved around in the van, like he was doing something.

The cop said, "Just wanted to warn you, better get ready. You think you're busy now."

"What happened?" Landry said, still rumbling around inside the van.

"Meth lab blew. At *least* five dead. Hear the sirens?"

Landry did hear them. They were far away. Coyotes sang along with them.

"Anyway," the cop said. "You're gonna get slammed. This'll be a very busy day for everybody. Good luck." He shifted the car back into drive and continued up the alley.

- — -

Landry got back to Jolie's place shortly after that. He and Jolie had a lot to catch up on, but right now she had to go into work.

She came back a half hour later. "I've got two weeks off minimum. But I'll be on administrative leave for the indefinite future. They've already made the determination that everything I did was well within the force continuum."

"So you're okay?"

"It was righteous. But I'm still supposed to go see a psychologist. Keeping the job is contingent on that. I told them I had to get away for a while, maybe leave town for a bit, but I'd be back bright and bushy tailed at the end of next week to see the psychologist."

"Will you?"

"I might go once. You know I had to go through all that before . . . after Florida."

"Did it help?"

She shrugged. "Kind of."

"So after you go to the psychologist. Then what?"

She shrugged again. "I don't know. I'll either stay on, or they'll find an excuse to let me go. Who knows? I'll find something, I guess."

Landry said, "What about the BATF? What about the FDLE?"

"Doubt they'd want a troublemaker."

"Troublemaker? You're a hero."

"I *attract* trouble. First, Florida. And now this."

Landry said nothing. She was a hero, yes, but there was something unlucky or at least "off" about her, and everyone knew it. First, Florida—a massacre of immense proportions. Helicopters, black-ops teams, firefights—the island had looked like a movie set for a dystopian action film. And then an audacious bank robbery, semiautomatic weapons and all.

And Jolie standing there in the street with her twelve-gauge shotgun.

Landry had seen the tabloids after Florida, calling Jolie "the Terminator" and "Annie Oakley on Steroids" and all sorts of ridiculous captions. And now here she was again, top of mind. A hero, again. And the fact was, most organizations despised heroes. They paid lip service to them, posed with them, medaled them, but what they really wanted was to get back to work, and heroes made that virtually impossible. Cops didn't want the light shined on all that they did.

He knew that deep down, they probably just wanted her to go away.

"So what are you going to do if they let you go?"

"Make a living. Somehow."

"How?"

"Private security, maybe. I'll figure it out." She looked at him. "I never told, you know."

"I figured that."

"But you had to check me out anyway."

"I read about the brother. I figured he'd be heading your way."

"You didn't need to worry."

"Apparently not."

"You know what I want to do?"

Landry didn't. Then he did.

She was not all that tall. She would fit comfortably against him, so he could kiss the top of her head. He reached out his arm and drew her to him, or she drew him to her, he wasn't quite sure, and before he knew it they were across the doorstep of the house and in the front room and then in the bedroom, the sun finally up and streaming through the window, and he liked that she had already made the bed, neatly with a quilt, and he thought, *Too bad we're about to mess it up again—*

And they fell into it.

- — -

Jolie was sleeping. It was already midmorning, and she was out like a light. Landry wasn't the best authority on human nature, but he'd seen a lot of war and he knew that she had been through a lot the last few days. She'd taken three lives, and witnessed him snap a man's neck like a pretzel.

He thought he might have taken advantage of her, but that was not the way it felt. It felt like a two-way street.

He also knew that their frantic lovemaking probably didn't mean much. It was in the aftermath of a killing. The adrenaline was up, they had recognized that they were of like mind when it came to the third brother, and more than that it became clear to them both that they needed some kind of release. All this he knew almost instinctively, because normally he didn't believe in delving into emotions. Too much overthinking.

But he had been in war and he knew what people were like. And she was acting like a lot of the men he'd seen over the years, after a dangerous mission. After a close brush with death.

He guessed that Jolie felt it, too, because afterward she'd popped up and said, "I have a great idea!" And then she'd padded into the kitchen and made them a late breakfast—a feta cheese omelet with hot sauce and some wheat toast on the side. And when they were almost finished with breakfast she'd said, "Just a minute" and "I've got to change clothes" (even though she'd just ten minutes before donned the clothes she had on), and then she went into the bedroom. He'd waited, finishing his eggs and drinking coffee. He'd waited some more, washing up and wiping down the table, and finally he went outside to enjoy the coolness of the morning. Eventually he'd gone back in and there she was, out cold.

She needed to sleep, and he needed to think.

His mind went back to the one kid, Devin Patel. The kid who only merited two lines in the *LA Times* "In Memoriam" section. Landry had Googled the kid and the only thing that came up was a mention that he'd won a radio contest a couple of years ago—an all-expenses-paid ticket to an Insane Clown Posse concert in Detroit, Michigan. The contest was sponsored by a soft drink company called Faygo and included an exhortation for "Juggalos" to "Watch this spot."

He went back outside with his new iPad and looked up "Juggalo." The Urban Dictionary described Juggalos as white kids who glorified the musical group Insane Clown Posse. Other descriptions included hip-hop (but not really), metal (but not really), and rap (but nowhere near good enough to qualify). The followers of the "horrorpop" group Insane Clown Posse (ICP for short) were described as "losers," "greasy fat teenagers," and "cowards." Apparently, anyone could contribute to the Urban Dictionary.

Juggalos were as low on the food chain as "wiggers." So he looked up "wiggers." According to Wikipedia, "wiggers" was slang for white people who emulated the "manners, language and fashions associated with the African American culture." Then he looked up "Insane Clown Posse." ICP was a duo of artists who emphasized death and clowns, using Joker memes along with their music to "tell their stories," and played to the lowest common denominator with violent themes and scary clowns. Maybe like an acting troupe with music.

He looked at the photo of Devin Patel again. In a way, Devin fit the description in the Urban Dictionary. His face was pasty white and his eyes were empty and his mouth was slack. He was overweight. The Juggalo crowd was not one of the most popular groups in school, which might explain why Devin Patel had only two lines in the *LA Times* "In Memoriam" section.

Landry stared at photos of the Insane Clown Posse, which didn't seem all that different from the old band Kiss. At least he couldn't see any real difference. Bad boys, lots of satanic stuff, lots of white makeup, lots of tight leather pants, lots of noise.

Was there an evil cult around the Insane Clown Posse? Maybe.

He heard the screen door creak open and footsteps on the wood planks of the low porch.

Jolie stepped out, wearing an army T-shirt and a pair of shorts. Her hair was pinned up in a bun, but this time it was loose and attractive rather than cop-like.

She came and sat down beside him. "Who's that?" she asked.

"Insane Clown Posse."

"And who are they?"

"Some band."

"They look like a Stephen King nightmare."

Landry shrugged.

Jolie pushed a strand behind her ear. "So what's going on?"

He told her about the school shooting. He told her about the kids, including his daughter and Luke. He told her about Devin Patel and his two lines in "In Memoriam" and his obsession with the Insane Clown Posse.

"So you think he had something to do with it? But he was killed, wasn't he?"

"He could have been the one. The one among many."

"What do you mean?"

"The rest could have been shot to make it look like a school shooting. The shooter was supposed to get away."

She frowned and rested her elbow on her knee and her fist under her chin. "You think?"

"I think. But I don't know." He didn't add that it was most likely that the "one among many" was his own daughter.

"It's a place to start, I guess." Then she looked into his eyes. Her eyes were clear and forthright. They were gray blue or gray green, depending on the light. He remembered that from their time on the island. "What are you going to do next?" she asked.

"I need to find out who's behind this."

"Behind the shooting? How do you do that?"

"I was thinking you could help."

"Help?"

"I was thinking you could take a look at the kids who were killed."

"Me?"

He showed her the pages torn from the newspaper. "It's online— easy to find. I thought you could look into their backgrounds, see if anything crops up."

She unfolded the two pages and looked at the memorials and the photos. "But they're in LA."

"I thought you could look into it—see if you can find any leads."

"I'm not there. I don't think—"

"Maybe you can narrow it down."

She pushed a strand of hair behind her ear and looked at him with her clear eyes. "That's a tall order, trying to do it just from what you have here."

"And what's on the Internet."

"And what are you going to do while I run down leads?"

"I'm going to do what I do best—find out who the shooter is."

A crease materialized between her brows. "How are you going to do that? I heard they can't identify him. The guy—"

"—was a pro."

"So? There are a lot of those around."

"There are ways to find people."

"Like how?"

"Make people come to me."

She looked at him, mystified. Finally, she said, "How do you do that?"

He said, "By going to Austria."

CHAPTER 15

Danielle Perez, 18: Danielle was a cheerleader who planned to become a doctor. She had her eyes set on UCLA's premed program. Danielle received several citations and awards for working with animal and children's charities. Her favorite musical group was Imagine Dragons and she recently saw them in concert. She spoke fluent Spanish, loved to ride in the Alameda Creek on her horse, Teddy, and lavished love on her dachshund, Tippy. She is survived by her parents and her sister, Jessica. —"In Memoriam" Special Section, the *Los Angeles Times*

Landry sat at an outdoor table at the Café Angelika in Graz, Austria. He was on display. He had dressed in a black short-sleeved tee that revealed his upper-body musculature and his one tattoo—a snarling mountain lion's head. He wore tan combat-style cargo pants with Velcroed pockets up and down the legs, combat boots, and aviators that both reflected the Graz scene and hid his eyes. His hair was short but not too short—he wasn't military, but he still adhered to rigid grooming. He sat by himself, his back to the shaded wall of the café, a steaming cup of coffee near his fingertips. His posture conveyed relaxed awareness—that he was cognizant of his surroundings, alert to possible danger, and watchful. This was what the people he was seeking would expect to see.

Even behind the mirrored aviators, beyond his stillness, it was clear that his eyes roved the square constantly.

Landry was telling them—the people who mattered, the people who knew—that he was available, and that they would have to come to *him*.

If you want a terrorist, go to Yemen.

If you want an assassin, float through Austria.

Using the Jeffery Peterman alias, Landry had booked a flight from El Paso, Texas, to Graz, Austria, at the bargain price of $1,195.

Landry knew that the right people would immediately recognize who and what he was. Austria was a hub—an easy jumping-off place to other countries. Civilians were used to strangers, people with unknown agendas, hanging around the cafés. They ignored him—live and let live.

He'd put out feelers since arriving yesterday. A few words here, a few words there. Most of those words were confined to the Reisebüro Fasching, a travel agency tucked inside the picturesque Gasthof, Hotel Sonnenblick ("Hotel Sunshine"), where he stayed. Hotel Sonnenblick was at the edge of the city, up a road that wound through a spectacular forest. The Gasthof had a fine view, good food, few tourists, and a beautiful open-air terrace. The travel agency tucked inside never seemed to have clients. It was a small cubby with posters of trams and scenic river trips and Alpine ski vacations. The man who ran the travel agency knew Landry from years ago when he had helped them move a client out of Bosnia.

A long time ago, but the man was still there, still working both sides of the fence.

Landry had presented his credentials—the clean passport and a United States DL for Jeffery Peterman. They were the real thing, as far as anyone who knew anything was concerned. If they weren't picture-perfect credentials, the people who mattered would see through them immediately. Landry had waited a long time to use Jeffery Peterman. He'd made sure to keep Jeffery's passport current.

And so he visited various cafés and waited.

People came by, checking him out. Sitting at a table next to him, striking up a simple conversation, a quick word here and there.

And then they were gone.

Graz was the second-largest city in Austria. It was also very old. The year Landry first saw Graz, circa 1992, he encountered a few old German Nazis on the *Strassenbahn*. These men wore the traditional lederhosen, smelled bad, and radiated hatred. He saw one of them kick an old woman down the steps of the tram and slash at her with his cane.

Later that night, the old man died of a stroke in the Gasthof where he'd been staying.

It looked like natural causes.

Graz was a sophisticated, culturally alive city with classically elegant buildings dating back to medieval times, many stunning modern buildings, incredibly efficient public transportation, and a thriving arts and music scene. But the crumbling underneath hinted at the not-so-secret story of Austria. Beautiful as it was, Graz—and Austria itself—was a Baskin-Robbins for specialists: there was something for everybody. Austria's law-enforcement entities were loosely controlled. It was a place where operators could always connect with potential employers. A reliable marketplace.

Most of the old Nazis were gone now. But in their place were hard men for the taking in Austria. Men with skills.

The police looked the other way. They wanted no trouble. They did not generally draw their firearms, no matter what the confrontation.

And so Landry sat on display in various cafés and waited, sometimes in the shade, sometimes in the sun, the ancient wall at his back, attentive to those who came and sat nearby to check him out. Sipping his coffee and watching the Strassenbahns load and disgorge their human cargo. The trams were more modern than he remembered, although the old ones—green and yellow—still plied the streets. They ran like caterpillars, fast and efficient, alongside the traffic, the whistle and hum of the lines above them a constant sound. Slowing and stopping and starting off again—endless. The indoor and outdoor cafés were plentiful. People walked through the streets and squares, shopping in the open air. Wares pulled out onto old stoneflagged walkways in the shadows of ornate old buildings. The young and the old alike going through racks and racks of clothing.

Landry had set his line and now he waited for a bite. He didn't need a cardboard sign to alert the people he wanted to meet with.

He was in excellent shape. You knew he was the real thing just by looking at him. By his stillness, by his attitude, he made his presence known. He struck up conversations in the open-air cafés, bars, and restaurants. He never mentioned what he did for a living; they always danced around it. Just general stuff. The waiter might leave a card for him along with the check.

Everything he did fit the mold. He walked with his hands loose at his sides but you could see that he was ready.

He looked at his watch. Just past one in the afternoon. He'd been on display long enough.

He took the Strassenbahn back to the Hotel Sonnenblick, aware of the eyes on him. Aware of the people who sat on the Strassenbahn with him. Most of them looked down—reading. Or looked out the windows. Mostly impassive, involved with their own thoughts and lives.

He walked from the tram up the short road to the Gasthof.

His room was in the back. He headed up the outside stone steps and went in through the side door, then up the hall to his room. He checked to see that the thread still ran from the doorknob to the jamb.

Listened at the door.

Prepared himself for anything.

He stood to the side and pushed the door open.

Nothing. The room was in darkness, except for a lozenge of golden light from the window. He could see the furniture. Everything as he had left it. The coffee cup on the little table. The book next to it. The bed still unmade, the quilt still sculpted in such a way that he could see a full sunflower emblazoned on the cloth.

As he reached to turn on the light, he felt it: almost like electricity. Displaced air. He had already tensed, was already turning, when the blow obliterated his thoughts.

CHAPTER 16

Mike Morales, 17: Mike belonged to the Gordon C. Tuttle HS Chess Club. He loved to work on cars. His pride and joy was a 1999 Ford Mustang he refurbished with his father. His little brother, Robert, was hit especially hard by Mike's death. Mike used to let Robert tag along with him, whether it was to a concert or Chuck E. Cheese's. Recently Mike took Robert to his first Comic Con. Mike was also a star athlete, participating in track and field. —"In Memoriam," Special Section, the *Los Angeles Times*

Landry lay on the floor, something crushing hard between his shoulder blades, holding him down. A knee? Or a foot? The lights in his brain blinked out for a moment, then came back to immense pain. The pain throbbed from his ear to the base of his skull and pulsated like a beating heart.

Someone kicked his legs apart and confiscated both handguns and the knife strapped to his leg.

A rough voice snarled, "Pussy!"

Landry strained to see over his shoulder, head hurting like a son of a bitch. "I know you," he said.

A light snapped on.

"Every night in your dreams, Pretty Boy," Eric Blackburn said.

Landry didn't laugh because he knew from experience it would hurt too much. Instead, he said, "That's why we called you Hard-on, sweet lips." He wished his head and neck would stop pulsing, but at least he knew he would live. "Can you take your foot off me now?"

"Sure thing."

Landry rose to a seated position and leaned back against the door. "If you knew it was me, why the hell did you hit me?"

"Because I could?"

The man looked broad and even heavy, but Landry knew he was all muscle. He had a day-old beard (he always had a day-old beard) and the red hair that wasn't in a ponytail flopped in his face.

Landry massaged his neck.

Eric held out his hand, helping Landry to his feet. "Good to see you, friend," he said. Then he opened his arms. "Come to Daddy."

They hugged and slapped each other in the way friends do when they haven't seen one another in years.

— · —

The two of them walked to the corner café, catching up on the way. Eric was no longer with SEAL Team 3. He was a consultant for a company in Nicaragua.

"But you're here."

"Had some unfinished business." Eric didn't elaborate, and Landry didn't ask.

They took a table far away from the other café patrons, ordered, and waited until they had been served.

"Glad to see I was noticed," Landry said.

"A parade through town would be more discreet."

"I wasn't trying to be discreet."

"Good thing." Eric had his phone out and started throwing it from one hand to another, more to occupy his hands than anything else. Eric's engine ran hot, and while he could do stillness, he preferred movement. He fiddled with the phone, his tanned face inscrutable behind his dark glasses. "You're supposed to be dead, is what I hear," he said.

"It's all relative. I heard the same about you."

Eric grinned, making him look like a friendly alligator, which was an oxymoron. Eric himself was an oxymoron: family man, devout Christian, SEAL, and hired mercenary. "Your picture was floating through the Toolshed, so I snagged it."

"Glad this wasn't all for naught."

"No way it was for naught. Got your contract, too." He set the phone down, leaned back, and stretched out his legs. He crossed his tennis-shoed feet at the ankles. "Seriously, dude, the people I work with wouldn't be happy about the way you're sniffing around."

"Oh?"

"They asked me to find out your prospective intentions."

"Who are your people?"

Eric smiled and shook his head. "You know I can't tell you that. So. What's the story?"

Landry saw no reason not to tell the truth.

After he was finished, Eric said, "You think the school shooter came from a Toolshed?"

"He was a pro."

"Not that good a pro. He's dead. So tell me about the guy."

Landry repeated what he'd learned from the special agent in California—the fly-fisherman. No ID. The shape he was in. His age. The missing fingerpads.

"No car?"

"No car. Unless they've found it since then."

"Someone dropped him off."

"What I think." An accomplice. An accomplice who got away.

Eric shook his head. "Man, this is gonna be tough. I heard you died in Florida."

"Somebody got that wrong."

"So what happened? I heard it was a clusterfuck—Whitbread Associates dissolved its partnership a little bit too rapidly, you know what I'm saying. Heard you ended up in the drink."

"I'm still here."

Eric grinned, his face thoughtful. "Yeah, you know the saying, right? 'Never assume a frogman is dead until you find the body.' No one knows you're alive?"

"My brother. He picked me up."

"No one else?"

Landry thought about the cop, Jolie Burke. "No one."

"I heard there were helicopters."

"Two helos, yeah. One got blown up on the island. The other one was gone by then. The storm."

"Could've seen you, bro."

Landry shrugged. "Could have, but didn't."

But was he sure about that? He'd swum for hours. There were times when he'd drifted, at the brink of unconsciousness. But there was no way the helo would be flying then. In the storm, in the night, especially after everything had ended and the only thing to do was escape.

No way the helo would fly during a cat-2 storm.

Eric said, "Damn. Who would hire a guy to shoot up a school? That's cold." He tilted his head sideways a little and regarded his old friend. "Tell you what I'll do. I'll leave your name and creds up and we'll see what happens. Who knows? Maybe you'll get a bite yet."

"Thanks, bro."

They split up after that. Landry headed back to the Gasthof, and Eric for parts unknown.

- — -

Jolie had a friend of a friend who had access to photos of the scene. They were not crime scene photos—those would be kept under wraps—but a TV news photog with a telephoto lens had shot them from a helicopter a day after the shooting. There were at least two hundred photos, most of them similar to one another, although they were shot from slightly different angles as the helo circled. All they showed were crime scene tape and tiny police markers on the asphalt—and those were blurry. The markers pointed out the spot where a shooting victim fell. Each marker corresponded to its own bloodstain. By then everything else had been gathered up—the kids' possessions, the spent ammunition, each round circled by shiny orange paint before removal.

The markers were distributed from the entrance to the parking lot about halfway through. A grouping of markers had been placed about two-thirds of the way in, and Jolie tried to make sense of the pattern—five grouped within a few yards of one another. She compared the photos to a schematic her friend's cop friend had drawn for her and sent by iPhone. It was not accurate, just a sketch from what she remembered at the scene, but Jolie had also compared these photos with the sketch in the *Los Angeles Times* and they were very close. She looked for discrepancies but found nothing major.

She blew up and pasted together sixteen squares shot from the helicopter and put them up on the wall of her den. She paired the names with the photos and saw that the center of the grouping were two girls and a boy: Danielle Perez, Taylor Brennan, and Hunter Tomey.

One car space away was a fourth victim, Devin Patel. The Juggalo boy.

Jolie read and reread the biographies. She grouped the kids by what they had in common. She grouped them by where they were in the parking lot.

Nothing she saw made goosebumps of recognition walk up her back.

There was no thrill in her gut.

She made calls. She got through to a police sergeant in Torrent Valley who spoke briefly, cop to cop. (She'd told him that one of the kids had a father in Tejar.) He gave her nothing. The only thing he let slip was his contempt for the story that the security guard had killed the shooter.

"Can you elaborate on that?"

"Nope, sure can't."

Frustrating.

She was on the outs. She was on leave, and although Jolie had used her full rank as a police officer, it didn't get her very far.

Thing was, it *looked* like a random shooting. Like your typical rampage shooting.

Except for what Landry had told her. He had seen the guy and he said he was a pro. He should know, because he'd seen the guy through a sniper scope—right before he bit the dust.

It was impossible to do anything from here. Jolie realized that almost immediately, even though she kept trying.

I could fly out there. God only knew she had the time now. Try and talk to the families. But she couldn't act in her official capacity.

And where would she start?

All that studying and she came back to the same conclusion Cyril Landry had come to.

Maybe it was Luke Brodsky and an attempt on Kristal Landry's life. But maybe it was Danielle Perez, or Taylor Brennan, or Hunter Tomey.

Or maybe, it was Devin Patel.

Or none of the above. Maybe it was completely random.

Just another school shooting.

- — -

Even though Landry had made it known where he was staying, no one contacted him. No one associated with the Toolshed approached him. His alias was excellent, his creds were beyond reproach, but he didn't get one bite. Landry didn't know the reason for this, but it seemed he had not made his case.

Either that, or he was suspect.

He was careful to watch his back. Every hour, every minute, every second.

There was no way to get back in touch with Eric. No way to access the Toolshed. The Toolshed was not a mom-and-pop store sitting on the corner of a quiet street. The Toolshed didn't exist on a physical plane. If no one was interested in Landry's wares—in his skills—they would pass him up, and he'd never know.

He wasn't surprised.

Anyone who needed access to a Toolshed was naturally suspicious and careful, and would prefer to connect with someone they'd worked with before.

At least he knew that Eric would keep his mouth shut. He didn't know much else, but he knew that. It was written in stone.

He waited one more day, just in case, then made his reservation to fly back to the United States.

The trip had not been for nothing. Jeffery Peterman was still circulating through the system. If someone did show interest, they would find him. He had set his lines, and now all he could do was wait—and hope—for a catch.

He would have to wait for them to come to him.

CHAPTER 17

Cam had just started to drift off when the truck gunner came into the tent.

"Sorry to be the bearer of bad news, Lieutenant, but we drew the short straw and we're on night patrol."

Good news and bad news. The scouting part was good. The flying bullets were not. As his cliché-spouting sister would say, you have to break a few eggs.

He just didn't want to be the egg that got broke.

He slid his vest over his head, pulled on his helmet, and chambered his nine-millimeter handgun. He holstered the weapon, charged his M-16, and was good to go.

The heat was constant, along with the flies. It was worse tonight, pushing back at him. He felt like he was trudging uphill. Rumors about "field money" were flying. He had no idea how that got started. No one believed it. Some of the guys he was with knew what he knew, and waited for the chance he waited for. Cam's mind worked overtime as he trudged through the heat and the darkness. His eyes went to his feet—a habit he wished he could break.

He heard it first: the loud clang of a bolt charging a .50 caliber. Close. Close enough to stir the hairs on his arms, enough to send his internal organs backpedaling into the center of his body.

He looked up from the desert floor at the Humvee, into the barrel of the .50 caliber.

"Thought I'd wake you up," the gunner said. The .50 pointed right at Cam's head.

Cam sucked in a breath and held it.

"Hahahaha! You should see your face!"

Cam was his superior, but he said nothing. The rules were different out here.

There was a group of borderline head cases and psychopaths in his unit. To face this shit every day, you almost had to be.

The guy cackled and another soldier joined him.

Cam knew that some of these guys called him "the Boy Wonder." Maybe because he was a commissioned officer, he was younger than them, and they had to take his orders.

He knew they despised him, but they depended on him, too. He was the brains of this outfit, but even so, he never turned his back on them.

They drove out in a funnel of dust. Cam and his boys. Jedediah, who came from a religious family, and Martin, whose family came from Mexico. The rest were not worth burying, except to worry they might shoot you in your sleep. Cam, Jedediah, and Martin. The Three Amigos. And guess who would come out of this deployment smelling like a rose? Not the psychopaths.

Pretty soon they were out in the godforsaken middle of nowhere. They had already gone far beyond the patrol perimeter, which was fine by Cam because he was always, always scouting.

The moon was full. In the distance Cam saw a small structure. An old farmhouse, out here where the farm fields had dried up and blown away and the few houses in the area were empty and blackened from fire. This place was no different.

He happened to glance over at Willets, the gunner who had tried to scare him. Who had scared him.

Willets caught him looking, and even though the man's face was mostly covered by his headgear, Cam could see the look the gunner gave him. Fear knifed into his entrails.

Willets pointed at him and nodded.

Coming up on the right was a slice of the river, and a shot-up palm grove.

Everyone in the Humvee suddenly clammed up. They seemed to draw into themselves, like snails into their shells.

The bad feeling spread over them.

Cam was aware that the gunner's finger was on the trigger. His M-16 casually pointing Cam's way. But there was nothing casual about the man's feelings. They radiated off him like heat from a stove. They came across the distance between them, and Cam knew the man's hatred was so deep that he meant to kill him.

"I hear you got something going," the gunner said.

Cam said nothing.

"Hey! Lieut, you hear me? I want to know what it is!"

The gunner opened his mouth just as a sibilant rush of air told Cam to get down—now! He did. The rifle crack came two seconds behind the sound, two seconds after the gunner's chest burst from the inside like a rotten pomegranate, juice flying everywhere.

The driver swung the Humvee around fast and they hightailed it out of there, zigzagging to avoid fire.

They made it past the doorless, windowless building, and around the back. The shooting had come from a palm grove. The driver pushed the gunner away and took control of the .50.

He shot into the grove.

But there was no screaming, no return fire.

They were fighting phantoms.

Then he turned the .50 on the Iraqi farmhouse—just in case.

The concrete block was maybe thirty feet in length, no windows, not even frames. No roof, just a skeleton of a house in the middle of nowhere, and the driver pulled the trigger and blew the thing to smithereens.

As the smoke and dust drifted away, Cam could see the house had been disintegrated into nothing but the first line of concrete block, only inches above the sand—nowhere for insurgents to hide.

SOP was to go forward, secure the area, and verify the kills.

But the driver scrambled back behind the wheel and they peeled away.

"Where the hell are we going?" Cam said. He was the superior officer, but the driver ignored him. "We've got some prodding to do!"

"Screw that," the driver said. "There ain't nothin' to check out. Hostile parties might be—"

"Turn around and go back now."

For answer, the driver put the pedal to the metal.

Cam could feel the eyes of the crew on him. The moonlight gleaming off the planes of their blackened faces, their eyes glittering.

If you knew what I knew.

But even his guys, even the ones he'd always depended on, were looking at him differently.

They'd turned on him in an instant. Their eyes gleaming like shiny bug carapaces. All of them.

Hating him silently.

Which wasn't true at all. He'd commanded respect and appreciation from his men, even though some of them were psychopaths and killers.

A whistling sound. Someone yelled "Duck!" and—

- — -

Something tickled his bare foot. Cam burst out of sleep, his heart chugging under his breastbone like a locomotive.

"This little piggy needs to get up right now," Duncan said, wriggling Cam's big toe.

Cam snatched his leg back. "Dammit! I wish you wouldn't do that! It's morning already?"

"Rise and shine. Those calls aren't going to make themselves."

They were in a hotel room that looked like every other hotel room. For a moment Cam forgot where he was.

Florida, wasn't it? Yes, Florida. Tampa, Florida.

Duncan had gone into the bathroom. He was already running the shower.

Cam sat up in bed and stared out the window of the hotel room. All he could see from this vantage point was dark sky through the sheer drapes.

Still sweating. Shaking. His heart revving.

So many bad things had happened. Terrible things. He closed his mind to them now. He couldn't let the past drag him down.

Steam billowed out from the bathroom. Room service knocked on the door. The day would be the same. Another state, another city, but the same. Another marathon in a string of marathons.

No end in sight.

The only thing keeping him going was the fact that he wanted it so badly. He wanted it more than he hated it.

He *needed* it. It burned him up like a candle but he would go through hell to get there, because he knew he was destined for greatness.

"You have enough Nicorette to get you through the day?" Duncan called from the bathroom.

"Kelli says she has a shitload in her purse."

"You two could get separated."

"I'll cadge some, don't you worry."

His body man ducked his head back into the bathroom, and Cam's mind went back to Iraq.

His men, their eyes glittering in their hollowed-out sockets.

The hatred in their eyes.

After all he'd done for them.

CHAPTER 18

James Schaffer, 17: James was your average high school kid. He had two brothers and a sister. Jim made friends easily. He loved skateboarding, parties, and hanging out with his friends, listening to groups and popular artists ranging from Robin Thicke to 2 Chainz. He loved to play practical jokes. Chances were you would see him on his skateboard more often than not. Everyone liked Jim, and his teachers will miss his impish smile. —"In Memoriam," Special Section, the *Los Angeles Times*

Landry flew back to El Paso and called Jolie Burke from the airport. "How'd it go?" he asked her.

"I got *nada*."

"That's because you were trying from a distance."

"It was impossible."

"You want to go to San Diego?"

"What's in San Diego?"

"Devin Patel's old school. He's the only kid not originally from the school district. There might be something from his old school— his life in San Diego."

And so they flew to San Diego and checked in to another hotel downtown. Landry liked to keep moving, and when traveling, he never stayed in one place more than a night or two.

He didn't know why Jolie agreed to come with him, and he didn't ask. They got along well, giving each other space and treading lightly. Even so, she was a cipher to him. Usually *he* was the cipher. For one illuminating moment on the plane ride to San Diego, when she'd gotten up to go to the restroom, he realized that this was how he must appear to other people. He really didn't know what she was thinking, and found himself wishing he did. He knew that was how people regarded him. Early in their marriage, Cindi was always asking him what he was thinking. She'd wanted him to express himself, and he'd dutifully done so. But it always came out by rote, because the truth was, most of the time he didn't feel like he had anything to say. After a few years Cindi stopped asking, and it all seemed to work out okay. Better than okay.

Since he went off the grid, he'd slept with a few women—like Barbara Carey. But this time around it seemed like the woman he was sleeping with didn't need him any more than he needed her.

This had the effect of keeping him off balance—and he liked it. He didn't know where he was with her. He didn't know how long this would last. Obviously, the endgame was to get back with Cindi and Kristal, but he wanted to enjoy their relationship for whatever it was.

After all, Cindi was seeing the comptroller.

Devin Patel's family had moved to Torrent Valley from El Cajon, a valley along the Interstate 8 corridor—part of the sprawl inching its way out into the desert to the east.

Landry had looked up the El Cajon school system on Wikipedia. The Grossmont Union High School District consisted of thirteen high schools.

Interestingly enough, there had been two separate school shootings in El Cajon. In the first instance, on March 5, 2001, fifteen-year-old Charles "Andy" Williams shot and killed two students and wounded thirteen others at Santana High School. This was in Santee, near El Cajon. He was sentenced to fifty years to life in prison. Apparently, Williams had been bullied and was suicidal. He'd used a .22.

Three weeks after that, there was another school shooting. An eighteen-year-old boy named Jason Hoffman used a .22-caliber handgun and a twelve-gauge shotgun to shoot five people—two teachers and three students—at Granite Hills High School. He was inspired by Columbine, had severe emotional problems, and had been turned down by the navy the day before the shooting.

He was twenty-five pounds overweight and had a skin condition.

Landry looked at the photo of Devin Patel. Overweight. Pasty complexion. Dead eyes. It would be easy to think that Devin Patel would consider Jason Hoffman someone he could look up to.

But that was where it broke down. Devin Patel was the victim, not the shooter.

Had he gotten in with the wrong group? Were the Juggalos really violent, or were they pretenders?

There were probably plenty of both types, just like anything.

Landry and Jolie found the list of GUHSD high schools in El Cajon on the Internet, and between them called the offices of each school. They varied their spiel. It was either very good news or very bad news. They posed as police, calling to say that Devin's father had been in a car accident and was at Sharp Grossmont Hospital in San Diego, and that his mother was coming to pick him up. Or that Devin had been suspected of stealing a bicycle and had lied about which school he'd gone to. Or that Devin's mother had just given birth and she wanted her son to come to the hospital. Jolie was very good at this. She had the cop stuff down. She was believable. Of course she was.

On the ninth try, she hit pay dirt: the receptionist at Desert Hills High School in El Cajon told Jolie that he had transferred out the previous semester, that he'd moved to the Los Angeles area.

"I'm surprised you don't have his current address," the receptionist said. She gave it out. "He lives in LA."

Jolie had used the car-accident ploy. "This is the address we
have on file."

"That figures," the receptionist said. "But we don't have his current address or phone number."

"Can you give us his old street address and phone number?
Maybe his neighbors have that information."

The woman paused. "We're not really supposed to . . ." Then
she changed her mind. "Okay, here's the address and phone."

"Thank you."

- — -

The neighborhood where Devin had gone to school was about
ten years old, and looked a lot like Landry's own neighborhood: a
maze of tan stucco houses with red Spanish-tile roofs, broad streets,
plenty of cul-de-sacs, a few lawns, a few trees, and almost no cars
parked on the street. Most of them were in their garages.

Landry had grown up at racetracks, and he'd loved the life—
even though it was messy and they'd often lived hand to mouth
on the low end of the spectrum. When he was twelve, his parents
bought a house in a neighborhood just like this—no more living in
a fifth-wheel. He'd grown up watching TV shows about kids who
lived in neighborhoods, and finally he lived in one, too. He'd liked
the broad, quiet streets. He'd liked the walk to the park to play
softball with his friends. Landry had realized that he liked order; he
liked these cookie-cutter neighborhoods.

But he loved the backstretch of the racetrack, too.

They went to Devin Patel's old address.

A young woman answered. She looked to be about nine
months pregnant. She had an open, friendly face, and didn't seem

to think twice about answering the door on a bright, sunny week-day morning.

But she knew nothing about the previous occupants. Literally, nothing. They knocked on the doors of the houses on either side of the house and across the street, but no one answered.

They went to the school and caught his English teacher, Max Caulfield, eating lunch in his room. The teacher uniform hadn't changed since Landry was a kid, at least not in this case. Max wore a short-sleeved button-down shirt and a tie and Dockers. He looked like a mix between white collar and blue collar, and it was hard to tell just what category he thought he fell into.

Landry experienced an instant dislike for him because he looked a lot like Cindi's fiancé, Todd.

Between mouthfuls of food, Caulfield told them what he knew about Devin Patel.

Devin wasn't big on hygiene. This seemed to be the thing that bothered Caulfield the most. He said it three times. "The kid had body odor. The others would tease him, leave deodorant in his desk, things like that."

Caulfield talked with his mouth full. Pot, meet kettle.

Jolie said, "Is there anything else that stands out? Did he have friends?"

"Friends? I never saw any."

"What kind of clothes did he wear?"

"The usual. Really, he was just kind of a lump here in class. The kind of kid who never did anything one way or the other, except for his personal habits. That's how I think of him: a lump. His grades were middling to poor. Everything about him was unremarkable, except he wore the same or similar clothes every day. Never any color. Just black. He just took up space."

"Was he a Juggalo?"

"A what?"

"Juggalo," Landry said. "They dress up like clowns and follow a group called Insane Clown Posse."

"I wouldn't know about that. All I know is he wore black from head to toe. Always."

"No friends?"

"He might have had, but as I said, I didn't see any."

- — -

"It's like he didn't exist," Jolie said.

"He existed," Landry said. "But somehow he didn't register. Like he flew under the radar."

"No friends."

"At least not at school."

They managed to talk to three other teachers.

The last one, his math teacher, a woman named Nora Gill, who was cute, small, blond, and looked a little like a doll in her pale chiffon blouse and pencil skirt, said she felt sorry for him.

"He was good at math, but I think he tried to play it down because he didn't want to be in the spotlight. So I was really surprised when I saw him dressed up like a clown."

"When did he do that?"

"He and some of his friends were on the sidewalk at the street fair we have every year—this was last fall—and they all had painted faces. You know, like white greasepaint? I knew him, though. He always wore the same big hiking boots. He was so big—he towered over me, even more than most. It was kind of scary, but he was harmless."

"What did the face paint look like?"

"He had these weird black triangles painted over his eyebrows. And under his eyes, too—those were upside down. I think he was stoned, too. The way he looked right through me." She shuddered.

"And now he's one of those kids who got shot and killed in that school shooting. Unbelievable."

Jolie nodded sympathetically.

"We've had our share in this district," Nora said. "I had a bad feeling about him. I didn't think he'd live very long. He just seemed to walk around with a cloud over his head. So he was killed in that mass shooting?"

"Yes, ma'am, he was."

"I missed that. I didn't want to know the names of those kids. Didn't want to even think about it. Not after the shootings we've had here." She paused. "So his family moved up there and this is what happened as a result. I guess that's fate."

— — —

Using cash, Landry bought a car at a used-car lot in El Cajon. It was a cheap, white, 1997 vintage Kia. He followed Jolie to turn in the other vehicle at the rental place, and then they headed to Torrent Valley.

They drove past the address they had for the Patels. It was in a down-at-the-heels apartment in a down-at-the-heels neighborhood in the low-rent end of town. A cars-on-blocks kind of neighborhood. The Patels lived in the Riviera Apartments, two one-story redbrick buildings and a parking lot in the front. Four units to each building, eight units in all. A pocket courtyard lay between the two buildings. The courtyard consisted of turquoise gravel and a bedraggled dwarf palm.

Jolie had made some phone calls to cop friends in the area and she learned that the Patel family now consisted of a mother, her sometime boyfriend, and Devin's fourteen-year-old sister, Willow.

"You think she's in high school yet?" Jolie asked Landry.

Landry shrugged.

"They'll be in mourning," Jolie added. "This is not going to be fun."

They drove past without slowing, parked the Kia two blocks over, and walked in. They followed the walkway up to the third apartment on the left and rang the bell.

A girl answered. She was dressed in jeans and a long-sleeved tiger-print top. Pretty, in an elfin way. Slender and delicate.

Hard to believe she was Devin's sister. Devin was big.

This girl was beautiful.

Landry looked at Jolie. Wrong house?

"We're looking for Mrs. Patel."

The girl stood on one foot, stork-like, looking diffident. "Mom's at work." She started to close the door.

Landry put his foot between the door and the jamb. "We want to ask you about Devin." He nodded at Jolie. "This woman here is Jolie Burke, a detective with the Playa Sheriff's Office."

On cue, Jolie produced her badge.

The girl looked confused. She bit her lip.

Landry withdrew his foot. He was a big guy and he knew he looked threatening, so he gave the girl some space and let Jolie take the lead. The girl seemed to respond to that a little, now looking at them with something akin to interest. They were so busy watching her face that they weren't watching her hand on the doorknob until she slammed the door shut.

They heard the rattle of the chain. Looked at each other. *Now what?*

Jolie knocked on the door. No answer. Landry tapped her shoulder and nodded to the car. They walked back down the cracked sidewalk past the turquoise gravel and dispirited palm tree and walked back to their car. They were parked on a low knoll beside a pocket park. The neighborhood was old and the park had seen better times. Now it was just grass and a couple of picnic tables, no restrooms, a few palms, and a couple of shade trees. A man was out with his dogs—he'd let them loose to run around the small patch of green.

They sat in the car facing down the hill toward the street the Riviera Apartments sat on. This was low-tech surveillance in the extreme: sitting there peering around the car's crinkly silver sunshade.

An hour went by. The windows were down but it was hot in the car. They were in the valley, after all.

Landry stretched his legs, squinted around the shade.

Took a drink of water.

Jolie was still. He was amazed that she didn't fidget. She was quiet. There was a calmness to her.

From where they were, if they used the binoculars, they could see the door to the Patel apartment.

Surveillance was boring. Landry had done it countless times, and he always had to work to keep his mind from wandering. He clamped down on his thoughts and concentrated on the ten-foot-square area around the front door of the Patel apartment.

Two things: There would be a back door, a kitchen entrance. The other: Why wasn't she in school?

"School's still in session, right?"

Jolie agreed that it probably was.

"Then why is she home?"

"Who knows?"

"Her mother working?"

"I don't know."

They didn't know anything about the Patels. Did the mother work? Probably. Most likely, since she was obviously not wealthy.

"She could be on disability."

It was as if Jolie read his mind.

The door did not open. Maybe the kid was inside doing what kids did. Probably on her smartphone. With these kids today, who knew?

There were a couple of people in the pocket park. One was a woman walking her dog. The dog seemed to want to poop on everything—he stopped at every bush. Landry wondered if the dog might have some issues with his bowels. The woman was reed thin and appeared anxious. As if she were waiting for someone, and the dog was just an excuse. Landry said to Jolie, "What do you think of the woman with the dog?"

"She's meeting someone."

"That's what I'm thinking."

"Not Devin's sister, though."

It was starting to get hot. The shade had moved.

Eventually a man showed up and met the woman. They got into a car and drove away.

"Look at those guys," Jolie said. Her gaze was directed toward the top end of the park, where there was a privet hedge and a large ash tree.

"Juggalos?"

A big kid and a skinny kid, the fat kid sitting in the shade from the ash tree, the skinny one on the picnic table with his combat-boot-clad feet on the bench. Working their cell phones.

"That's what Devin was," Jolie said, even though it was obvious.

The kids could have been any age from middle school to high school. The skinny kid had his back to them. His jeans were at half-mast, his boxer shorts—red and yellow print—peeking out above. Landry could see the crack of the kid's ass. Disgusting. The kid was shirtless, his torso a dirty tan—he was skinny but unformed, with no muscle mass. Like a stick of caramel. His back and shoulders were marred by several tattoos. He had a greasy ponytail. Landry carefully raised the binocs. The biggest tattoo on the kid's back was easy to read: "GO TO HELL," in an Old English font—the type you might see penned by monks.

The fatter one was blond and had a buzzcut. He wore a long black shirt over dungarees. The armholes of the shirt were cut out and revealed fleshy arms—huge but without an ounce of muscle. His bicep (if you could call it that) was tattooed with a weird running man holding an ax. Landry knew it was a Juggalo tattoo, very popular. There were studs on his chin, his lip, and his nose. Two pieces of hardware snared his eyebrows like fishhooks.

Landry spotted a shocking-pink liquid in a clear jug between them: Faygo.

Jolie muttered, "What are the odds?"

They waited. Their chances of seeing the kid again had gone from fifty-fifty to sixty-forty, or better.

It could be that Juggalos were everywhere. They'd just have to see.

They waited.

And waited.

It got hot, so they drove away, hit a dollar store, and bought a tablecloth and a couple of paperbacks and something to drink.

They parked a block or two away and walked out to the opposite end of the park from the Juggalo kids, in the deep dark shade of a eucalyptus tree. They spread out their tablecloth and sat under it and took turns watching through the binocs.

Just after noon, Jolie stiffened. "I see something at two o'clock," she said.

Landry leaned close. He inhaled her perfume, which was, in his opinion, light and tropical. "Is it the sister?"

"I think so. Different clothes."

Landry squinted at the sidewalk alongside the road, and saw the stick figure in the distance. "It's her."

She still wore the jeans, but had changed to a black sleeveless top that looked long and sloppy—like the one on the big kid—and chunky, blinding-white athletic shoes. Her hair was loose and looked uncombed, hanging in her face.

Jolie said, "That's a lot of ink."

She had several tattoos. There were holes in the tank top. They looked like they had been cut into the material on purpose, kind of like holes in Swiss cheese.

Willow joined the boys under the tree, climbing up onto the picnic table and assuming the position: feet on the bench, elbows on knees, hands propping up her chin.

Landry soon figured out what the dynamics were. It didn't seem like Willow was the girlfriend of either one of them, although he wasn't completely sure about that. He looked at Jolie. He'd been known not to peg relationships correctly, a time or two. "What do you think about their situation?" he asked her.

"Friends?"

"That's my guess." That made two of them, which was better than one. Both having come to a similar conclusion.

The girl was eating candy out of a bag. M&M's, Landry thought. In the vernacular, they were "hanging out." Landry wondered if the kids today had a different term for it. He remembered being in high school and just hanging out. Usually he and his buddies were up to no good. Small stuff, though—nothing serious.

The serious stuff had come later. After he joined the military.

The girl stood up and shouldered her backpack. One of the boys reached into his wallet and handed her some money.

Landry couldn't tell how much it was. It could be hundred-dollar bills or just a few bucks. "What do you think?" he asked Jolie. "What are they giving her money for?"

Jolie shrugged.

The girl walked off. Young, slim, pretty, her whole life ahead of her. Except her brother was dead and she lived in a dump and hung out with Juggalos.

Landry smelled marijuana about the same time Jolie said, "They've got a joint."

Landry shrugged. "Maybe it's medicinal."

"Uh-huh."

They waited.

"She'll come back," Landry said, although he didn't have to. They both knew the boys had given her money, they both knew that they were "hanging out," and they both knew she would come back with something. Legal or illegal, they had no idea.

Fourteen years old.

"You think she has a drug connection?" Jolie said.

"Probably."

"Big brave boys, sending a little girl to do their dirty work."

"If that's the case."

"Yeah, if that's the case."

He glanced over at her, sitting there in the shade, for all the world just a happy woman with her lover, resting her elbows on the ground, face tilted toward the few places of sunshine spattering through the leaves above.

A good-looking woman.

He leaned over and kissed her.

"You want them to notice us?" she said, after returning his kiss.

They'd just avoided a makeout session. Landry tried to get his mind back on business. "I'm sure they've seen it a thousand times before," he said. "Right here in this park. We fit right in."

"Uh-huh." Jolie shaded her eyes and looked in the direction of the road Willow had taken. It ran downhill to a stop sign. She'd turned right, and had disappeared behind a row of houses.

"The Quik Mart is two blocks down that street," Landry said.

"Not city blocks, though. Two short blocks."

"Yeah. All the blocks are short around here."

The two boys seemed oblivious to Landry and Jolie. They were joking around. One of them—the skinny one—brayed like a donkey. He drank the last of the Faygo and set the jug on the picnic table bench beside him.

They waited.

It was pleasant. There were grackles in the trees across the way, loud and obnoxious. Water sprinklers came on, but nowhere near them. Droplets of water shimmered in the sun.

But Willow did not come back.

The sprinkler was the kind that rotated, shooting streams of water in a long radius.

"Rainbow," Jolie said, pointing at the spray.

Landry checked his watch. Twenty-five minutes. "You think she's coming back?"

"Maybe not."

"You think she's doing a deal for them?"

"What do you think?"

"I don't know."

The Juggalo boys pulled out a Frisbee and threw that for a little while. Not long. The overweight one lost interest quickly enough.

"I think they're passing time," Landry said.

"Waiting for her to come back?"

"Is that what you think?"

"Uh-huh."

"There she is." Jolie nodded at the sloping street. The girl had just made the corner and was walking along.

They followed her progress up the street. Had she done a drug deal? Did she go to get them more snacks? She swung a plastic bag in her hand, a grocery bag. Maybe there was a grocery store down around the corner.

She came closer.

The boys were now sitting side by side on the picnic table, their feet on the bench.

She reached the one-lane street that fronted the park. It was uphill. There were several parked cars, nose to tail, on the street. Parked out front of the houses, which looked like they had been built after World War II.

She was partway across the little street when a car door opened.

A guy said something to her.

She stopped.

Middle of the narrow street, but there were no cars coming either way. It was a neighborhood street, no traffic to speak of.

Bag dropping to her side, she stepped toward the man and the car.

Landry pegged him as midtwenties to thirty. He looked like a young father. Wore shorts and a tee and athletic shoes. He leaned down to talk to her, and for a moment it looked like an earnest conversation.

Then he grabbed her arm.

She struggled, pulled away.

The boys on the bench took off like a pair of rockets.

Landry and Jolie were twenty feet behind them.

The man was wrestling Willow into the car. He was winning. He looked up and saw four people pelting down the hill toward him.

Willow managed to shake herself loose, dropped her bag, and ran for the two Juggalo kids.

She launched herself into the arms of one, legs wrapped around him, head buried in his neck. The second kid took a roundhouse punch at the guy, but missed, tripped, and fell on his butt.

The guy half-in, half out of the car, the door open, tried to start the car. The car caught, then stalled as Landry reached the car door and slammed it hard on the man's bare leg.

He screamed like a banshee.

Landry opened the car door and dragged him out. The guy fell onto the asphalt and curled up in a ball, holding his leg. The foot above his athletic shoe had been crushed and partially severed. Blood soaked the white athletic shoe and smeared the asphalt. The man's screams were manic.

Landry pulled his head back by his hair and slammed his forehead against the pavement.

The screaming stopped.

Landry looked at the Juggalo who wasn't holding on to Willow. The guy who wasn't stroking her hair and telling her it was all right. The guy who wasn't squatting down beside her and talking softly.

Landry looked down. The car guy, kidnapper guy—whatever you wanted to call him—was squirming on the ground. Murder in his eyes. "I'm gonna *kill* you, man!" Landry saw the empty knife scabbard just as the car guy raised his arm. "Knife!" he shouted as he raised his foot to stomp the man's arm. But Jolie was ahead of him. She grabbed the car guy by the arm and wrenched it around hard. There was an audible snap. The knife clattered to the pavement. "You don't want to do that," she told him.

"Who are *you?*"

"Someone who doesn't want to see you go to jail."

The fight went out of him like air out of a tire. He was too busy writhing in pain.

Landry ripped the car guy's T-shirt off him and tied a tourniquet just below the knee. The man was heading into shock, but Landry didn't care. He opened the back door of the car and dragged him into the backseat and laid him out. He took the man's phone out of his pocket and snapped a photo of him with it. "Here's something to remember the occasion by." He threw the phone on the guy's chest.

The man was babbling something. He was also crying. Impossible to tell what he was saying.

"You might lose that foot," Landry said. "So if I were you, soon as you can manage, dial 9-1-1. You're at . . ." He glanced at the street signs. "Olive and Trelawny."

The guy swooned.

Landry slammed the car door shut.

The overweight Juggalo said, "Holy shit, dude. Did you kill him?"

"Not yet."

"Oh, man. Who *are* you?"

"I'm the Lone Ranger," Landry said. He nodded to Jolie. "And that's Tonto."

- — -

It was a quiet street and apparently no one was looking out their windows. Or if they were, they chose not to do anything. There were no sirens. Landry figured they might have to call it in themselves to make sure the guy got the medical help he needed.

First, though, they needed to get away from here. They walked back across the street to the park and all got into Landry's rental car.

"Any place you want to go so we can talk?" Landry asked.

"We can go to my place," offered the skinny one, whose name was Luke Conaboy.

Luke—small world. Even though Landry still considered himself a Catholic of sorts, he wasn't religious. But the fact that the kid's name was Luke made him feel that something powerful had happened. Kismet, fate, or whatever you wanted to call it.

Luke said, "But the name I go by is Eezil."

"Easel? Like for artists?"

"E-E-Z-I-L."

"What's it mean?" Jolie asked.

"Like I'm the illustrated man or something—put me on an easel 'cause I'm art, right? Only it's spelled different."

"Yeah, that's fresh," said the other kid, whose name was Brian Swinney.

Landry was confused. "You spell easel like 'fresh'?"

"No! Fresh! What would old folks like you say? Cool. Fresh. Got it?"

They ended up at a small stuccoed-over block of a house. It looked like it had been built in the thirties.

The front room was dark and old-fashioned. Lace curtains in the windows, heavy dark furniture. "My grandma likes antiques," Luke-Eezil said. "Don't touch anything."

He led them to his room.

The room was like a den—crowded and very dark. It had been painted deep plum, and the shades were drawn. There weren't a lot of places to sit down—just the twin bed and a cheap desk chair that had no desk to go with it. The walls were covered with art of sorts, including a black running hatchet man (Landry'd read about that) stamped into the wall at intervals in ink.

Landry sat cross-legged on the floor with the young men while Jolie took the desk chair and Willow sat on the bed. Jolie sat quietly but expectantly, and Landry assumed that she wanted him to ask the questions and she would observe the reactions to whatever was said.

"We won't get in trouble, will we, man?" Eezil said.

"Hey, what do you think?" Brian said. "They're piggies."

Landry said, "I doubt anything will come of this. Just don't boast about it."

"Hey, ninja, you know the truth. We were trying to save her. Look what *you* did!"

Ninja? Landry wished he had a translator handy.

"Piggy can do that, ninja," Brian said.

"You go to the same high school?"

"Yeah. So who are you? You police or something, right?"

"Or something," Landry said.

"So we're all on the same page, dude. We weren't there, didn't see nothing, didn't do nothing, right?"

"Fine with me," Landry said. He turned to Jolie.

"Fine with me," Jolie said.

"Awesome!"

"So how do you know Willow? She's a freshman, right? You hang with freshmen?"

"Not usually."

Brian fidgeted. Eezil looked away.

Landry turned to Willow, who had sunk into the deep burgundy chenille bedspread and thin pillow. "Willow? Did you know that guy?"

"No." Her voice was tiny. She sounded sleepy.

Landry looked at Jolie. Jolie leaned forward, so she was on a level with Willow. "Willow? Have you ever seen that guy before?"

"No."

"*Ninja*. She's been through a lot," Eezil said. He was clearly the spokesman for the three of them.

Protective.

"How do you know Willow?" Landry asked.

"We're homies—were homes with her brother. Devin," Eezil said. "Hey, you want something to drink? My grandma makes sun tea. Ninjette, go get some tea, will ya?"

Willow just looked at him.

"Some sun tea, for our guests here. Come on, Willow!"

Willow got up. She wandered past them, slow and unfocused.

"What's with her?" Jolie asked.

"She gets sleepy."

"Sleepy?"

"Yeah, you know, like nighty-night?" He put his palms together against his cheek.

"In the middle of the day?"

"Yeah. Sleeping Beauty."

"Is she on drugs?"

"Nope, doesn't touch drugs. We wouldn't let her even if she wanted to. Devin and me were close. Like that." He crossed his fingers. "It sucked when he got shot."

"Were you there?" Landry asked.

"Nah, we skipped last period. Lucky for us, huh?"

"Very lucky for you."

"Devin was my *homes*."

His voice cracked a little, his throat full of tears.

"What do you think about the shooting?" Landry asked. "Who did it?"

"Some rat's ass."

"Yeah," Brian chimed in. "Weak. He better not come around here, we'll put a hurt on his ass."

"The shooter is dead," Landry said.

"Oh."

"You didn't know that?"

"Oh, yeah. I forgot."

Landry wondered what kind of drugs they were on. He didn't care, though. They were good kids in their way.

Willow came in with the jar of sun tea and a stack of plastic glasses on top, holding them fast under her chin. Landry had once seen the opera *Lucia di Lammermoor,* where Lucia, a beautiful woman with long hair, wandered around the stage in her nightgown, distressed and out of it at the same time. Willow set the sun tea jar and glasses down on the little desk next to Jolie, then ambled over to the bed. She sat on it, smiled vaguely at them, and slumped sideways into a faint.

"Is she all right?"

Eezil shrugged. "That's her way, man. Out like a light. She'll wake up in a few."

"Yeah," Brian Swinney said. "Like those fainting goats, you know? I saw it once on TV."

"So she's okay?"

"Oh, yeah. Any little thing, and she goes down. That fucker must've scared the shit out of her."

Landry said, "Did you know Luke Brodsky?"

"Brodsky?" Eezil said. "Yeah, I knew him. He was one who got shot. Ninja was down-ass."

"That's good, right?"

"Oh, yeah. You better believe it." Eezil lit up a cigarette. "Mind if I smoke?"

"You know him well?"

"Uh-huh. He and his ninjette, Kristal? She's so hot." He saw the look on Landry's face. "Hey, you aren't his dad or anything, are you?"

"Just interested."

Jolie said to Eezil, "Do you have any idea why that guy would shoot up the school?"

"No, that's seriously whack." He rubbed his tattooed arm. "Gave me nightmares."

"Ever see him before—the shooter?"

"No! At least not like he was dressed up in the vid. Like a ninja. A *real* ninja. Then he got *his* ass shot up. Talk about poetic justice yo."

Landry leaned forward, elbows on knees. Looked Eezil in the eye. "So what do you think happened?"

"I dunno, man." He had backed up a little. There was perspiration on the sketchy little smudge above his upper lip—what some people would call a mustache.

"No theories?"

"Sounds like somebody went crazy. You know, like they do on TV? I mean like how many schools are getting shot up?" He shrugged. "We just won the lottery, dude."

Landry said, "So you're good friends with Willow. She's only a freshman, though, right?" He remembered what he thought about freshmen in high school when he was a senior.

Eezil glanced over at Willow. "We're, like, her *uncles*. We look out for her 'cause Devin can't. Anybody messes with her, they mess with us. Don't fuck with a Juggalo!"

Jolie said, "*Do* people mess with her?"

"Not anymore. At least not till now." Brian laughed. A maniacal laugh—jagged and with a hint of terror in it. "Like that guy in the car? He messed with Willow. Guess *he's* not a problem anymore!"

Landry noticed the kid was shaking. Adrenaline setting in.

Everyone dealt with it differently. He looked at the girl, passed out on the bed. *Narcolepsy.*

"Any talk around the school? Anyone know who the dude who shot up the school was?"

"Nuh-uh."

Brian shook his head, too. They looked scared.

"It could have been *us*," Eezil said. "If we didn't cut that last class. We *always* park there."

Landry said, "Tell me about Kristal."

"Hey, I only knew her to say hi to."

"You said you knew her."

Brian nodded. "We hung out with them some, but as far as we were concerned, she was just some chick."

Some chick.

"Luke we hung with in middle school. Then they got hot and heavy. That was kind of a new deal."

"They weren't together long?"

Eezil shrugged. Brian didn't add anything.

"Luke have any enemies?"

Eezil said, "None I know of. He was solid—even if he wasn't a Juggalo. He respected us. He treated us like we *were* something!"

"Nobody threatened him?"

"No."

"Did he ever mention that he was worried about someone?"

"Like what?"

"Like someone maybe was after him. Or had it in for him?"

"I don't think so."

Jolie said, "What about Devin? Did Devin have any enemies?"

"Just the usual. The bullies and Juggalo haters an' shit. Some people, man."

"And Willow?"

"She gets bullied, too. Girls, they're mean. Nothing meaner than a mean girl. They make fun of her."

"Like how?"

"Like they're glad Devin died. Calling him all kinds of shit. No kidding, girls are *mean*." His cigarette between his fingers, he rubbed his forehead. "Bitches! But me and Brian made a pact. If they want to get to her they have to *go through us*!"

- — -

They left not too long after that. They drove up onto the hill by the park and looked down and saw the ambulance and police cars on the street looking at the car belonging to the man who'd tried to kidnap Willow.

Jolie said, "Juggalos aren't so bad after all."

"Those Juggalos," Landry said.

"Just kids, trying to make it through a hard time."

Landry said nothing.

"I was bullied when I was a kid."

"You were?" That surprised him. If anyone he knew was strong and knew herself, it was Jolie. "What did you do?"

"First, I avoided them. It was easy to do back then, before social media. I just faked an illness and stayed home from school."

"Sneaky."

"Survival. I stayed out a whole semester. These days they can get to you through Facebook or other social media and make your life a living hell."

"You said that *first* you avoided them."

"Yeah. I went back to school—I had to at some point. But by then I made a decision."

"And what was that?"

"I decided to pick the biggest, meanest torturer in the school, the one who made my life a living hell, and first day of the new semester, I walked up to her and punched her in the stomach."

"Really."

"Yeah. You should have seen the look on her face. Charlene Morrisey. She sat down on the ground and cried like a baby. I got detention, but it was the best thing I ever did."

Landry nodded. "Always take the early advantage."

"Hit 'em swift and hard. Were you bullied as a kid?" Jolie asked.

"No."

They lapsed into silence.

As they passed the exit for Santa Anita, Landry's eyes strayed in that direction.

Jolie said, "Do you still think the shooter came to the school because of Devin?"

"No."

"Me neither." She stared straight ahead at the police cars. "So who does that leave?"

Landry said, "It leaves me."

CHAPTER 19

Cameron Mills sat opposite a man named Jeremy Cleeves at a small table in his hotel room. There was always the small table in every hotel room in every city they had stayed in, and they always sat across from one another, their knees nearly touching, from six a.m. to eight a.m. They started at six on the dot, as they did every day.

He'd come a long way from the stinking sand hills of Iraq.

On the Eastern Seaboard it was eight o'clock in the morning—late enough in the day for Cam to make his calls to people there.

Cam's nickname for Jeremy was "The Ogre." Jeremy might or might not have been aware of the nickname, but if he was, he didn't seem to take offense. He simply did what he was supposed to do, pushing sheets of paper at Cam one at a time, impervious to the moans, the sighs, the rolled eyes, and sometimes, downright rebellion. Cam only used rebellion when he felt it would get him what he wanted and needed—some free time. He had learned that the bigger the temper tantrum, the more time he got.

But the tactic also had to be portioned out at the right time. They owed him time to himself, and he would get his time, but not now. If he wanted to get where he wanted to go, he had to do The Ogre's bidding.

Right now The Ogre sat across from him with the same short stack of paper at his elbow, and handed Cam the first sheet.

Cam dutifully read the sheet, which listed a man, his wife, and his children, how much to hit the man up for, and what to settle for.

Always ask the maximum.

He punched in the number and said, "Hi, it's Cam Mills." He made his pitch. He was good at it. He knew how to massage the wealthy and the important and make them want to be a part of it all. He knew how to tailor his pitch to the particular person he was talking to, knew what to offer them and when. It was easy, actually, because if he could convince them that they had a shot at being a part of Greatness with a capital "G," that they might—*might*—have a shot at sleeping in the Lincoln Bedroom, they were happy to play along. If only they got in early enough, if only they were someone he could depend on no matter what, they would pay gladly. *If* he could convince the potential donor that he and *he alone* would be Cam's right-hand man, his kingmaker, his rainmaker. The one man who had the ear of the candidate.

And Cam was a good candidate. He had a high profile. For one thing, he was not a congressman, but a senator. The junior senator from Arizona. And he'd made some waves recently, gotten some press. They called him a "Gunslinger"—a new kind of Democrat with an appetite for a fight. The kind who shot from the hip. He had gobs of potential. At forty-four years old he was not too young and not too old. Yes, he was a Democrat, but he was a *conservative* Democrat—a very conservative Democrat. He reminded a lot of people of their fathers' Democrat, back in the day. Yellow Dog, Blue Dog, whatever was farther to the right, that was what he was.

So he had two hours. He asked for the maximum and two times out of three he got it. He was that good. He always asked them to do more. "Jim, will you talk to your friends? If I could get one, or even two, of your friends to donate . . . honestly, the sky's the limit."

The Ogre pointed to his watch.

Cam had time for three more calls, tops. Then it was on to the next thing.

He had spoken to seventeen donors and netted $10,000 to $20,000 from each donor. Many of those would put the touch on their friends.

The trick was to get in and out as gracefully as he could, as quickly as he could.

And think about it. All day, every day, he worked exclusively to get money. Six a.m. to eight a.m. he worked the phones—every single day. And another two hours later in the day. Four hours. In between that, he went to fund-raisers. He solicited a lot of money but he needed a lot, too.

He would need approximately $6 to $8 million to run a successful presidential campaign.

The irony? He had three times that amount stashed away, but he still had to go through the charade of pulling in money.

The money was a virtual albatross around his neck. When he'd found it—*found money*, seriously—it had turned on a light somewhere inside him.

He'd grown up in politics, helping his uncle. Licking envelopes. Making up signs. Being a messenger. It was in his blood. He'd learned the ropes like few others had, had developed a keen sense for bullshit at an early age. As an only child, he always got along better with adults than with his contemporaries. And he had a gift for politics—everyone said so.

The money was what had opened up the possibilities for him. But now it sat there, unused, waiting to catch him up.

And so here he was, hitting up donors from six to eight every morning, eking out $20,000 here, $50,000 there. His whole day doled out by his body man and his other handlers, in increments, down to the minute. His body man, Duncan Welty, never left his side.

He was thinking about the money. Always thinking about the money. It would help so much. He needed every penny. He had to use some of his own money for the campaign, he was working like a dog from early in the morning to late at night, and Kelli didn't work. Not only that, but their kid was on the junior show-jumping circuit—that took a lot of money. But he could access only a little at a time.

Although the money was laundered, his family, friends, and the people in the political realm knew too much about his financial history. There was no way to explain the obscene amount of money he had sitting in the Cayman Islands. After he became a senator, after more donations poured in and he was running for president, that could change. But not now. Right now, he was Jeremy's slave.

As he washed his hands in the bathroom sink, he called out to Jeremy.

"What's next?" he asked.

But he barely heard Jeremy's reply. He was thinking about Iraq.

- — -

They had been on an endless loop of patrol—looking for trouble—and stopped near a bombed-out farmhouse in the boonies somewhere south of Nasiriyah. These houses could shield enemy combatants—something they had to worry about as they patrolled the Mars-scape of Iraq endlessly and for no reason.

But now, Cam didn't care. His bladder was full and he couldn't hold it any longer. They had a female photog with them and she'd been cracking dirty jokes all along to show she was one of them. Asshole.

He was sick of it all. His second skin was granules of dirt that poked their way into every crevice. He could smell himself. It was so fucking hot he couldn't stand it one more minute, and he hadn't been able to stand one more minute since he got there. His mouth was dry—always. Cam sensed that Martín, one of the Three Amigos, had turned against him for some reason. Sometimes he felt like he'd fallen into a nest of pirates.

Jedediah—he was a true friend. But Jed was in the sick bay with a fever. Without someone who had his back, commanding this crew was an uphill battle.

He needed quiet, and taking a leak was a good enough excuse.

Cam realized he wasn't even nonstop terrified anymore. If some raghead wanted to blow his head off, so be it. "No skin off my nose," he muttered, and then laughed at the image. His head blown off but no skin off his nose! Hilarious.

Was he going just a little bit crazy? He wondered for the hundredth time if he was a candidate for the puzzle factory. "Humpty Dumpty," he muttered. "That's me."

There was the bombed-out house, under a listing Aleppo pine tree that had been scorched halfway up, branches and pine needles rust colored where they weren't singed.

"I'm gonna take a leak," he said to his men. "You stay here."

Nobody argued with him. They didn't like him any more than he liked them.

He knew they laughed at him behind his back. Even his friend Martín.

He walked through the dirt, thinking, *Go ahead and shoot me now.* But no shot came. No mortar came. Just the sand crunching and blowing under his feet, the desert grit in his teeth, and ahead of him the blackened walls of the bombed-out house, which looked like every other bombed-out house he'd seen in this godforsaken shithole.

Keeping the woman in mind—not that he was a prude or anything, but he'd been raised to be private—he decided to go around to the far corner of the house, where the pine was.

The blackened wall was about waist high.

He unzipped.

He could hear them laughing in the Humvee and wondered if they were laughing at him. Hyenas. Jackals. He hated every single one of them. The wind carried their voices. He heard no mention of his name.

The problem was, his bladder was so full it had become balky. He looked around. Try to think of something else . . . Just let it happen . . .

He noticed that the door was set low. It had been blown open. It led down a few steps covered with debris and dusty cement blocks. He could feel the coolness emanating from the place, underground.

Something down there. Boxes. Munitions? He knew there were stashes of weapons all over the goddamned place. Mostly, they were dumped—or stolen. People out here stole everything that wasn't nailed down, and the stuff that was nailed down they used a blowtorch on.

Finally, his bladder loosened up. He was drenched with relief, inside and out.

His eye wandered to the low-cut doorway, the basement, the junk-littered steps going down. It was dark but there was a gold bar of light partway across from another opening—a half window, probably.

He looked back at the Humvee.

Their voices drifted out to him. Talk, talk, talk.

Not even aware of their surroundings, the dumb fucks. Always yakking. And he'd been reprimanded more than once for their actions. How could you control a pack of dogs?

The way they looked at him, as if they couldn't contain their mirth another moment. "Pretty Boy." That's what he'd heard his name was.

Their eyes.

Like wild pigs in the darkness.

Let 'em wait. He zipped up and started down the steps.

CHAPTER 20

"If it's not Devin, it's you?" Jolie said to Landry. "How can you be sure? There are a lot of victims. It could have been random."

"No."

"Okay, the shooter was a professional, but that doesn't mean he was after Kristal."

"The shooter was an operator."

"Is that what you people call it?"

"Among other things." Landry looked for the exchange. "Desert or mountains?"

"What?"

"Do you want to go to the desert or mountains? It's almost four p.m."

"And you think we should lay low?"

"*Lie* low."

"Didn't you ever get it that correcting someone's grammar is rude?"

Landry said nothing. He realized he was making it too hard on himself. He had two town houses. Might as well just hole up at one or the other. Few people interacted in either of the neighborhoods, but the handful who had seen him saw him enough to know he belonged there. They kept to themselves and he kept to himself.

He exited the freeway and drove into Lake View Terrace.

The street was empty. The townhomes, usually beige, were yellow in the late-afternoon light. Nobody was outside, as usual. No kids on bikes, or people walking their dogs, or neighbors chatting in their front yards. That was the way the neighborhood was. Maybe there were people looking out their windows, but one drive past showed him the blinds were closed in all the houses on both sides of his street. People would be coming home from work soon, but Landry had a detour he needed to make.

He checked his watch. The post office was closed. He wouldn't be able to pick up Betsy, his sniper rifle, until tomorrow. He drove past the neighborhood, and turned in the direction of the boonies.

"Where are we going?" Jolie asked.

"You'll see."

They drove up into the hills. The sun was lower in the bright blue sky. It wouldn't be that way for long, though. Already one side of the hill was in deep shadow. The road turned to graded dirt, and then to washboard gravel.

They turned onto another road, even narrower. It was getting darker all the time. They were only seven or eight miles from his townhome.

The hills here were covered with manzanita and scraggly trees. The city seemed to come right up against the rural area, like surf up to a beach. Landry always liked it out here.

"Where are we going?"

"Almost there."

Landry parked in an area that looked like every other, the little trickle of a dry wash meandering through a small valley between chaparral-clad hills, the dirt road bottoming out in it.

He checked his GPS.

Here.

He recognized it. Not far from the trail was a stack of stones. "Ducks," he said.

"Ducks?"

He pointed at the cairn of stones.

"Oh, ducks. Hikers' cairns."

"You hike?" he asked her.

"Sometimes."

"Hope no one's coming back from a hike now."

It was getting cooler now. The sun was behind the hill that separated them from the city and the ocean. A light wind set the manzanita bushes quivering.

Landry parked on the edge of the road, making sure not to block other vehicles should they come along, and got out of the car. He walked along the side of the road, which had several small turnouts where people had driven off and parked.

"What's this place?" Jolie asked.

Landry hunkered down at one of the pullouts. The tracks of tires on the dried, hardened road pan. But here there was gravel and dirt on top, a natural indentation in the road that ensured there would be loose gravel. Creekbed sand and rocks. He wiped his hand across the dirt. "It's a nonparallel ground trap."

"A what?"

"A ground trap. In the military, we called it a mono vault."

"Oh. Well, that's illuminating."

"It's a military drop point." He reached down and screwed off the lid to the plastic vault. "See? Polyurethane."

"What?" She bent forward.

He heard her gasp. Inside were three assault rifles and several handguns.

Landry nodded to one of them. "It's a SIG Sauer. You want it?"

Jolie said, "Sure. That's what I use anyway."

"A P-226."

"Uh-huh." She rubbed her arms. "It's getting cold out here."

"Like the desert. It's the breeze, too." He screwed the top back on after retrieving an assault rifle and the handgun. Handed her the P-226. He took something else for himself: one of two garage-door openers.

He kicked dirt and rocks back into the shallow pan of the road. Stomped it down some.

The vault's cover had been painted like the road, a camouflage job Landry was proud of. Beige, white, gray white, gray, some red-brown pebbled spots. But he always made sure to tamp sand and rocks down on top.

They drove back to his neighborhood. There was a pullout just above his subdivision (one reason Landry had bought the town house—because he could spy on anyone who might be coming to spy on him). This pullout was a lover's lane kind of deal. They lay on their bellies and watched the town houses through binocs—like watching paint dry.

One car drove onto his street. The car turned in five houses away, its headlights throwing their beams on the garage door. Kind of like two spotlights on a stage. The door rose, and the car pulled in. The garage door rolled down.

They waited. No cars came or went.

They got back in the car and Landry drove down the hill and turned onto his street and turned again onto the driveway pad. He pointed the garage door opener and the door rumbled up, just as the other garage had opened up for the other car five houses down. They drove in and parked, and the garage door shuttled down behind them.

"Tomorrow," Landry said, "we can pick up our own weapons from the post office. But these should be okay for the night."

- — -

They drew the blinds and ate frozen dinners Landry kept in his freezer for such occasions.

"So what happens next?" Jolie asked, toying with her Michelina's spaghetti dinner.

"I have to find the guy who hired him."

"The man who shot up the school? You sure he didn't do it for himself?"

"He was a professional."

Jolie gave up on the spaghetti and set her fork down. "Maybe he had his own beef with the school."

"Possible."

"But you don't believe it."

"I think it's more likely that he was a hired gun. You're not eating."

"I'm not hungry." She paused. She was beautiful even under the dull glow from the overhead ceiling light. But there were shadows under her eyes. She looked washed-out—he thought that was due to the light.

"You should eat," he said. "Keep your strength up."

Her chin dipped in a small, tight nod.

He knew what she was going to say before she said it.

"I think I should go back."

"To New Mexico?"

"Uh-huh. I think it's the right thing for me to do. If I want to keep my job, that is."

"Do you?"

She went back to toying with the spaghetti. Stabbed a meatball with her fork but didn't raise it to her lips. Kept her eyes down. "I think so."

Landry wanted to ask her why she'd come in the first place, but suppressed the urge. It was what it was. He hated it when women asked him something like that, and he suspected Jolie would feel the same way.

She looked at him. "It's not that I don't like being here . . . with you, but . . ."

He waited.

"I like it there."

"New Mexico?"

"Yes. New Mexico. My place. It's the first home I've had in a long time."

"So it's not me?"

She gave up on the spaghetti and pushed the cardboard container away. Looked at him. "Oh, it's you, too. You're a killer."

"So are you."

"But I'm a cop."

He shrugged. "Same thing."

"No, it's not. But you look like you want to argue about it. So, say it: You were a Navy SEAL. You had permission."

"I was a Navy SEAL. I had permission." He leaned his elbows on the table. His dead mother wouldn't approve, but he had become lax in his table manners over time. He had to view his mannerisms in the light others might see him. He couldn't afford to stand out in any way. "What's all this leading to?"

"Remember you told me about the safe house. Your team. When we were on the island? You said they were all dead." She turned her eyes full on him. "Did you kill them?"

He dabbed at his lips with a linen napkin. "Yes, I did. I think I told you that."

"The kid—I read about him. He was nineteen."

"Soldiers are nineteen. They die all the time."

"No one knew who did it. But I thought it was you. Was he on the team coming to kill us?"

"Yes."

Jolie's great-uncle, the former attorney general of the United States, had gotten himself in trouble with some bad people. Bad people in the form of Landry's boss, Mike Cardamone, who ran Whitbread Associates. Whitbread Associates was one of many government contractors that popped up like mushrooms after a rain. The rain, of course, was Iraq.

But Landry's relationship with Mike Cardamone ended in a firefight on a private island off Cape San Blas.

Landry had had to choose sides. He'd elected to fight on the side of the angels. He'd known that to survive, he would have to disable the threat before the enemy had a chance to kill him—he'd had to strike first. That was his mantra. And so he had killed the three other unsuspecting members of his team in a suburban house in Port Saint Joe.

It was the right thing to do, but he'd made a mistake. One of their team was a younger man. Really, he was a kid. He was an operative but he was in over his head. His name was Green. Landry had planned to kill him quickly—an icepick to the base of his skull—but the pick had slipped and Green fought back.

It was bad. Ugly.

Landry held Jolie's eyes with his own. "Why did you think *I* killed them?"

Jolie shrugged. "You'd have to. You'd be the only one who'd have access."

"I did it to save you, your cousin, and the two girls."

"I know." She kept her eyes steady on his. Her serious gray-green, gray-blue eyes. Only in this light they were gray yellow.

"No need to thank me."

He realized he sounded like a prim schoolteacher with her nose out of joint. He reached out for her hand and trapped it under his own big paw. She looked at him.

"Let's eat," she said.

She slept in the guest bedroom. He understood, laid out fresh towels on the bed, turned down the covers, made sure the room temp was cool enough for sleeping. He would have laid a mint on her pillow if he'd had one. His condo was now a hotel like any other.

In the middle of the night she came into his room. He awakened instantly. Just a sound outside his consciousness, a whisper of a sound, would wake him.

She stood in the doorway, silhouetted against the hall light, arms crossed around her chest, hugging herself. "I have to go."

"Why?"

"Because I don't want to be who I am when I'm with you."

He said nothing. But in whatever soul he had left, his heart crumpled, just a little, at the edges.

He wished he had the tears.

But he did not.

CHAPTER 21

He was up early, three a.m. early. He needed to be outside in the dark; he needed to walk. The house had cameras to the outside from every angle. Landry checked all of them. Nothing stirred. Standing in the dark, he looked out the windows. No strange cars. No cars at all. All of them in this neighborhood were buttoned up in their garages.

He dressed in dark clothing. Jolie was out like a light, beautiful in sleep. She snored slightly. Landry figured she would be over what they'd talked about last night. She was strong and she was smart.

And she'd killed enough to understand what he'd done.

They would be all right. If there *was* a "they."

He would have to figure that out, and soon. Jolie meant a great deal to him, but he loved his wife and daughter. He loved his family. He wondered if going to look for Jolie, and finding her, and having her take off with him—if those actions had been a way of saying good-bye to his wife and his daughter.

Gary could be right, that he had been gone for three years and they believed he was dead and he would never get them back now.

He had not wanted to face this possibility before, but in the dark, in the morning, after his talk with Jolie about the things he had done, he wondered. Was he delusional? Would Cindi take him back, the way he pictured she would?

He decided it wasn't the time to think about it, not now.

He went out into the cool dark morning and walked up behind the townhomes into the hills. There was a dirt road beyond, leading up into chaparral and a little place where he could look down on the city.

This was a time not to think, but to *be*. To take in anything and everything that drifted in through his transom. It was important, at times, to be empty. To try and drop thought, so that new ideas— fresh ideas—would have the room to come in.

But his thoughts were all snarled together. He tried to make his mind a blank, but something intruded.

Something had changed.

It was a tiny alteration on an invisible scale. Negative and positive ions switching places, maybe.

Some people might describe it as the hair rising on their arms. Landry felt it in his jaw. Tightness. Like some people might feel before an incipient heart attack. The feeling would start there and then ping off every part of his body. Like a tuning fork.

He even had a name for it, taken from a childhood book he'd loved, and the Shakespeare line that had inspired the title. "By the pricking of my thumbs, *something wicked this way comes.*"

He went back to the house, crept into the bedroom, and shook Jolie's shoulder. "Wake up."

She did.

"Get dressed, now. We're getting out of here. No sound."

She didn't argue. She pulled on her clothes and grabbed her small duffle and stuffed her purse inside. Strapped on her weapon. All fast, all quiet, as Landry did the same.

Over the years, especially in tense military situations, Landry knew when he needed to tighten himself up. When he needed to be ready. He heeded the firing of molecules in his jaw, the ache in his teeth, its connection to the electric grid of his body. The grip he needed to keep on his bowels. Through umpteen combat missions and close to twenty covert operations he had trusted it. *And the only person he could trust completely was himself.*

Jolie filled up bottles of water and grabbed a fistful of energy bars and fruit while he checked the street. All quiet, still dark. Landry didn't know how much time they had, or who was ranked against them, or how it would come. But he knew it would be soon.

"What's going on?" Jolie whispered as they rounded the Kia and opened up the Econoline van.

"Something's changed," Landry said.

"Changed? What about the Kia?"

"We leave it."

Jolie looked at him. "This is serious."

He loaded two motorcycles into the back of the van. One was a Honda. It was a recreational motorcycle. The other was a Harley chopper. Landry had clothing for each of them. He looked completely different depending on which bike he chose to ride— a different person. He had his cotton balls for his mouth and his pin-on ponytail, his leathers, his man-on-the-street casual clothes. All stashed in a good-sized duffle. His eyeglasses and sunglasses and caps and hats and boat shoes and motorcycle boots.

Jolie said, "What is this? Summer stock?"

"You could say that. If we need to get away in a hurry, you okay riding the Honda?"

"I've ridden a motorcycle before. Don't you worry."

But she sounded only half-believable.

The garage door rumbled open. They backed out, and the door lowered after them.

They encountered no cars, no dog walkers, no one at all as they drove under the orange sodium-arc lights of the neighborhood. Just another anonymous townhome on an anonymous block in an anonymous housing development in an anonymous neighborhood.

They hit the freeway driving south.

"What happened back there?"

"Something changed."

"What changed?"

"Something."

Jolie said, "*What? What* changed?"

Landry said, "I told you. Something's turned against us. I don't know what it is, but I know we had to get out when we did."

"That doesn't make any sense."

"Someone may know about the town house. Hard to figure out how. But someone's coming for us."

"And how do you know that?"

"I know."

"Unbelievable."

Landry said nothing.

"I should go back to New Mexico. My job is on the line."

"That's where we're headed."

"To New Mexico?"

"No. To the airport. You're flying back."

She said nothing.

"You said that was what you wanted to do."

She said nothing.

He said nothing, either. Not for a few miles. Then he said, "Take a look at my iPad. Look for up-to-the-minute news."

She powered up and looked. "I don't know the channel here."

"Look it up. Just do it."

She found CNN. "I don't know what you're looking for . . ."

"Just keep looking."

"It might not be news."

"Fifty-fifty," Landry said. "Worth a try."

They zipped along the freeway from pool to pool of orange sodium-arc lights, the night still dark but a blush showing above the mountains to the east. A woman anchor was speaking—reading the news.

"Turn it up," Landry said.

- — -

Barbara Carey wasn't paying attention to the little television set in the tack room. She was too busy trying to keep the two-year-old from biting her. His official name was Mia's Fotobomb but she called him Dummy, because he was the dumbest horse she'd ever known in her life. He was obsessed with the flowers on her T-shirt. Even cross-tied, he gave her fits. Resentment in every bone of his body, stamping his feet, trying to rear up, pulling this way and that, pinning his ears back and snapping at her. You did not turn your back on Dummy because he would take a chunk out of you.

So when she decided to leave him there for a while to think about it, and she stepped into the tack room for a gulp of Coca-Cola and a handful of tortilla chips (her breakfast), she had only half an ear tuned to the TV. She kept it on CNN all the time, because of the school shooting.

Although at this point she had begun to second-guess herself about Joe Till's involvement. There could have been a number of reasons he took off. If she were truthful with herself, she'd cop to the fact that she'd been *expecting* him to take off. She knew the type. He was a rolling stone. She'd seen enough of them to know. It was like they all thought they were in the old-time westerns on Turner Classic Movies, the ones where they kissed the girl, got on the horse, and rode off into the sunset. She'd come to the conclusion that a lot of men had somehow or other been brought up on westerns like that, no matter how young they were, and reveled in the idea that they were independent and free. Always yammering about "wanting their space." That's what her boyfriends would say when she was in high school and even her two years of college. "I need my space." And Joe Till was single, as far as she knew, so he was probably used to pulling that kind of crap.

She'd regretted talking to Justin about him. Justin thought she should send in the photo, but she didn't.

So when she saw his photo—her snap of him with the horse—on television, she aspirated the Coke she was drinking. Coughing and spluttering, she stared at the screen.

She barely heard the newscaster. Something about a "person of interest" who might have been at the scene of the school shooting.

How did this *happen*?

(You know how it happened.)

And why wasn't she surprised?

Her heart chugged, hard. She stepped out into the breezeway, rested a hand on the colt's neck. He stepped on the toe of her boot, barely missing her actual toes, and she jerked his nose chain. "Quit!"

Added, "I'm trying to think here."

The colt must have understood, because he raised his muzzle up to her ear and blew in and out of his nostrils. She pushed his head away and tightened her grip on the chain.

- — -

Driving through the predawn light on the way to the airport, Landry and Jolie lapsed into silence. The sound emerged from the iPad. A woman anchor's voice, babbling on about a second suspect in the shooting at Gordon C. Tuttle High School.

Landry glanced over and saw the photo of himself and the horse. "Barbara Carey," he said.

"Who?"

"The woman who had the farm where I worked. That's where this was taken."

"You didn't know?"

"Not at the time, but I recognize it. She must have sent it in."

"But why would you stick out? People must have been sending in thousands of pictures."

"I don't know."

"How'd they plow through so many photos and find *yours*?"

"I don't know."

"What now?"

"The airport's going to be problematic. They have to assume I saw myself on television and they'll have cops there."

"Feds, too."

"You want me to drop you anywhere? They're looking for me, not you."

Jolie was silent.

"I want to ask you something," Landry said.

"Go ahead and ask."

"Do you think I am capable of shooting up that school?"

"No."

"It's not at the back of your mind? Even a little bit?"

She said nothing for a moment. He thought she was second-guessing her answer. Then she said, "Because of the way you were on the island—how you saved my cousin's daughter. You wouldn't shoot your own child. You wouldn't shoot in the *direction* of your own child—you wouldn't take the chance."

"You're sure of that?"

She paused. Finally said, "I am not sure of a lot of things. You're a hired killer—"

"Jolie—"

"Hear me out. I know there's a lot you would do, but you wouldn't take a chance of killing Kristal. You wouldn't kill kids. Warriors don't kill kids."

First things first, Landry sent Jolie in to pick up his mail. To pick up his sniper rifle, Betsy, and whatever else was in the box.

After that, they cruised a parking lot outside a movie theater and switched license plates with a car out in the hinterlands. From there, they went looking for a down-at-the-heels car dealership— one in a bad side of town where plenty of drug dealers plied their trade. She bought a van, quick and dirty, for $4,000 cash. She'd altered her appearance to biker chick, thanks to some of the stuff he had in the back of the van—including cotton balls in her mouth. She'd spent twenty minutes in a gas station bathroom chopping off her hair and dyeing it black.

There had been no trade-in. She'd gone in on the Honda and loaded it up into the van and driven it off the lot.

Landry had attached the ponytail and rolled up cloths and stuffed them in his pants so that he had a pretty good pair of love handles. Mirrored shades. Leather vest. Biker leathers and a bandana tied around his head, Apache style. Grizzled goatee.

Everyone would see bikers. Everyone would see a whole subset of humanity in shorthand.

"Now what?" Jolie asked.

"I call my brother."

- — -

Barbara Carey thought: *Justin.* Her brother Justin must have got hold of her phone and sent the pic to his own phone, and then sent it to the FBI.

She put the colt back in his stall and ran back to the house and called Justin, but he didn't answer. She left a message, her voice shaking. "You had no *right* to send that photo. That was mine to send, not yours. My property. You went behind my back. I trusted you! What if he's innocent? You just ruined . . ."

She couldn't continue. She was too angry, too embarrassed, *betrayed*. Her brothers had always been like that—paternalistic—even her younger brother Ben. Like she didn't have a brain in her head.

The day had gone by, slow as a traffic jam. She had the channel turned to one of the news channels and periodically the picture would go up along with a description. The man in the photo was "a person of interest."

She was jumpy as a feral cat.

She *knew* she shouldn't have shared her thoughts about Joe Till with her brothers. Just because they had been in the armed forces, did that mean they knew anything about something like this? No!

Barb stared at the screen. The story had moved to something else—farm subsidies and the constant bickering in Washington. The last couple of days the tragedy had begun to fade, like a digital photograph of her daughter she'd framed and put on the tack room door. Only four months gone, and that picture had faded almost to white.

The world had moved on. It was a tragedy, yes, but the argument had moved on to gun control and mental illness.

But why did they pick out this photo of all the photos that had no doubt been sent in? Why Joe's?

That was the thing that worked on her mind. Could there be a grain of truth to it after all? Could Justin in all his sexist I-know-better-than-you-do self-righteousness be right?

There must have been thousands of photos. Thousands of tips.

So why was Joe Till's photo on the television?

Had she really been sleeping with a killer?

She thought about the way his hand caressed her jaw, as if . . .

As if he could snap her neck in two without half-thinking about it.

CHAPTER 22

Cam looked down into the basement of the bombed-out farm-house. The wind whistled through the doorway. Paper rattled under a brick on one of the steps leading down.

The dead palm tree fronds clattered. The Aleppo pine's branches stirred and were still.

The basement floor was awash in trash and other debris—including large chunks from the ceiling and walls. He was about to turn away when his eye caught sight of the corner of something. No, not just one corner, but two precise corners connected by a straight line.

A box?

No—not one box. Several—he could see the lines intersecting, repeating themselves, under the collage of mortar and junk and diapers and congealed food and bricks.

He thought he knew what they were: boxes of standard US-issued rifles, cached here by one side or the other—or more likely, left behind. The United States often left caches of rifles where they were—it was too expensive to transport them back.

Either that was the case, or the rifles had been stolen.

He bent down and pushed the top off one of the boxes—

And got a huge surprise.

There were not rifles in the box—there was money. US money. Millions—no, make that billions—of dollars in cash, if he was right.

If this was what he thought it was.

Like everyone else, Cam knew about the $6.6 billion in US dollars stolen from the Green Zone. Fucking jerks just left stacks of shrink-wrapped money on pallets in plain view of everybody. Billions and billions of dollars to help rebuild Iraq. They'd used guards around the clock but $6.6 billion had turned up missing somewhere along the line. There were a lot of jokes about that.

Everyone talked about the money. What they'd do with it if they had it. Because somebody did—somebody had it.

Could this be the missing $6.6 billion?

They were stacked in the box in bricks, each of them wrapped tightly in cellophane. Cam had heard that the bricks each held a hundred one-hundred-dollar bills.

He picked up a brick and peered at the bill on top.

One hundred dollars.

And he thought: *This is meant to be*. It was his destiny.

He opened the other boxes. They all contained stacks of bills the size of bricks. Each brick had been shrink-wrapped.

His for the asking.

Cam knew if he wanted to cash in, he'd have to act fast. No way he could take all of it out with him now. He needed to hide the money here, in plain sight, and come back for it as soon as he could. Today, or tomorrow at the latest.

How would he transport the money? How much could he take? Was there really $6.6 billion here? He couldn't take that much, but what if he could take even one-third? One-third would be what? If all the stolen money was stashed here, that one-third would come to $2.2 billion. Billion!

A billion would do it. No need to be greedy. Two billion would seal the deal.

He would need a lot of money to run for office. First he had to get a senator's seat or a House seat. That would take money. And then the run itself.

Cam walked through the rubble to the other side, peered out through a hole in the wall. He stared at the men and the one woman in the Humvee. They were having a smoke. He could hear them laughing and joking.

He sat down on the debris-covered step to collect himself, had to shake off the shock. His extremities tingled and he felt light-headed, his brain snared into an incessant loop between what this money could do for him and his future, and how in God's name he could work out the logistics of stealing it.

He would need transport—soon—just in case whoever stashed it here came back.

Move! his mind urged him. *Make a decision.* Like a sleepwalker, he reached down and picked up a kilo-sized bundle of money, opened his vest, and stuffed it in one side. Then he reached down for another bundle and snugged it into the other side. He zipped up his vest and patted it down. Too obvious? No—those assholes wouldn't notice anything. He wished he'd brought a duffle, but if he came walking out holding a heavy duffle, dumb as they were, one of them might notice.

Another thought. He didn't want anyone thinking this place was special. He realized he'd have to treat the farmhouse like a piece of shit. Make a show of it. Explode the floor above, cover the basement in rubble.

Blow the walls down on top of it.

First, though, he needed to protect the money. If he did it the right way—and he was an expert at setting explosives—the money would be just fine where it was, in the rifle boxes.

He set a C-4 charge and detonated the area right next to the house, watching as the rubble crashed down into the basement below. Then he trudged back to the Humvee.

The female photog said, "What took you so long?"

"I was having a wet dream about you."

She gave him a dirty look.

"At least you got to see some fireworks."

- — -

There were a few more hours of patrol, and Cam counted the minutes until he could get back to the base. He could barely think, for all the white noise in his brain. He could feel the money pressed against his chest, and suppressed the desire to hug the bundle hard against his body like twin infants of his heart.

Back at base, Cam went to his bunk. He had the place to himself—he usually did. He cleaned out his duffle and dumped the two bundles of cash inside. He tucked it underneath his bunk and stuffed miscellaneous stuff—jackets and such—around it. Then he opened his computer and searched for a business card program, his plan solidifying. He configured a sheet of business cards for a security contractor and made himself the CEO. Keep it simple; he typed in, "High Risk Protection Services."

He emptied another duffle and filled it with items he'd need for the task ahead. He'd be good to go in fifteen minutes, but he waited for the rest of the base to be at its calmest before he completed his tasks—to collect everything he needed for his own private op.

The night patrol was out. The rest were sleeping. This was when he needed to be careful. He went to the munitions dump and scavenged as many .50-caliber ammo cans as he could. He couldn't clean them all out—had to make sure they wouldn't be missed. But he managed to take two dozen. He'd come back later if need be, since this mission, "Operation Windfall," would take more than one trip. He dumped the ammo in a secluded area in the back of the camp and buried it, then loaded the empty cans onto his bunk. Now he was good to go for the next action.

Cam knew he had to do this right—no mistakes. Fortunately, he came from a family of bullshitters.

He drew the air in through his nostrils. Shook his hands and kicked his legs out, just to get loose. Time for the acting job—he needed to be in a panic.

Panicked, but not crazy enough to get himself shot when he barged in on the CO.

He went to his commander's billet and stood in the doorway. The commanding officer was already sleeping.

"Sir," Cam said, sounding desperate but reluctant to wake his CO up. Feeling it in his gut, letting the nervousness spread throughout his body.

Agitation.

The CO stirred, turned on a light, and opened his eyes. Those eyes were a piercing deep blue in daylight—but now they were flat black. Cam spoke quickly. "Sir, I have an emergency I need to deal with."

"What kind?"

"Family emergency, sir."

The CO sat up and rubbed his neck.

Cam knew the CO trusted him. He'd worked from the beginning to win that trust, just in case. This was the time to collect. "May I requisition a vehicle? I want to get going ASAP."

"It's serious?"

Cam said gravely, "It is, sir."

A pause. Then, "I can give you five days."

"Thank you, sir!"

Back at the barracks, making sure to sound panicked, he rousted his staff sergeant. He begged him to pull his paperwork for leave and travel as soon as possible. Then he trotted to the car pool and took his commandeered Humvee and returned to the barracks.

He loaded the ammo cans into the rear of the vehicle, covered them with a tarp to keep them from rattling on the trip, and stuffed the duffle holding the rest of his money under the seat. He tossed a hastily packed bag into the passenger seat, added his M-4 (with grenade launcher and a few grenades), and put them all on the passenger-side floorboard. From there he drove cross-camp to pick up his leave papers, and was gone.

He drove back to the bombed-out farmhouse and extinguished his lights about a half mile away. By now dawn lit up the horizon. He had a lot of work to do.

He loaded twenty-five ammo cans with as many bricks of cash as he could fit into them, stacking the cans neatly across the backs of the Humvee seats, and covering them with the tarp. He stuffed as many of the remaining bricks of cash into the open rear of the Humvee, covered them as well, and drove away from the farm-house.

The sun was up now, and it was hot and humid. The river wasn't far away, a sluggish brown rope fringed with green. There were more bombed-out houses strung out along what used to be a road, most of them just foundations. He found what he needed almost right away: blast craters in the sand, approximately a hundred meters away from a farm outbuilding that had been shredded to bits. He backed the truck up to one crater at a time and carpeted the bottom with bricks of cash. The flies buzzed around his lips, his nose, his eyes—seeking moisture. "Fuckers," he muttered, stacking in the bricks. "Even *you* can't bother me."

It was eight a.m. by the time he was done placing the C-4 charges to the side of each crater of money and drove back to a safe detonation point. He took a GPS reading of the craters, scribbled the coordinates inside his wallet, and rummaged through the other duffle for his civilian clothing. He'd packed them neatly: a button-down long-sleeved shirt, chinos, belt, and loafers. He donned the clothing and voilà! He was transformed into a private security specialist. A handsome Rolex knockoff completed the outfit.

He reached down to the floorboard of the Humvee, picked up the detonator, flipped off the safety, and ignited the C-4.

Several blasts shook the area in quick succession—flames spouting up through the black smoke, sand and dirt and dust dissolving and falling back to earth, the debris settling down over the cache of money. It would also cover any tread marks and footprints he'd left behind.

On to Kuwait.

CHAPTER 23

Jolie drove while Landry pulled the packaging off one of the new burner phones and texted a message to his brother Gary: "Chernobyl Ant," which was code for wanting to talk. Chernobyl Ant was their one-time shot at the Kentucky Derby. The colt hadn't been a Derby hopeful for long. He'd injured an ankle during the running of the Santa Anita Derby and was retired to stud. But what might have been.

Landry got Gary's voice mail and left a message. "Call me."

Ten minutes later, Gary did. "What happened? You're all over the TV!"

"Do they have my name?"

"You haven't been watching?"

"I've been driving. We've been listening to different stations."

"We?"

"A friend of mine."

Silence.

Landry said, "I haven't heard a name but maybe we missed it."

"From what I saw," Gary said, "there's just the photo. But that doesn't mean they don't have your name. Good thing, though, you can barely make out who it is with the sun behind you."

"I recognized it right away," Landry said.

"Yeah, but you remember where you were and what you were doing. If I was them, I'd withhold your name right now, too. It looks like you, but there's no way they can be sure."

And if they did put a name to it, Landry thought, it would be Joe Till. That was what his DL said. Still, his face, while blurry, might be recognizable to some. People who knew what to look for.

"The man in the photograph is a person of interest in the shooting at the Gordon C. Tuttle High School," Landry said. "Have they seen it?"

"You mean Cindi and Kristal?"

"Who else would I mean? Have they seen it?"

"I don't know. I haven't talked to them. It's only been an hour. I've been with the shoer all morning."

"Does James know?" Landry asked, thinking of their older brother.

"He didn't call me. He's at Churchill already."

"So they made it okay?"

"Yeah, he flew the horses in day before yesterday."

"I mean Cindi and Kristal. Did *they* make it okay?"

There was silence on the other end.

"Gary?"

"Look, there's something—"

"They're in Kentucky, aren't they? I told you to contact Tom. You got ahold of Tom, didn't you?"

No answer.

Jolie said, "Something wrong?"

He held the phone closer and tried to stem the cold feeling of dread spreading through his vitals. "Gary, they're in Kentucky, aren't they? They're staying with Tom, right? Tell me they're staying with Tom."

Tom was former military elite and ran a PSC—a private security company. He was not only a friend, but also an ally. One of the only people Landry knew he could trust completely. Tom would do anything a relative of Landry would ask. That was a given. He wouldn't ask questions, and Landry knew he would protect Cindi and Kristal with his life.

Landry was about to ask again when Gary said, "There's been a change of plans."

A Corvette put on the afterburners and swerved in front of them. Landry let the van slow a little. Checked his side mirror for police. Change of *plans*? "What do you mean, a change of plans? Haven't they left yet? Gary, you can't fool around! You need to make them go."

"Look—"

"It's Kristal, isn't it? She doesn't want to go?"

"Look, everything's changed—"

"Nothing has changed. Not on the ground. She *has* to go. You have to convince her."

Another pause. Finally: "She's not here."

"What do you mean she's not there?"

"Cindi and Kristal aren't here in town. They're gone. Like you said, we had to get them to someplace safe."

If it weren't for the traffic, Landry would have stopped the car. He could feel a humming in his gut, like a low-grade fever. "What are you saying, Gary? Spit it out! Why haven't they gone yet?"

"Because they're *not going at all*!" Gary blurted it out.

Landry's hand tightened on the phone. He didn't trust himself to drive, so he eased over into the breakdown lane and brought the van to a stop. "What are you saying, Gary?"

"They decided to stay in California." Gary sounded scared. Scared and defiant.

"Cindi and Kristal did? Did you tell Cindi that she needed to go find sanctuary?"

That was the phrase they had always used. "Finding sanctuary" in Landry's trade meant to go underground.

"We've got it covered."

"You've got it covered. You and Cindi? Are you telling me she's decided not to go to Kentucky where she'll be safe?"

"Look, I'm not like you. I can't boss her around—"

"I never bossed her around." Cindi knew when he wasn't fooling around, knew that when he told her he had to go to ground, or that she needed to watch her back, it was gospel. Then it dawned on him. "Was this *your* idea? You think you're better equipped to make that call?"

"She's an adult. Not only that, but she's been a widow for three years now. She can run her own life. You have no idea what she's been dealing with all this time. How bad it's been—"

"Don't you get it?" Landry tried to keep his voice low and reasonable. "This is what I do. This is my life. I know what I'm doing."

"One thing you do real well," Gary said, "is ruin lives!"

Jolie touched Landry's arm. He waved her away. "I am trying to *save* their lives now." His teeth gritted together. His heart was pounding, the same adrenaline rush he felt when he prepared to go into battle. Wound up, and ready for action.

Ready to kill. "You call her or I will."

"You're—"

"—dead? Not anymore I'm not. Now I can finally talk to my wife and—"

"Your wife?" Gary sounded incredulous. "She hasn't been your wife for three years! You let her and Kristal go through all that shit, because you didn't have the courage to tell them you were still alive? You didn't even trust your own *wife*? Are you living in a dream world? You honestly think you can just pick up where you left off and everything'll be just hunky-dory? Are you *that* full of shit that you think she'll take you back?"

Landry stared at the freeway, the cars rushing past, rocking the van. He couldn't look at Jolie. But he could feel her eyes on him, knew that she understood what he was going through.

Gary's voice sounded tinny. "Look, bro. It's over. She's moved on—like you moved on. Or you *should*. She's engaged, she's happy. Happy as she can be except for the fact that Kristal's boyfriend is dead."

Landry said, "Why don't you say it? You think it's my fault Luke died?"

"Don't you?"

Landry's jaw ached. He tried to push his blood pressure back down from the boiling point. "You know everything, Gary. Am I right? You know everything about our marriage. I'm telling you, and I'm going to make this as clear as I can make it. They need to get out of here *now*. Maybe I'm to blame, but I am goddamn going to make sure they're safe."

"They're safe, you can count on that."

"And who's going to keep them safe? *Todd?*"

A pause.

"Todd?" Landry felt a lot of things. Anger at Gary's betrayal. Determination to keep his wife and daughter safe. But he also experienced something he wasn't used to feeling. Helplessness. It felt as if his heart were dissolving.

"Yes," Gary said. "Todd. He took them somewhere safe."

"Where, Gary?"

"She doesn't want you to know."

"Did she tell you that? Does she know I'm alive? Have you talked to her today?"

Silence.

"I thought so. You're full of shit, Gary. Give me her number and I'll tell her what she needs to do. Because if you don't, you'll regret it. We'll all regret it."

"Bite me."

And he hung up.

Landry looked at the phone in his hand, disbelieving. His little brother, the kid brother who looked up to him—the one person in his family he could count on—had betrayed him. For a moment, Landry wondered if Gary'd had something to do with the photograph, but no—that was on Barbara Carey.

It made him want to visit her.

It was a thought that was unworthy of him.

He stared through the windshield, feeling the bleakness of the situation sinking into his bones.

Jolie touched his arm. "You okay?"

"Fine." He started up the van. "I'll call him later and find out where she is." He took the entrance ramp, but this time heading back in the direction of LA.

"We're going west again," Jolie said. "LAX, right?"

"Don't you think that's best?"

Jolie crossed her arms over her chest. He couldn't see past her sunglasses. "You going, too?"

"I would."

"But now—with the photo everywhere—you could be recognized."

"It's a possibility."

She kept her arms crossed, looking out the window. Hard to tell if she was angry or not.

She said, "You think I'm going to argue with you?"

"Are you?"

"No. If, God forbid, we got stopped, and I was with you? Good-bye Tejar Sheriff's Department."

"Good-bye any police department," Landry agreed. "Still, it's a trade-off. You could be famous—a femme fatale. Like in the olden days. Ever see *High Sierra*?"

"*High Sierra*?"

"An old movie starring Humphrey Bogart and Ida Lupino—a crime drama."

"Oh, I think I remember. There was a dog in it?"

"Yes—Pard."

"There was a manhunt. Bogart got chased up into the mountains and they shot him. Didn't he die in Ida Lupino's arms? You think that's what's going to happen to you?"

"Not if I can help it."

He dropped Jolie at the airport—at the curb. They kissed long and hard—clutching tightly before letting go. He felt guilty for dragging her along on this adventure and opened his mouth to say so, but by then she had turned and walked in through the sliding doors.

He thought that maybe he and Jolie were better suited for each other than he and Cindi—a thought that disturbed him.

He drove out to the exit and got back on the freeway.

Cindi had been a medical health technician when he met her—she'd been studying to be a nurse. She'd just gotten her degree when she became pregnant with Kristal. Cindi wanted to stay home with Kristal and she did.

It was a traditional marriage; at least that was how it looked from the outside. He was gone a lot. On deployments, and later, on missions. Cindi kept the home fires burning. She was very capable. She would have made a great nurse. She'd wanted to be an operating room nurse, but that hadn't panned out because she was determined to stay home with their daughter. She had friends—mostly wives of other service members, especially in the early days—and when Kristal got older she worked at a doctor's office.

They had fun together as a family, but it was always the things he wanted to do. There was his surfing phase, his bicycling phase, his running phase. Camping trips—that was her idea. They went all over the western United States, staying at public campgrounds and in national forests. It was an incredible education for Kristal.

By the time she was about to start her teenage years, she was eyeing the boys at the other campsites.

No more camping.

All these things they did, but they had to crowd them into short spaces of time. Because mostly, he was gone. He always came back home to familiarity. And he loved his wife and daughter. He loved them to distraction. He missed them—he and Cindi were soul mates. They were a beautiful family, the three of them.

But he never thought—and she never mentioned—what it must be like for her to see him go away and wonder if he might not come back.

She always kept her feelings close to her chest. Even more than he did—and that was saying something. They'd had their share of arguments, but it was always about little things—nothing earth-shattering.

But now, sitting in the van, he thought about what Gary had said. He thought about how she must have felt when the worst happened. When he packed up for the trip to Florida and left the house and this time he *didn't* come back.

She never shared her feelings. She was easy to be with that way. Everything had been easy. He could just go off and do his thing.

It wasn't as if he didn't do wonderful things for her. He did. He never forgot a birthday. When he was home, he would plan elaborate parties for her, or romantic getaways or dinners. He had a flair for surprising her. And she knew he worshipped the ground she walked on.

But now he wondered if that was enough. How did *she* feel about the life they had? Was Gary right?

He looked at it from her point of view. Or at least he tried—his mind kept wanting to shy away. The thought she might not have liked the idea of a husband who could be killed any moment made him uncomfortable. He'd avoided thinking about it. Maybe because he felt she should have just sucked it up, trusted him. She was a military wife . . .

In her mind, he was dead.

But if that were true, if she was that tough, *wouldn't* she be tough enough to cope? Wouldn't she just . . . move on?

He would have.

The only thing that had kept him from moving on completely was the knowledge that he could get everything back the way he wanted. The three of them would have to go someplace else; they'd have to stay under the radar. But always at the back of his mind, he'd been convinced they would be a family again.

Maybe she really was serious about Todd.

Maybe, she loved him.

He decided not to think about that.

CHAPTER 24

It took Cameron Mills three hours and forty-five minutes to reach Kuwait City. He drove to the business district, a mixture of onion-domed minarets and towering office buildings. The bank district was gold plated—the sun shone off phalanxes of windows rising into the deep blue sky.

He walked into the tallest tower in the largest bank building in the city and rode the elevator up to Barrett International. The fact that Barrett International was US based would be a help. Cam was keenly aware of Kuwait's very strict banking policies. For the average citizen, especially an expat, it was virtually impossible to open a bank account unless several hurdles were cleared.

Fortunately for Cam, he had friends employed by the big guys, Blackwater and the Brits with Aegis Defence Services Limited. They'd respected him and thought he'd go places, drank with him and shared stories. They'd told him which banks were accommodating, who should be avoided, and who could be "financially encouraged."

Even though Kuwait had very strict banking policies, this was a time of war, which meant a time of great opportunity. There was always a way around the rules, if you were a contractor who would bring in millions of dollars.

After a short wait, Cam was ushered into the office of the bank president and greeted cordially. Their introductions preceded a dainty dance—a fucking *minuet*—but there was little doubt that the president wanted High Risk's business. Speaking in generalities, their discussion touched on the requirements for depositing and transferring the cash High Risk had earned from its security jobs. They discussed the types of accounts necessary to keep his money liquid, and to facilitate wire transfers. After a friendly handshake and an awkward hug, Cam returned to the Humvee with a hand truck. This was the way money was transferred in this war-torn part of the world.

On his last trip to the Humvee, he heard a car horn blare—another near miss.

He glanced up and saw a man waiting for the light across the street. From his camo gear and his posture, loose limbed but alert, Cam pegged him as a Navy SEAL.

Hard to tell, with the mirrored sunglasses, but Cam thought the man was looking at him. And why wouldn't he be? Cam was directly across the street, piling stacks of cash into a handcart. "Nothing to see here," he muttered. "Move along."

Even after he turned away, he was aware of the man watching him, so much so, he found himself glancing back. *Paranoid much?* Guy was waiting for the light—big deal. He stacked ten more bricks before glancing back again. Still there—the light hadn't changed. Cam tried to shut him out and returned to the work at hand. But for an instant paranoia got the best of him and he wondered if his CO knew what he was doing. If he was laying a trap for him. But that was ridiculous.

He'd worked hard on his relationship with the CO. It was solid. The guy across the street was just your average bad motherfucker. He knew this by the way the man carried himself. Cam had been around long enough to know a bad guy when he saw one.

205

Then the light changed and the man walked on, down the busy street. Cam had filled his hand truck by then. He carted the money into the lobby and hit the elevator button.

The twenty-five cans had previously held .50-caliber ammunition. He'd even weighed two cans—one filled with the ammo, and one with the money—just to make sure they were equal, in case anyone, maybe a guard at one of the checkpoints, got it into his head to heft one. They were almost identical. To be precise, the money weighed 59 pounds, and the ammo, 58.2. Anyone picking up a can would never suspect there was anything but .50-caliber rounds inside the cans.

Each can was worth $660,000.

Each brick of money held a hundred one-hundred-dollar bills. He was able to fit sixty-six bricks per can: sixteen million, five hundred thousand dollars.

A lackey led him to the count room. There, the man lifted out a brick of cash, hefted it, and slit the cellophane. He peeled the shrink-wrap away, slipped the band off the bundle, and dumped it into the money counter. Cam watched as the first brick went through. The counter moved at high speed. A divider would pop up, smooth as glass, every time the counter reached $10,000. Incredibly fast and efficient.

He'd already done the sums in his head—many times—and so there were no surprises. When all twenty-five cans of cash had gone through the money counter, he had $16,500,000. Sixteen million, five hundred thousand dollars.

And he knew that was only the tip of the iceberg. The money stacked in the craters—he figured there would be at least another $2 or $3 billion—and maybe the whole $6.6 billion!—remained.

Cam would be a very rich man.

By two p.m. he had headed back to the craters by the river to pick up more. And so it would go for the next week. He would reload the cans, and return to Kuwait to make more deposits. The bank president was pleased, especially after taking his cut.

A win-win for everyone.

- — -

By the time he returned the Humvee at the end of the week, Cam had transferred some of his money to a bank account stateside. Only a little at a time—he would continue to siphon off the money in a conservative way. There was still close to $2 billion in cash buried in the craters, and he often thought about the GPS coordinates, and the possibility of picking them up. But his emergency pass was over, so it would be a while. He couldn't raise suspicion—he'd already made up one story that could easily be checked. No need to tempt fate.

But the money was there, waiting for him. After his deployment was over, he would go back and arrange for transport (with a generous cut for the transporters).

The money that would make it all possible.

Next stop: the White House.

CHAPTER 25

It had been a long day. At eight thirty this morning, Cam had spoken at a press conference and fund-raiser—three to four hundred people who cheered after his short speech and could be relied upon to open up their checkbooks. On the drive to the fund-raiser, he'd had a policy briefing on the calamity du jour—Syria again—and spent some time working with his speechwriters on his prepared statements. He had something for everybody: brief comments—usually they took only five minutes—and the lengthier policy speeches. Meanwhile Duncan was working the phone, making sure everything ran smoothly as they were limoed from pillar to post. He worked with military precision. Duncan had been in the military, himself—air force mission support. An administrative position.

Duncan was the one who had coined the term "to limo." He said it sounded much better than "driven."

Duncan made sure that Cam had a bathroom break before the next speech. This was the rule: Cam never went into a bathroom alone. He always had his body man with him. His body man was an extension of himself, his Man Friday, who handled public restrooms, clothes, the mail, paid the bills, and ran interference. He practically held his dick for him.

Cam was getting used to it, and he wondered what it would be like if he lost in the primary and had to go back to depending on himself.

He'd still be a senator. He could still run for reelection. But the band would have passed him by . . .

"Focus!" Steve Cray, his campaign manager, said. "The remark about the air force base, remember? You went off topic again! You weren't supposed to mention the air force base. They're gonna close it, so you don't want to talk about that. Remember, you *voted* to close it. *Focus!*"

"Fine, I'll focus," Cam muttered.

They reached their next destination, a Chamber of Commerce meeting at a major law firm. He could sit down, get off his feet, relax a little as he worked the small but exclusive room, getting commitments from bundlers and for fund-raising events—massaging the best-connected people in the state. He offered one of them, an investment banker and social climber, the position of "finance chair," an honorary job.

The man practically kissed his feet.

Finally—lunch, although he wouldn't taste it, and the food would be crappy if he did. Hotel food. He had to avoid anything "ethnic," especially dishes cooked with garlic or onions or curry—there was a whole list of foods to avoid. He could not have it on his breath. He couldn't smoke: hence the Nicorette gum. He could drink, but very little—just enough to be sociable but never enough to be drunk. And so the food ran the gamut from tasteless to unpalatable, and the liquor was a pale shadow of what Cam had been used to before he became a presidential candidate.

He would shower again or at least strip-wash, and change clothes. He changed clothes two to three times a day. Besides his body man, deodorant was his best friend.

At two p.m. he was back in the hotel making calls again.

Cam had a half hour before another meet and greet, so he kicked off his shoes and lay on the hotel bed while his wife took her shower. Duncan sat in the corner by the window, entering something or other into his laptop.

Cam switched from news channel to news channel. He was still under the radar, still in the second tier. He desperately wanted to be in the first tier. But he also knew he needed to be patient. *Be patient and work hard.* He'd known the drill since he was eight years old, when he stuffed envelopes for his father's campaign for the Apache County Board of Supervisors.

There was nothing on him today. There never was. The press followed the front-runners.

Duncan looked over at him. "Don't worry," he said, reading Cam's mind. "They'll know about you soon enough."

"I'm not worried."

"You don't want to catch fire too soon. Otherwise you'll burn out. The front-runner *never* wins."

"I know that." Cam cradled his one drink, Cutty and soda, on his chest, and felt the chill dampness from the glass leak through his shirt. "I'm sick of this," he said. He switched the channel to the national news.

Duncan said, "Seriously, you're doing great right where you are. You'll hit at the right time. We're doing all the right things."

He got this pep talk every day at some point. He tuned it out. He was so tired.

Just veg out and watch the nightly news . . .

And that was when he saw him.

The man from Kuwait.

The man he had run into three times. The first was in Kuwait City, when he'd carted his money into the bank. The guy looking at him had set off alarm bells, but it was just a chance encounter with

210

a bad guy. Cam knew dangerous men when he saw them, but those men had not been focused on *him*.

There had been two more times since then.

The second time he'd been on a stretch of road with his men on the outskirts of Basrah—must have been six months after he'd banked the last of his money. They'd been out on patrol and had come to a checkpoint. Vehicles were lined up waiting to pass through. As they moved up, he saw a Humvee parked along the side of the road. A group of men leaned against it, shooting the shit and watching the vehicles drive by. One of the men, leaning against the door of the Humvee with his arms folded, was the man he'd seen across the street from the bank in Kuwait City.

Cam recognized the Humvee and its driver—they both belonged to Whitbread Associates, a private security company. The man was talking to his friend, but Cam could tell that behind his dark glasses, he watched everyone who passed. Even though he looked casual, he was not.

Cam, of course, was in military gear.

The last time the guy saw him, Cam had been dressed like a civilian—very much like a military contractor. Almost identical to the man leaning against the Humvee with his pals.

They'd locked eyes. Even behind the shades, it was obvious that the man was looking right at him. The guy tipped his head slightly, spoke sideway to his partner, his eyes never leaving Cam.

The encounter had worked on his imagination. Running into the guy twice.

The third time, though, that was the charm.

Fast-forward a few years. He was a state congressman who had made a name for himself, running for the United States Senate. Because he was brash and had cultivated that quality (brash *sold*!), he often rubbed people the wrong way. That was okay, because it appealed to his constituency—they appreciated a certain swagger in their candidate. He was already beginning to receive national attention, so he decided it was time to have a bodyguard. This led him to a conversation with Mike Cardamone, head of a private security company called Whitbread Associates.

It never occurred to him that he would run into the man *again*.

But there he was: the first man he met. Cyril Landry picked him up at the airport.

Turned out the man was one of Cardamone's best operatives—Cardamone's right-hand man.

The trip from the airport had been excruciating.

The man had said not one word.

They had reached the Whitbread offices, and the man had held the door for him, silent as a cigar store Indian.

He could see it like it was yesterday, Landry standing in the office, arms folded, fit and tall and impassive. Those eyes. *Jesus!* They were icy blue and pierced right through him. His mouth crooked up at the corner, just a tad, but it wasn't really a smile. There was no doubt in Cam's mind that Landry recognized him. Cardamone had talked for the most part, telling Cam that Landry was the best man he had. And Cam had stood there, trying to look impressed, trying to look at Cyril Landry, and his eyes just seemed to . . . slide off the man's face.

It was as if the man knew all his secrets. Like the guy knew what he'd done, how he'd gotten to where he was now. This was all bullshit, of course. But he'd now run into him three times, *three chance meetings*, and each time he could tell the guy had taken note of him. The man had looked at Cam clinically, as if he could see past the jovial smile and the open hand to something underneath.

He knew about the money. Cyril Landry had seen him, dressed like a private military contractor, loading bricks of money into the hand truck and carrying it into the bank.

Hold on.

Why did he think that Landry would know that he stole the money from that house? No way he would know that.

No way would he know anything—except perhaps by the guilty look on Cam's face. And yes, he guessed that a guy like Landry could *smell* fear.

The guy was a killer.

After Landry had left, Cardamone told Cam that Landry would be perfect for the security job. Cam said he would prefer someone else.

"Why?"

"I just would."

"If you think he'd do anything out of line, think again. You can trust him with your life. He doesn't care whether you're a Democrat, a Republican, or a Jehovah's Witness. He'll protect you. He doesn't care what he's asked to do. He'll do anything—if you're in danger, he'll kill for you or die for you without blinking an eye."

Cam told Cardamone he would think about it. He'd walked out of Whitbread Associates, feeling much the way he did when he'd spotted Cyril Landry across the street in Kuwait City and Landry had walked away down the street. He felt as if he'd dodged a bullet. Closing the door behind him, standing on the step outside, he was weak-kneed and trembling. Cam had good instincts and he trusted them. He did not want to get crosswise of the man.

He hired another personal security company instead.

Months later, Cam learned what had happened on the island in Florida. The gun battle, the conflagration: a miniwar on the attorney general's private island. Other than Mike Cardamone, the names of the missing and the dead didn't ring a bell—until he'd heard the name "Cyril Landry."

He was sure in his heart that Mike Cardamone had died at the hands of Cyril Landry.

- — -

Cam was watching one of the cable channels when he saw the photo. It was a bad shot, backlit by the sun, taken on a smartphone. Just a man's head mostly in profile. He turned up the sound.

The newscaster was talking about a school shooting. The one that just happened, in LA.

Cam had been asked about the mass shooting on one of the news shows—and had condemned the shooter, although he'd been careful not to call for any kind of gun control. No need to anger the NRA.

The photo disappeared as the news channel switched to the latest celebrity's brush with the law.

Cam's eyes remained fixed on the TV screen. Thinking, thinking, thinking.

Landry.

He'd always had a bad feeling about the man. That Landry had somehow known what was in his mind. That Landry knew he'd stolen the money. The *idea* of Landry had grown bigger and bigger over time, instead of diminishing.

Cam was the type of guy who always followed his instincts. He'd hired a private detective to look into Landry's death on the island, and the results were inconclusive. No body had ever been found.

The private detective had sat in his office, reeking of cigarette smoke, his fat fingers laced over his belly, a self-satisfied grin on his broad face.

"He's dead, you can take it to the bank," the detective had told him. "Don't you worry about that. No way he could have survived that storm. No way they'd find the body, either. He was just so much shark food."

But Cam hadn't been satisfied.

He'd paid the guy what he was owed and found someone else. A harder character. Someone who was former military, like himself. Only this guy was the type who knew other hard people—the kind of guy who could make things happen.

The guy had told him an interesting story about a place that wasn't on any map. He called it the "Toolshed."

Cam remembered their conversation, almost word for word. How hard it would be to find out if Landry was, indeed, alive. "If he's alive, he'll be very careful. If he was Special Forces, he has discipline." Then the guy said, "But there is *one* way to lure him out."

When he told him what it was, Cam recoiled.

But he'd had second thoughts about that.

Oh yes, he did.

He'd had second thoughts.

CHAPTER 26

Marcella Rouch knew she'd hear from her sister-in-law, Barb Carey. She knew Barb would feel angry and betrayed. Marcella didn't have much use for Barb anyway, so that wouldn't pose a particular problem. Marcella also knew that Barb suspected that Justin had swiped the photo of Joe Till from her phone. She would assume that he'd shared the photo with Marcella, and boom! More family drama.

Now the photo was all over the news—on TV and the Internet—and Marcella had already ignored two calls and deleted three text messages from Barb. Barb was no dummy. She knew there were hundreds, possibly thousands, of photos that the Gordon C. Tuttle School Shooting Task Force had to go through, and she knew that one way to narrow it down was to rely on sources in law enforcement—from other cops. In other words, trustworthy sources. Marcella was all cop; she worked Crimes Against Persons with San Diego PD.

Yesterday, Marcella had received a phone call from a member of the Gordon C. Tuttle School Shooting Task Force. An FBI special agent on the task force took her statement. Marcella told him about Joe Till's odd hours, and her sister-in-law's own conjecture that Till drove someplace every weekday and returned by early evening. Barb herself had done the math, how he could have driven five days a week to Torrent Valley to familiarize himself with the school and the kids there. She'd suspected as much—that he had gone there day after day, on weekdays, when school was in session. It didn't take a rocket scientist to make the connection. Not to mention, Barb had also said she'd had a bad feeling that day, even calling Marcella to check to see if Joe Till had been injured or killed or—God forbid—jailed when he failed to come back.

Deep down, Barb knew. Marcella was sure that Barb knew exactly what had transpired. Joe Till knew that there would be a school shooting—knew it would go down. It was her opinion that he had kept that knowledge secret.

Why, she couldn't imagine. But she'd always thought there was something wrong with him. Maybe he'd been damaged by the war. She'd had no qualms about submitting the photo to her sergeant.

But so far, as far as Marcella knew—and they could just be withholding info; in fact, they were *probably* withholding info—they had not been able to identify the man she knew as Joe Till.

Then the FBI special agent working the case called her. He'd kept his cards close to his vest, just asked her where she'd obtained the photo and when it was taken. That was yesterday. She suspected that law enforcement might very well converge on her sister-in-law's place—and soon.

She hoped Barb wouldn't be held as a material witness. She hoped that she wouldn't be arrested. But justice was justice and the school shooting task force needed to know. She was a cop first, and family, second. Barb Carey wasn't much of a sister-in-law, and now Marcella was returning the favor.

If she could prevent this guy from going off again and killing more people, she would be happy. It was the way she rolled.

- — -

Landry awoke in the darkness of the hotel room. It was the middle of the night. For a moment he forgot where he was. He was back in Afghanistan. Or maybe Iraq. No—Afghanistan. The Korengal Valley. It was bad—he'd lost two good friends that day. Then he realized he was in another hotel room, another anonymous hotel room, and nothing had awakened him except his own mind. Jolie was gone, back to New Mexico. His wife and daughter were gone, too, and Gary refused to tell him where they were, except to say they were "safe." He doubted that. What would a pansy comptroller know about safe houses? Would he fight off the bad guys with a briefcase and a spreadsheet? Fortunately, Landry had made sure that both Cindi and Kristal knew how to protect themselves. If they took their weapons with them, they would know how to use them. *If* they'd kept up their practice. He hoped they had. They'd also had martial arts training, but he knew Cindi and Kristal would be no match for whoever was coming for him.

The person behind this had used Landry's family once to try and draw him out. He would have no qualms about doing it again.

Right now, though, he could feel that something—or someone—was closing in on him. It wasn't just the photo on TV, but the idea that someone, somewhere, had turned an eye on him.

He knew it was personal.

Again, he felt it in his jaw. He felt it in his whole body, which had tightened up, like a violin string to its breaking point. He took a deep breath. Closed his eyes. Let the white noise in his head subside into silence. He'd had years of practice letting go of his fears—war had done that for him.

Whoever it was—one person or an army—he would be ready for them. He knew how to evade, and he knew how to fight, and he knew how to kill.

- — -

He allowed himself to drift back into sleep and awoke again at four a.m. Rested. Ready. He ordered room service. Turned the shower on and left the bathroom door open. Called out to the hotel employee who brought it to leave it outside the door. He waited ten full minutes and then retrieved the food.

He turned on the television. The "news" had moved on. There were more pressing and important things in the world than a poor photo of one person of interest.

There was nothing about Gordon C. Tuttle High School. Already it was old news, fading like that photograph would if it were printed up and exposed to the light. Presidential, global, and local politics took the spotlight, the same flames fanned over and over again.

But Landry thought about the school. He wondered where his wife and daughter were. He wondered how Kristal was handling Luke's death. He wondered if she suspected it had something to do with her father.

He wondered how she had taken the news about him—that he was alive.

What would she think? Would she think he had something to do with the deaths of those kids? With Luke's death?

He couldn't believe that. Kristal would know he loved her. She had to know he loved her and her mother more than anything else on earth. She had to know that he would never shoot up a school.

From what he'd seen on the news, they were still leaving out details on the shooter's death.

In fact, they had ignored that whole aspect. More than a week had gone by and there was very little on the shooting, if anything. When his picture popped up on the screen yesterday, Landry assumed that they were thinking he was an associate of the shooter. Maybe an accomplice.

They would assume that a sniper of his caliber would be a professional. These were no dummies, these cops. If he were working the case, he would have guessed that the two had worked together—himself and the shooter—and that he had shot the shooter to keep him from being captured and questioned.

Caught and interviewed—those were the nonmilitary terms for it.

The problem was, they were looking at it the wrong way. Landry was convinced that someone had shot up the school to lure him out. Someone already suspected he was alive.

And all those kids were dead because of it.

He had to stay at large. He had to figure out who had tried to draw him out. And he had to find his wife and daughter and make sure they were safe.

The restaurant, Sam's Place, was on Wilshire Boulevard in Los Angeles proper, a busy part of town with plenty of high-rises, businesses, four lanes of traffic, bistros, shops, and hotels lining the streets. Not too upscale but not down in the mouth, either. Sam's Place was a chain with four rooms chock-full of talking people. It was lunch hour, the noise level was high—a loud babble, people leaning forward and conversing earnestly with one another. The waiters were young and attractive, probably college students, friendly but busy. They couldn't afford to linger. Taking orders was down to a science. The kind of place where the young server tried to sell them an appetizer by rote.

Eric wore blue. Landry wore gray. Just like Landry's favorite film of all time, *Casablanca*, a heady cauldron of war, betrayal, spies, sentimentality, patriotism, and outrageous heroism. Sam's Place fit the theme.

Eric the Red had cleaned up nicely. He wore a blue shirt and a blue tie and navy-blue slacks. Good shoes. Reasonably good slacks, a nice watch. Eric could afford a nice watch. He had the requisite iPhone and the get-down-to-business-after-the-first-drink attitude. Busy, busy, busy.

Landry, likewise. He wore a gray shirt, a darker gray tie, charcoal gray slacks.

There were plenty of others who wore those two colors, but the uniformity of the presentation made them stand out across a crowded room.

Of course Eric the Red would stand out in any room.

They made it easy on the server. Generic food. Generic drinks. Earnest conversation—and the server knew from experience that the best thing he could do was leave them alone, popping up only to put down a plate or sell another drink or dessert.

They'd managed an out-of-the-way corner at a two-top where the weak and unobtrusive sound system played "As Time Goes By" through the speaker above. Eric had set his briefcase on the small table, had a printout under one hand.

"Got some news for you, bro," Eric said, leaning forward so he could be heard over the rush of sound. "It's from the Toolshed."

Landry had known it was coming. "I'm a mark?"

Eric nodded.

"You know who put out the paper on me?"

"No idea."

Landry absorbed this. He'd been prepared for this eventuality, ever since his photo was put up on TV.

The trip to Austria had yielded results, but not the one he'd expected. He'd expected to be hired for a hit, thought that he would get into the network that way, as—Peterman.

"The pic, man. They're taking it seriously."

"Who's taking it seriously? Is there a way to find out who put the paper out on me?"

"No idea and no way to find out. *Somebody* got a nasty surprise when you showed up on TV."

Landry reflected that it would be a lot of people. Hard to narrow down.

Eric leaned forward. "I do have a marginal framework—a hack. He may be able to get you what you need."

Two questions. Landry asked them. One was "How long will it take?" and the other was "How much?"

"Might be a couple of days, or it could be like that." Eric snapped his fingers. "You know how it goes." And he named a price.

Just then the waiter, who looked to be all of twelve, came by with the food. "Careful," he said. "These plates are hot."

－ — -

Andrew Keller, FBI special agent, Los Angeles field office, had figured out within a few hours that the man who spun stories about a brother with a fishing lodge in Montana—and had extracted information from him—was a fake. And Andrew could thank his lucky stars that the information the man had extracted was minimal.

Think about it: how easy it was. The man who called himself Jim Branch from Kalispell never replied to the message Keller'd left on his cell, and when Keller had finally called the municipal number, he got a message saying he'd reached an office in human resources on the first floor. He called back later and got a receptionist. The receptionist said she'd never heard of Jim Branch, homicide detective from Kalispell, Montana—or his son—and as far as she knew there was no one named Branch working in the building. She'd added that if Jim Branch's son was indeed a police officer, he would have called from one of the three offices in the Las Vegas Municipal Police Department, or used his cell.

Which made Andrew feel like an idiot.

No doubt about it; he'd been played. And whoever had played him was good at it.

Now, though, he had a photo, and what do you know? They had facial-recognition software.

He'd discovered something amazing. Ground shaking, to be more accurate.

The man in the photo was Cyril Landry, a former Navy SEAL, last employed by Whitbread Associates, a private security firm out of Washington, DC, that no longer existed. And neither did Cyril Landry.

Landry had been an operator—a professional killer—and that went a long way to solving the problem Special Agent Keller had with the shooting at the school.

The shooter was a pro.

And the shooter who shot the shooter was a pro as well.

That was pretty sweet shooting. The shooter who took out the guy they were now calling "Mystery Meat" was a top-notch sniper. He had shot Mystery Meat in the perfect place, the base of the skull. This had the effect of cutting a marionette's strings. The guy dropped in place, instantly dead, without even the *possibility* of jerking the trigger and killing any more kids.

In one way, the second shooter was a hero.

But Keller had wanted to know what Cyril Landry was doing there that day, and why he'd had all that firepower with him. He knew there was a girl who went to the school named Landry. Kristal Landry. He drew up her file and the photo.

There's your reason right there.

Truth be told, Keller didn't blame the guy one bit. He would have done the same thing himself, if he'd had the chops to do it. Which, he readily admitted, he didn't.

But after reading up on Landry and seeing what a bad guy he was, Keller had less sympathy for him.

If it *was* him. Facial recognition was fairly reliable, but not perfect.

But it felt right. Maybe Landry was there by coincidence and shot to protect his daughter. Or maybe he shot the shooter for another reason. As a father of three, Keller wanted it to be the former. He wanted Landry to have protected his daughter. But he couldn't rule anything out. It could just as easily go the other way. For all he knew, Landry could have wanted his daughter dead, for some reason.

There were a lot of sick people out there.

Keller pulled up information on Landry's death—the firefight on a tiny private island off the Florida coast. He knew the basic outlines of the story. The private island belonged to the former attorney general of the United States. He had fallen in with some bad associates—namely, Whitbread Associates, a private security contractor that did plenty of outright illegal things, including several killings. Several killings had been ascribed to Whitbread, but they had never been proved. The attorney general was prosecuted for some crimes, but there were rumors that the time he was serving (three and a half years—the rich *are* different) was just the tip of the iceberg.

There had been allegations . . .

Crazy stuff, like dead superstars. He tried to remember the name of one of them, some country singer, a stunning blonde. His daughter had her songs on her iPhone.

Mostly, what was written about the star's death was tabloid stuff—but you never knew.

Cyril Landry had died on the island. Or rather, drowned during the storm. That was Keller's recollection of the incident. There had been a firefight. Whitbread Associates' assets were essentially "liquidated" that night—literally. Including three dead operatives in a safe house.

He looked at the photo again. He was convinced he was looking at the face of Cyril Landry.

The only thing now was for them to decide what to do next. Use his name? Or just leave the photo out there as it was and see what cropped up?

For the moment, Keller decided to keep it quiet. Horse out of the barn and so forth.

Part of it was the idea that Landry had played him for a sucker. He had done his homework, leading him on about High Mountain Outdoor Adventures and his brother's fishing prowess. Keller was embarrassed—he admitted that now—that he'd given more information to Landry than he should have. Not a big deal, now that he knew who and what he was dealing with. But he couldn't help but project ahead a few scenes to the moment Landry was arrested—and hopefully he would be arrested, not killed—and they would come face to face. *You thought you had me measured,* was what he'd say. *But you were wrong.* Now *who's got the last laugh?*

That evening he stopped at the Safeway and bought his wife flowers and a box of candy. When he got home, he told her they were going out to dinner. At first she demurred, because she had worked hard all day—she was a schoolteacher—and all she wanted to do was veg out on the couch and watch another episode of *House of Cards.* But he jollied her into it and they had a great time. They went to Tosca for dinner, and drank a whole bottle of wine between them and an after-dinner drink. She asked him what the occasion was and he said he had a lead on the school shooting. He usually confided in her, but this time he just gave her the general outlines. She was relieved, and then happy. Clasped his hand in hers and said, "If you can get to the bottom of this . . ."

"It could be a promotion."

A little voice saying: *If only I hadn't fallen for that song and dance about the fishing lodge!*

"You think he shot the man to keep him quiet?"

"Could be." Although there was that small, sane voice in the back of his mind that said Landry had probably shot to save his daughter's life. He willfully ignored that voice. The man was a stone-cold killer. "We've always been operating under the assumption that the shooter was a hired gun."

"I thought so."

"But I'm going to get him."

She looked into his eyes. "I know you will."

Like it was a done deal.

He felt like a bloodhound on the scent. It was a great feeling—the best feeling in the world. The FBI's reason for not releasing the name of the second shooter, Cyril Landry, had plenty of good points to it, but for Andrew, it was like manna from heaven. He had a second chance to even the score.

You're mine, he thought. *I have you all to myself.*

That'll teach you to fuck with me.

- — -

Landry and Eric the Red met again the next day. Different restaurant, same noise. Better than the same noise. Right after they sat down, restaurant employees marched out of the kitchen clapping their hands rhythmically and singing "Happy Birthday" at the top of their lungs, the waitress in the front of the line carrying a cupcake with one candle on it. Almost every eye turned in the direction of the happy birthday boy, who looked to be around sixty years old.

Eric the Red took a big draft of beer and spoke under the din. "As you can see, these are the results on that in-house promotion." He pushed a folder across the table.

Landry glanced at it, peeked inside, then put it in his briefcase. "That's great—looks like we're gonna be up this quarter."

"You know it."

When the birthday song ended, the place erupted in applause.

Business done, they discussed various things. Eric had a wife and three boys. The oldest boy was in high school, a football player. "My wife's worried about concussion. The kid's great. Tight end. But you know, sometimes, at night, I think about his future."

Landry's own mind turned to Kristal. Where was she now? He'd put out feelers—very carefully—but there was nothing. It was as if she'd disappeared from the face of the earth. Hard to believe an ass-hole like Todd could pull something like that off. He'd find them, though. "The sport's changed," he said. "All those big guys. Steroids. I wouldn't want one of them coming at me. Concussion's nothing to fool around with. It's a real and present danger," he said. "Could mess him up for the rest of his life."

Eric nodded, his expression glum. "You should see the suicide rate in former pro football players. Good money, though, you know that. Fame, fortune. Be able to take care of your wife and kids. A good, solid life. And there's the camaraderie—we know about that, don't we? But the price, man. The price is so damn high. In other news, do you have any idea who would put you up on the chalkboard?"

"More people than I can name."

"Hey, yeah, I get that. You also know the board usually discusses it within a twenty-four-to-forty-eight-hour time frame. But this time—"

"—they moved fast."

"No shit. *Somebody* wants you dead right quick. You've got all the life span of a burnbag print."

Landry smiled. A "burnbag print" was a highly combustible carrier bag that contained important info. To ensure it wouldn't end up in the wrong hands, the bag had a high oxygen content, which created enough turbulence to destroy whatever was inside—turning the contents to ash. It was an apt description of Landry's chances.

He said nothing. He was thinking.

Eric said, "Wouldn't underestimate the guy even if he *is* young. You of all people know they're meticulous in who they choose."

Landry knew that was true. After the bulletin went up, they were very careful to find the right guy—the most capable of a half dozen or so candidates.

He also knew that once you were offered a contract, you took it. Always. You didn't say no to the agency, even if it was a suicide run. Even if it was a major assassination. You would be off the call sheet and out of business.

Landry thought about the guy who had shot up the school. The one lying on a slab just north of here. He thought about Devin Patel, the Juggalo kid, who left behind a sister with narcolepsy. As strange as he'd seemed, the boy had good, solid friends. He'd cared about his sister. Landry thought he must have been a good kid.

Like Luke Brodsky. Luke Brodsky—hero—who had pushed his daughter under the car and took the bullet meant for her.

- — -

Landry didn't look at the information Eric gave him until he reached the hotel room. There, he took off his shoes, sat on the made bed, and opened the folder.

The shooter's name was Zachary Smith. The last name was kind of obvious, but it was just possible he *was* a Smith. There was no law against it. "Smith" was a common name for a reason.

It sounded made up, though.

Landry decided to call him "Zach."

Zach Smith was twenty-eight years old.

He was well trained and well skilled, but Landry read between the lines. Smith wasn't heavily experienced. Sure, he had been in the military, but he wasn't elite military. Sure, he'd been a hired operative, but not for very long.

It didn't pay to underestimate someone who was coming to kill you. But what you *could* do was probe for potential weaknesses and come up with two or three game plans. The fact that Zach Smith was young and hadn't had elite training might have led Landry to believe he was just another kid, a thuggish killer, and that would be a big mistake. There was *some* reason he'd been chosen for this hit.

The fact was, though, Landry had the keys to the kingdom, and he knew how to use them. He might be in his late forties, but he had the one thing this kid didn't have: experience. Thousands of miles under his belt, two wars and a military action, and countless kills. He'd seen just about every possible situation, or at least knew about them.

Landry now had the assassin's contact info and had received the communication key. Now he could communicate with Zach Smith. He could tell Zach where to pick up his instructions. Whom to kill, and when and how to do it.

All Landry needed to do now was come up with the right place.

CHAPTER 27

For this mission—and Landry saw it as a mission—he needed a remote meeting place. He had made a habit of running through many canyons in the Angeles National Forest near his home base in Arcadia, so it was easy to narrow it down to the one most favorable for this op. After weighing the pros and cons, Landry decided on the Devil's Canyon in the San Gabriel Mountains.

It wasn't perfect, but it was good.

There were a few things that recommended the area. One, it was a harder hike than many others, so few people. The farther down you hiked, the more remote it became. And the trail was difficult in places and would require some concentration on the part of the mark.

The biggest worry was that Zach Smith would pause often to look behind him on the trail. Smith would automatically worry that a large part of the trail was downhill. He would know that if anyone was stalking him, the shot would come from above high ground—and he'd never see it coming.

Landry had planned for this contingency. He had set the drop point down on the canyon floor, an area entangled by vines, shrubs, and undergrowth, hidden from view by a canopy of trees. There would be running water and hidden rocks to add to the distraction.

The idea that the drop was on level ground would bolster Smith's confidence in the mission. As for the effort to get there—these guys came to believe nothing in life was easy.

Landry would set up behind him in the creek, on the same level ground. He had already found the place, and made sure he could be completely hidden there.

He made a dry run and timed it. The drive there, how long it would take to jog to the place where he would set up, the places on the trail where Smith would be in his line of sight. He knew exactly where he would bury the packet: in the dirt against a massive boulder where an oak tree encroached on one side, and a berm on the other. The mark would have to present his back to Landry as he crouched down to dig up the packet. This was of the utmost importance, because Landry had planned his shot for the back of the head.

It had to be the back of the head.

On that point, there was no ambiguity.

- — -

Landry called the hitter. It was a very short phone call—just long enough to introduce himself as the man tapped by the person ordering the hit to give him the GPS position where the packet would be buried.

The next morning Landry watched through binocs as Smith drove to the trailhead and parked. It was just dawn. There were no other cars. Smith wore a T-shirt, shorts, hiking boots, and a large pack on his back—probably containing a high-powered weapon of some sort. There was a firearm on his hip as well.

As the TV ad said: "Don't leave home without it."

Landry didn't move from where he was. He watched as the

man disappeared from view, reappearing here and there along the trail.

After letting him get a good head start, Landry trotted down, stopping every once in a while to glass the trail ahead.

The kid was making good time. Landry made sure to stay in cover as much as he could. The farther down they went, the more cover: chaparral, woody trees Landry didn't recognize, oak, plenty of rock formations, snarls of grass and wildflowers, and a few puddles of brackish water here and there.

Landry didn't have to get close. He had already picked out the best place and waited for the mark to reach the spot.

Rarely did it work out so perfectly.

The kid (he couldn't help thinking of him as one, even though Zachary Smith was twenty-eight and an adult) worked his way to the water. There, he pulled out a GPS, correlated the coordinates for the package's placement, and followed the trail to the foot of the boulder.

Smith looked around first, using his binocs and scanning the hills above him. That was where the threat would come from—above. Finally, he crouched down and took a knee. He swept the dirt and oak leaves away from the base of the boulder and pulled out an earth-brown envelope. Abruptly, he froze. His body was taut, on alert. He scanned the mountain range above, looking for possible threats. Looking, Landry knew, for an odd glint of light on a rifle barrel. Anything out of the ordinary.

Smith decided the area was clear. Still on one knee, he tucked the envelope inside his jacket.

Landry pulled the trigger.

The kid's head recoiled—Landry imagined he could hear the thwack as the bullet hit, followed by the faint spit of the silencer screwed onto Landry's rifle.

The kid fell forward and lay facedown in an awkward slump, legs crumpled partially underneath his body, partially behind him. Head down, pressed into the base of the boulder.

Landry kept him in his sights. He did not move for ten minutes. Down here in the canyon, there was no wind. It was quiet, except for the birds. The kid in the scope did not move. Landry listened for car engines in the distance, but heard none.

He was alone.

Waited another ten minutes, watching the trail in and out of the canyon, listened for car doors, glassed the hills and rocks and high ramparts, just to make sure no one was coming. Then he made his way down to the canyon.

- — -

He jumped down from the berm and rolled the body to one side to snap the photo with his new burner phone—making sure the kid's face was still planted in the dirt. Even if he had displayed the face, there wasn't much left—the shot had been placed so that the bullet obliterated Smith's features when it blew out the other side, making him virtually unidentifiable. Landry paused, and looked down at him, said, "Dumb kid." The kid was a killer, but it was still a shame—they should have hired someone who knew what he was doing. Landry spared the kid a moment of regret. Then he roped Smith's feet and dragged him downstream to a grave he'd dug the day before, a hole tucked under an overhang of rock in an area filled with brush. Using the folding camp shovel he'd left there the day before, Landry covered Zach Smith with dirt and pulled more rocks and brambles down on top. The grave was high enough and far enough that water would not reach, even during a flash flood. The operator who had come for Landry was now dead at Landry's hands.

At the post office, he forwarded the photo of the corpse along with his own fingerprints and saliva sample to the Toolshed, using the envelope they had kindly provided Zach Smith for that purpose. The saliva sample would be used to confirm the corpse's DNA, and the fingerprints would be corroborative: proof positive that the operator they'd hired—Zach Smith—had completed his mission.

Cyril Landry was dead.

Again.

CHAPTER 28

Back at the hotel by midmorning, Landry showered and changed. He kept the TV on, listening for his name, but didn't hear it. He checked his iPad—all the Internet news sites—but Landry's photo had been replaced many times over. In fact, there was nothing on the school shooting, which was old news.

He called his brother and got his voice mail. "Call me," he said, and disconnected.

He called Tom, his old friend in Kentucky. One of the few people in life he could depend on.

First thing out of Tom's mouth was "So what they said on TV is true. You're still here."

"So far," Landry said.

"I heard someone put out a paper on you."

"They did. Someone killed me."

A pause. "Well, that's good news. So what now?"

"This worked for a while, but it's possible whoever put the paper out on me will want to make sure."

"You mean, take a victory lap?"

"See for himself. But that's not my real problem. The real problem is I don't know where Cindi and Kristal are."

"Gary won't say, huh?"

"No."

A pause. Then, "Damn."

"You don't know, do you? Any idea?"

"Nope. Just got the call from Gary saying they wouldn't be coming out here. They made 'other plans.'"

"He didn't say anything about her fiancé?"

"Nope." Tom Davis was a man of few words. He worked for a pinhooker outside Lexington, training young horses to run. He had seen a lot of action, mostly in Vietnam, and had his own place, thirty acres covered in junk. Landry pictured Tom in his trademark overalls, his long white hair and beard—he looked like Santa Claus, not one of the best pinhooking trainers in the business. Tom was what Landry called a "scattered genius." He'd once built an airplane from scratch in his barn—not from any specs; he'd just built it and built it right—before realizing there was one last part of the puzzle he couldn't fix: he couldn't get it out the door. Tom had come up with an unusual solution—he'd told Landry about it but he still didn't get it—and the plane made one maiden flight before Tom just gave up on it and it became another pasture ornament. Whether it was training racehorses or building something in his shop, he was all about the project. Once he was done with something, he was done.

Tom was also former Special Forces, and the most trustworthy man Landry knew. He was the only man in the world Landry would trust with his wife's and daughter's safety except for himself.

And now Tom was out of the loop.

"Could you call Gary again? Find out why there was a change in plans?"

"I could. You think it will help?"

Landry thought about how Gary had dug in. "Probably not. But I need to know where they are. Have you met Todd?"

"The boyfriend? No. Haven't even talked to him on the phone. Only talked with Gary."

"You have no idea where they went, then?"

"Well, I assume they went to Big Bear Lake."

Landry felt the spark, like someone had connected a jumper cable to his chest. "Big Bear Lake? Why?"

"Heard Gary mention the boyfriend has a cabin there."

"Where?"

"That, I don't know. He mentioned it once, is all."

"But you think that's where they'd go?"

"You said for them to get out of town, right? So that would be my guess."

- — -

Landry called Gary and got his voice mail. He left a message, asking Gary to call him.

"Don't mention I called," he added. "Somebody put a hit out on me. It's okay now, but no one knows I'm alive."

He disconnected, feeling as if he'd been cut loose from the world. Heard his own words. *Somebody put a hit out on me. No one knows I'm alive.*

What kind of crap was that? Was that supposed to sway Gary into telling him where Cindi and Kristal were?

Gary had the power. Gary and, to a lesser extent, Cindi. What would Cindi think about what he'd just said? *Just another day at the office. Somebody put a hit out on me, and it's all worked out, but for all intents and purposes I'm dead.*

He couldn't think about it right now. He needed to know where they were, needed to protect them. Needed to get them someplace safe. They couldn't depend on *Todd.*

He glanced at the TV. The caption option was on.

Landry didn't watch a lot of TV, but he liked to read newspapers. He followed the news. And this news concerned him.

It had taken some time for some of the bodies from the massacre at Gordon C. Tuttle High School to be released. The first to be buried was Devin Patel. The Juggalo kid. His funeral was at the end of the week.

A reporter on the news channel was interviewing a man who planned to protest the funeral.

Landry recognized him. He was one of those preachers in the news all the time. The kind who capitalized on anger, fear, and misery.

When you got to that level where you were on television all the time, it was all for show. To be more specific, for show and money.

Pope Francis was the only exception to the rule Landry could see. But then he wasn't really what you'd call a preacher.

Most of the preachers Landry had seen on TV were charlatans at the very least, and soul-stealers at their worst. They made their money scaring people. As far as Landry was concerned, a lot of these high-profile preachers with their massive cathedrals and expensive limos were con men, and they made their money on pain. They sucked money and pain into themselves and grew bloated on it, and spewed out more grievances, insults to God that their flocks had never heard of until they brought them up.

Like Devin Patel—the Juggalo.

According to the man on television, he wasn't just a Juggalo. He was a *gay* Juggalo.

Landry didn't know if Devin was gay. He didn't care if Devin was gay. What did it matter to him?

What mattered was, Devin had looked after his sister. What mattered was, he had friends who cared about him, friends who looked after their side of the pact they'd made, and watched after his sister now that he was unable to.

What Landry felt as he stared at the TV screen was animus— very unusual for him. Landry prided himself on being even-keeled. Even-keeled and efficient.

He had seen the face before—you couldn't miss it if you watched TV, or read a newspaper, or used the Internet. It was a mean face, scored with cruel lines running down from hard-apple cheeks to a hinged jaw that made Landry think of Howdy Doody. A clown face gone awry. Piggy little eyes stared out at the world from behind round wire-rimmed eyeglasses, the kind bankers and politicians and big businessmen wore during the Great Depression.

He seemed to have come to the present from long ago. Not the Great Depression, though: the Gilded Age. Large girth, three-piece suit.

Well fed and pompous.

He was standing outside a university called Mount Loyal Independent Christian College—a religious institution Landry had never heard of—located in Pasadena. The sun shining on his glasses, his mouth opening and closing like the lips of a large-mouth bass. Quoting Bible scriptures and thundering death and destruction to those who did not obey God's law.

Melvin Fortun. President of Mount Loyal Independent Christian College. Mel to his friends? Landry wondered. Landry remembered seeing him once before. He had a memory for strange-looking people. Fortun had gone hunting with one of the US House members—Landry remembered a gray day, the man dressed to the nines in hunting gear that looked like it had come directly from Rifleman Warehouse. So new it crunched. Hunting rifle tucked under his arm. High up in the National Rifle Association. Landry himself had had a membership in the NRA, but had to let it lapse, due to the fact that he was dead.

Fortun thundered about homosexuals and keeping and bearing arms, and the two issues were so consistently linked together, for a moment Landry wondered if he was in favor of homosexuals bearing arms. He railed about the Juggalo lifestyle. Satan worshippers, fiends, evil incarnate. He slipped and called Devin "Devil" Patel.

When the reporter corrected him, he said, "Devil isn't far from the truth. He should not be buried on hallowed ground."

The reporter asked about the shooting. Melvin Fortun was a little more circumspect there. "It was a sad occasion, but no one should read anything into it more than a madman with a gun."

He cited the brave security guard who had shot the bad guy.

Landry was never one for pride of ownership. His mouth turned up a little, thinking how easily the press had been snowed. That anyone could believe a security guard with a pistol could have made that shot . . .

It had become common knowledge, though. The security guard had been made a hero. And meanwhile, people like that FBI special agent Landry had talked to on the phone—they knew that it had taken an expert sniper to kill someone like that. Which was why they were looking for someone like him.

Fortun was actually stupid enough to say the words "collateral damage."

Landry turned the TV set off.

He thought about Devin Patel, and Luke Conaboy—"Eezil"— and Brian Swinney, and Willow. Willow, wandering around like Lucia di Lammermoor.

One person he avoided thinking about was Luke Brodsky. It was still too close. It was the one place he could not go.

- — -

Mount Loyal Independent Christian College was a sprawling, lively campus full of kids who looked like college kids everywhere. The grounds were particularly inviting. Plenty of grass, shaved close to the ground like felt on a billiard table. Big shade trees. California sunshine. A few palms. Redbrick buildings that looked a century old but up close were clearly built to newer standards. There was

Sermon Hall, square in the middle of campus, complete with a white cupola with a bronze angel on top. Gabriel, blowing his horn.

Landry walked the campus and got a feel for it. He had dressed in a business suit and held a briefcase. He sat down on a stone bench in the dark shade of a tree opposite the administrative offices, opened his iPad on top of his briefcase, and looked absorbed. At twelve noon on the dot the doors to the admin building opened and people started coming out, ostensibly heading for the student union for lunch, or at least a cigarette break.

Landry recognized Melvin. He looked like a fat shark in a suit. Light bounced off his gold rims. He walked close to the woman with him—someone in the administration, but from here it looked like he was too close, as if he were trying to feel her up. The woman ignored him and kept to a businesslike pace.

Landry had seen enough. He already had the man's address, and now he'd seen him in the flesh. After watching six video clips of him—three TV interviews of short duration, microphones basically thrust into his face, a sit-down address on his cable show, *Praising God* (ChristWorks TV), and two short clips of his sermons—Landry had confirmed that while Melvin Fortun threw his weight around, he had a strong sense of personal space. It was clear he didn't like to be touched.

Melvin Fortun's house was easy to find. Very easy to find. There were photos of the mansion all over the Internet, especially the infinity pool. There had been many photo ops and interviews outside on the front steps of the massive house, which looked a little like an upside-down egg carton made of glass and wood.

The street boasted some of the most expensive mansions in Los Angeles. The homes were elegant and massive—old school—set like jewels on broad lawns facing onto broad avenues. Apparently Melvin Fortun didn't get the memo, because his brand-new egg-carton house on Oak Knoll was completely out of touch with the neighborhood's sensibilities. Landry imagined he was hated by his neighbors.

He wondered how the good reverend had gotten around the zoning restrictions.

Melvin Fortun ranked number eight on the *Forbes* list, so it was entirely possible he'd managed an end run by sheer bribery and promises, with a little strong-arming thrown in.

Landry spent two days and nights surveilling the reverend's compound. It might seem like an inordinate amount of time to someone not familiar with his profession, but it was always better to be safe than sorry. He could watch the comings and goings, see what the security was like, get an idea of Melvin's habits.

Which were lax.

But Landry always played it safe. There were still security cameras and a security guard or three. A little before four a.m. was the best time for a raid. Four a.m. was the optimum time for *any* raid. The target was more likely to be in the deepest part of the sleep cycle at that time. Landry knew that the good reverend's wife lived in a suite of rooms on the opposite side of the compound. There was virtually no interaction between them. (Landry had picked this up and other bits of information about the family from the tabloids on the Internet. He took everything with a grain of salt, but he knew that tabloid claims were usually pretty close to the truth. They used their own investigators, and that kind of focus generally paid off.) Fortun's children were grown, and only one lived on the compound. Jacob Fortun: twenty-eight, unmarried, and an avid mountain climber. It was quite possible that Jacob wasn't on the property at all, since he traveled a great deal and had a home in France.

Fortun had bodyguards. Landry had seen them. But from what he'd gleaned, the bodyguards stayed away from his personal apartment, remaining closer to the perimeter.

Landry was quiet. He came up behind the first guard, clasped his hand over the man's mouth, and jabbed a needle full of triptascoline into his neck.

The man fell in a heap. Silent, like the proverbial tree in the forest. In this case, a giant redwood.

Triptascoline for the second guard, too.

It was as easy as picking ladybugs off a screen. He needed to make sure he didn't let it go to his head.

And Landry had plenty of triptascoline, a hallucinogenic drug derived from scopolamine. It was his favorite drug of choice—three times the strength of scopolamine. Over the years, he had used triptascoline many times. He had found the exact strength of the drug he needed. Too much, and it would knock you out for hours. Too little, and you'd hallucinate a good deal. Side effect: you'd get silly. In this case he'd gone full bore. He'd given enough to the guards that they would be out for probably five or six hours. He'd overdosed them so they would be knocked out completely.

Landry had other plans for the good reverend.

He made his way up the grandiose stairway. When Landry was a kid, he watched lots of reruns on the old TV set in their trailer off the racetrack. One of them was *The Beverly Hillbillies*. Their taste and the good reverend's were similar. Ostentatious and vulgar. Bling on a grand scale. He checked the hallway, the other rooms, all of which were empty. Finally, he focused on the master bedroom—a massive suite. The bed took center stage in the room—massive. Landry moved quietly but quickly to the bed. Aware of their even breathing.

Both of them were naked, the sheets pushed down to the foot of the bed. Landry stood there for just a moment, trying to figure out what kind of animal Reverend Fortun resembled. A stoat, he decided. A fat stoat.

The woman was attractive—at least her body was. She had the largest breasts he'd ever seen. Like balloons. Perfect, round balloons.

They slept as far apart as possible.

Landry wondered if she was paid for or if she was his mistress.

The reverend lay on his back, snoring like a gas generator.

Usually, he'd take out the biggest threat first—almost always the male. But he needed to be careful how much triptascoline to give him. He didn't want to knock him out. He didn't want to give him too little, either. It was a lot like the Goldilocks fable. The strength of the drug had to be just right, and that took precision.

He administered a shot of triptascoline to the woman. Her eyes fluttered open, and she started with a tiny gasp.

He put his finger to his lips. His lips that were distorted by cotton balls, his now-blond hair shorn close to his skull. He also wore wire-rimmed glasses, and there was a large mole near his mouth. He wore a dark business suit, shirt, and tie. A Secret Service earpiece to complete the look.

In the muted amber glow of the night-light, her eyes shined with fear. He gently patted her arm, keeping his finger to his lips. She seemed to take comfort from that and relaxed.

Then she was out.

Fortun stirred. Even in sleep, he must have sensed something. Landry was already at his side of the bed, and administered the triptascoline to him.

"What—"

Landry hadn't given him a lot. "Get dressed," he said. "I'm Agent Johnson with the Secret Service. There's a plot to kill you, and we have to get you out of here."

"The *president's* Secret Service?"

"No talking. We have to get out *now*. Move."

The man just stared at him, his mouth open like a Mars crater—reddish and crumbly in the light from the hallway.

Landry prodded him. *"Move."*

Naked as a jaybird, the reverend waddled toward the doorway. He didn't spare a glance for the woman on the bed. She could be dead for all he knew, but it didn't affect him.

He didn't look too well.

Actually, he was already starting to sweat.

"What's going on? Is someone out to kill me? I know those fucking heathens want me dead! Is the president involved? Tell me he's okay."

"He's fine. It's you we're worried about."

Suddenly he sagged in Landry's grip and sat down hard on the floor. Gripped his head in his hands, and crossed his legs, Indian-style.

It was not a pretty picture.

Landry touched his ear. "We have to go, sir," he said. He hunkered down before the man, who was now visibly agitated. Even in the semidarkness, in the light thrown from the bathroom night-light, Landry could see the man's face had turned beet red. His eyes were red, too. He looked lost. Lost and scared.

There would be paranoia.

And hallucinations.

And an irregular heartbeat.

Dilated pupils—Landry shined his light in the eyes and they were very dilated.

"What's that?" Fortun asked.

"Just checking to see if they drugged you, sir."

"Drugged!"

"It's the Juggalos, sir. They're coming for us."

"They're coming for *us?*" He grabbed at his chest.

"Could be an incipient heart attack, sir," Landry said. "We have to move. Get you to an ambulance. They're coming."

"Who's coming?"

"The Juggalos, sir. There's a plot to kill you."

"*Kill* me? Oh, God, no!" He grabbed at Landry and missed. "Juggalos? Where have I heard that name?"

Landry pulled a magazine photo out of the inside pocket of his suit. "The plot is to kill you." He spread the photo out on the floor. Melvin Fortun looked like a bilious Buddha cross-legged on the floor. He leaned forward, squinting, and fell over sideways.

Landry set him back upright and held the torn magazine picture under the reverend's eyes.

"Clowns! Oh, dear God!"

"They know you're going to picket the funeral."

"Funeral?"

Confused. Apparently, he was having trouble thinking.

"Devin Patel's funeral."

Fortun licked his lips. "Oh." He looked at Landry. "He was a clown, wasn't he?"

And then he threw up.

— — —

The sun was a ball of fire in the eastern sky beyond the tall trees of the minister's estate. There was a rushing sound of traffic on the 110. Landry loaded Fortun into his black late-model Suburban with tinted windows. Landry had dressed him in a pair of gray velour sweats he'd found in a chest of drawers. Didn't bother with the underwear, just the sweats and some flip-flops. Like a prisoner. And he was a prisoner of sorts. Landry's captive was scared, and restless, moving around in the seat, continually swallowing.

Occasionally, Landry had to point a gun at him.

He drove Fortun around for three and a half hours, buying time until the protest, mostly driving the freeways. Every once in a while he'd force the man to drink from a bottle of water—didn't want him too dehydrated. They needed to put on a show.

Finally it was time.

Landry stopped on a quiet side street and administered more of the triptascoline. This dose—if it didn't kill the man outright—would send him into orbit.

He would be highly impressionable. He would believe anything Landry had to say. This was good for control, and it was also ideal for what Landry had in mind.

When he reached the campus, Landry drove in through the open gates, between imposing stone walls made to look old. The sun slanted across the mowed green grass along with the shadows.

The protestors were already beginning to gather outside the admin building on campus, and a news truck was already there. A slim woman in a dark pantsuit stood outside the van, someone touching up her hair. Landry recognized her as one of the local newscasters. A satellite truck from another station was driving in, followed by more cars. Pretty soon it wasn't just the local news affiliates. Pretty soon, the CNN bus cruised in.

This was big. There would be a huge show of force.

Landry noticed some of the men in the crowd were older—and armed. Armed to the teeth. Dressed in camo. He wondered how many of them ever wore camo in the real world. Signs were everywhere. Some were printed up by the church. Others looked like they'd been painted in first grade. "FAGGOT" was the most used word, followed by "HELL," and the ever-popular "YOU WILL BURN IN HELL."

Landry could feel the Christian spirit from here.

It would take them time to get going. There was quite a crowd. Landry continued on. He had the fright wig and a rubber clown mask, under the seat. He drove around three or four times, just another black Chevy Suburban SUV in a crowd of them. The procession through the narrow college lanes reminded him of a president's motorcade.

At the moment, his companion was curled up into a little ball, whimpering. "My eyes. They hurt. They're bleeding! My eyes are *bleeding*!"

"You'll be all right," Landry said. "Once you hit the ground running."

"What?"

"S'okay. You don't want to miss the demonstration, do you?"

"No! No! I have to be there."

"You will be," Landry said, and drove on.

- — -

Landry decided to make a delayed entrance. The rally should have started at 9:00 on the dot. He and his passenger rolled in around 9:05.

He pulled up to the area where the forest of microphones was set up. They bristled in the sunshine.

Landry said to Fortun, "This is your big moment."

The man's face lit up like a Christmas tree when he saw the adoring crowd. "I've got to lead my flock!" Added, "But I'm so thirsty."

"You'll be all right." Landry reached across the reverend, unlocked the door, and pushed it open. Fortun squirmed his way along the seat. Dry and dehydrated, but raring to go.

"Just one thing," Landry said.

Fortun turned to look at him—and blanched.

Landry regarded him through the eyeholes of the clown mask he'd just pulled on. "Boo."

Fortun backed up hard against the seat. "What are you—"

"We're going to get you," he said. "Be afraid of us. Very afraid."

Fortun grabbed at his chest and backed up even harder against the door frame. His eyes bugged out. Landry had rarely seen eyes bug out, but this was one of those times.

Remember, the man is highly susceptible to suggestion.

"Something else," Landry said, glancing at Fortun's lap. "Your clothes are on fire."

"What?"

"Your clothes are on fire! *Run!*"

Fortun looked down and slapped at his clothes, high little barks coming from his throat before he launched into full-fledged screams. Landry had to plug his ears. The reverend managed to open the door of the SUV, at the same time divesting himself of his sweatpants. Wearing only flip-flops, he ran toward the cameras screaming. Slapping at his legs, his hair, his backside.

His *naked* backside.

Zigzagging across the grass.

Screaming, howling, sobbing, jabbering, *yipping*—in front of the two hundred people gathered there.

In front of a whole lot more on television.

Hundreds of phones popped up in the crowd.

"Clowns! *Juggalos!*" he screamed. "They're going to kill us all!"

Landry reached over, pulled the door closed, and drove away.

He doubted anyone saw him leave.

All eyes were on the good reverend.

CHAPTER 29

From Mount Loyal Independent Christian College, Landry drove to Arcadia for Devin Patel's funeral at Saint Clare of Rimini Catholic Church.

Today he had one of the vans, the newer model. A white-panel van—a worker's van. Inside was a change of clothing and the Harley. Just so he had options.

He parked up the street at a strip mall outside a 99-cent store and walked in, late enough that most people had already gone into the church. The church itself was inner-city modest by Catholic church standards—sixties-era, a mellow gold-colored brick, fronted by tall Italian cypress trees.

Landry had changed out of his "Secret Service" agent suit. Now he was dressed casually but respectfully: dark blond hair, clip-on ponytail, and wire-rimmed rectangular shades. He wore a long-sleeved shirt and a tie, but paired them with jeans. He looked like a youngish professor or teacher who had taken time off for the funeral—the kind of guy that kids in college would call "Professor Dan," instead of his full name and title.

A few people remained outside, including some of Devin's Juggalo friends. Eezil and Brian did not leave Willow's side. Willow looked better than she had when he'd last met her. In fact, she was ethereally beautiful.

Landry said a silent prayer for her and for her two Juggalo guard dogs. They'd even given it their best shot, dressing up for the funeral in what looked like borrowed suits. Sure, there was Brian's new look—a bright orange Mohawk—and the lip studs and the eyebrow studs and the tattoos crawling up their necks. But at least they'd made the effort.

Landry spotted a white Hyundai Tucson Fuel Cell. His wife and daughter were already here. They had to be inside already.

He felt a hitch in his chest.

Their SUV was parked in between two other SUVs. Landry walked over to the Armada parked on the passenger side of his wife's car, and paused to light up a cigarette. He hated smoking, but it came in handy on rare occasions, and this was one of them. He dropped what passed for the lighter but was actually a GPS tracker—a seventy-five-dollar "Slap and Track." It worked, so why spend more? He leaned down as if to pick it up and affixed the magnet side to the inside of the rear right-side wheel well of Cindi's Tucson. Straightening, he tucked his hand in his pocket, then worked his way over to the church steps and brushed past the ragged group of protestors—the ones who hadn't gotten the memo. Four, to be exact. Kids holding signs at their sides, scanning the street anxiously, waiting for backup that would never come. A sad little bunch—a body without a head. As he walked past them he said, "The reverend's not coming. Look it up on *Gawker*—you'll be glad you did."

Then he was past them, up the steps of the church, and in at the back.

Place was crowded.

He scanned the pews. Didn't see them at first. But license plates don't lie. Landry could feel the carnival-ride dip in his stomach. He'd faced a gun barrel shoved against his cheek, right under his eye. He'd fought for air when his larynx had been squeezed off in a death grip. But it paled in comparison to the moment he saw his wife and daughter.

They looked the same.

He remained at the back of the church. People praying, kneeling, standing up, sitting down, hymnbooks open.

A pall of sadness over the whole affair.

Cindi sitting strong and upright, smaller than their daughter, Kristal. Kristal's head bowed in grief.

He wanted to reach out, to touch them, to embrace them, to comfort them.

He left early, parked on the side street to the church. Watched his girls come outside. Cindi beautiful in navy, her long blond hair curling down her back. Dark stockings even on this warm day, heels. Kristal in a dress, too—which surprised him. It was a short dress that showed her legs. Bordering on disrespectful, but what were you going to do? Kids today.

He felt a pang. A mixture of sorrow, regret, and hope. Thought about walking up to them now. He couldn't make himself do it. This was not the time. At least Todd wasn't with them. He was hard at work at his comptroller job in Torrent Valley, no doubt.

Landry thought about what it would be like when Kristal went to Luke's funeral. He shut it out of his mind, got the van while people were still milling in the parking lot, and waited to fall in line with the cortege.

He parked way back in the line of cars along the one-lane asphalt drive.

There were a lot fewer people who made the trek to the cemetery. The graveside service was solemn and sad. The mother looked strong and determined. Landry knew from the way she kept looking over her shoulder and at the cross streets that she expected someone to picket the funeral.

A different group of picketers showed up—three to be exact—and parked at the edge of the cemetery. A dispirited little group, they held their signs up halfheartedly. Landry noticed they were checking their phones, just as the first batch at the church did. Awaiting the troops? Within ten minutes, they were gone, even before the mourners had trooped all the way to the gravesite.

Landry saw the relief, palpable, in the mother's posture.

He stood in the dark shade of a tree on the brow of a sun-bleached hill—the cemetery wasn't the best kept in the world—and watched the solemn graveside service. He was thinking about Luke, not Devin Patel. Thinking about Luke and what that kid had done to save his daughter's life.

Which led to his own culpability.

Landry, the absent father—beyond absent. Nonexistent. Worse than nonexistent, because Luke would not be dead if it were not for him. None of those kids would be dead, if not for him.

No going back now. He couldn't change anything. Better to concentrate on what he *could* change. What he could salvage—he needed to protect Cindi and Kristal.

He'd put the tracking device on Cindi's car. Tom had said they were staying at Big Bear Lake. He typed Todd Barclay's name into his phone, along with the words "Big Bear Lake."

And got nothing.

He looked at the Google map of Big Bear Lake. Scrolled along the lakeshore. There were a lot of cabins. A *lot* of cabins. It was a big lake and a large surrounding area. Here he was, multitasking at a funeral. Modern life had become complicated, and concentration, fractured. Landry saw it in himself. And yet there was so much to think about—especially when it came to his wife and daughter. He needed to stay on top of the situation.

He wondered if Cindi and Kristal would go back to Big Bear Lake right after the funeral, or if he'd have to track them all over town. It would be easier if Gary would just tell him. If Gary would step up and do the right thing.

One eye on the graveside service, he punched in his brother Gary's number, and waited through two rings. The call went to voice mail.

"Call me." He was aware that his voice sounded grim. Grim and frustrated.

He heard a car turn onto the drive toward this part of the cemetery—the deep rumble of a muscle-car engine—probably a 426. A black car arrowed up the lane between poplar trees and then turned in their direction. A 2013 or 2014 Camaro.

The Camaro slowed along the curve in the road near where the small group gathered by the gravesite. Rumbled along, idling, before speeding up and driving away. Landry watched as the Camaro followed the road back to the main highway and turned north.

Someone from the church?

Landry felt a prickle on the back of his neck, as if someone was staring at him. He looked below—he was on the highest ground in the cemetery. He scanned the area for anything out of the ordinary.

Nothing. Nothing he could see.

He found himself thinking about the vehicle the shooter, Zachary Smith, had left at the Devil's Canyon trailhead.

Landry had moved it to another trailhead not too far away and had hiked back to his own vehicle. He'd been very careful, had run into no one on the road, and no one at the other trailhead. The Jeep was the only vehicle in the parking lot. Landry was almost sure no one had seen him. But of course he couldn't be sure.

He'd suspected the vehicle, an older-model Jeep, had been stolen. If it was recovered, it was probable the police would dust for prints.

Landry had used gloves. He'd wiped the Jeep down, but it was possible he'd missed the door.

Too late now.

The black Camaro did not return.

The casket was lowered. The crowd broke up and started walking to their cars. Landry watched as his wife and daughter walked to the Hyundai Tucson.

He took one last look at Willow and her "uncles." He knew they would take care of her.

Satisfied, he went back to his car—

—and followed his wife and daughter to Big Bear Lake.

CHAPTER 30

Landry let them get a good head start. He didn't need to be anywhere near them to track them.

He spotted a florist and stopped to buy roses. Pink roses, for them both. A massive bouquet. It smelled cool and slightly dank, as roses did, the moist petals resting for a moment against his cheek when he opened the door. He made another stop, this time at a Walgreens, looking for chocolates. Something nice. He chose a Whitman's Sampler. And a card. They didn't have any blank cards, so he picked out an anniversary card because it was beautiful—embossed and romantic, with a peacock and a heart. He scrawled a note inside to his girls.

Actually, it wasn't really a note. Just "Love, Cyril." He couldn't think of anything else to say.

He followed the tracker, and realized he was taking the easiest way to Big Bear Lake from Torrent Valley. The path of least resistance: Huntington Drive west to Santa Anita Drive; Santa Anita Drive to the San Bernardino Freeway, CA-210 east to CA-330, north. Merge onto CA-18. Turn left on Big Bear Boulevard and you were at Big Bear Lake.

He followed the transmitter driving east on Big Bear. Getting warmer. He slowed near Mill Creek Road. Hot now. Following the winding road between tall pines and through the Aspen Glen Picnic

Area. The pines were tall and imposing, their boughs ragged against the deep blue sky. He'd never been to Big Bear Lake, so he'd looked up the flora and fauna in the San Bernardino Forest: ponderosa pine, knobcone pine, Jeffrey pine, sugar pine, Coulter pine, lodge-pole pine. Many of them looked similar to one another. Landry realized he was cataloging the flora and fauna because he was getting close now and he didn't want to think about what was coming.

He assumed it would be all right despite what Gary'd told him. Gary was always the dour one in the family. His brother had definitely taken sides, although Landry couldn't fathom why he'd take that pale little comptroller's side against his own brother.

He reminded himself that Gary was easily led. He was the type of person who was prone to hero worship. Landry's younger brother had always worshipped Landry and now he'd fixated on someone else. He'd imprinted himself on Todd like a duckling on its mama.

The road seemed to have turned into Tulip Lane. Very strong signal. But it lessened the farther he drove along Tulip Lane. He turned around, drove back, and picked up Mill Creek Road again, slowing for a curve. Way out in the boonies now. The beeping became loud and manic. Not just hot, but burning hot! Scalding. Up ahead he saw a green-roofed cabin through the trunks of the tall pines. He turned onto the pine-needle-covered lane and drove the short way up the hill. The GPS tracker going crazy.

The cabin was new but made to look old. It had the varnished-pine-log look—rich, honey color. There was a closed garage attached, the green roll-up door the same color as the roof. The dark green of pool-table felt.

Cindi's Hyundai Tucson was out front. The sun glistened off ponderosa needles and the blue sky was saturated so much that it had taken on a neon glow. He looked out toward the lake and saw a slightly darker blue through the trees.

He pulled up beside the Tucson.

The curtain flicked in the window—he guessed it was the kitchen.

A dream cabin. The kind Cindi had always wanted. Even the curtains were right: yellow-and-white gingham. Old-fashioned, but new.

He sat in the car for a moment, his heart beating hard. This was the moment of truth. He couldn't imagine his wife turning him down. Couldn't imagine Cindi and his daughter—his only child—turning their backs on him. Unimaginable. But his heart still beat hard. There was still a sinking feeling in his gut. He sat there in the van.

Was he nervous?

He'd been on TV. She had seen him. She knew he was alive. Gary had confirmed that. Yet she had not reached out to him.

Was Gary right? Was she finished with him? Had it been too long?

Landry was used to success. But now that he was here, he realized he might be on the brink—the brink of the dissolution of their marriage.

He couldn't believe that. Not after everything they'd shared together. All those years. A child they had raised together.

He sat in the van. He could hear the engine ticking. The curtain in the cabin window had not moved. What were they doing? Hiding in there? Were they afraid of *him*?

The sun bore down through the windshield. It was the high altitude. The air was thinner up here. The colors were lurid. He noticed pansies and daisies and hollyhocks and all that sort of stuff hanging in baskets from the eaves. A home, not a house. Did Cindi plant those? Was this now her home?

The engine ticked.

Could it be she really loved Todd? That wimpy comptroller with the comb-over?

He opened the van door. It squeaked. He shut the door and stood there in the sunshine, feeling it beat down on his head. Pins and needles fuzzing up his vision, then clearing.

Get a grip, he told himself. *This is your wife we're talking about. Your daughter.*

He walked up the shallow stairs onto the porch and knocked on the door.

CHAPTER 31

"About what you saw in the paper," the voice on the phone said. "The SUV they found at the trailhead, that was *another* trailhead. Not the Devil's Canyon trail. In fact, it was several miles away."

"Yes, the Jeep Cherokee. But was it *his*?"

Silence on the other end of the line.

"I'm sorry," he added. "I didn't mean to imply that you don't know what you're doing. You do think it was his, though?"

"Actually, we think he stole the Cherokee, but in the scheme of things, that hardly matters, does it?" A pause. "For my own edification I'd like to ask you: What part of 'mission accomplished' don't you understand?" The man on the phone waited for this to sink in. Then he said, "DNA doesn't lie. Fingerprints don't lie. You have the envelope, right? There is your proof."

"Yes, I know that, but you're sure you have no idea where the body is? Shouldn't we at least find out?"

"You shouldn't have called."

"I'd like to talk to—"

"Sorry, you can't talk to anyone. We have now concluded our business." And he hung up.

The man in the Ritz-Carlton sat there, stunned for a moment—at a complete loss. He tried to call back. The number he'd just dialed had been disconnected. He tried to absorb what little he'd learned. There really wasn't anyone he could discuss this with. It was simply a transaction, and now it was finished. He could go back to the man who gave him the phone number, but he didn't want to do that.

That man—the first man he'd contacted—was dangerous. A psychopath. He'd said, "What I can do is give you a contact number. If there is interest in pursuing a transaction, they will contact you. Don't ever call this number again."

Now the man sat perched on the edge of the beautiful-but-generic hotel chairs, spine straight as a die, staring out at the city skyline and feeling oddly disconnected. As if he'd been to a smorgasbord and eaten every last delightful thing he could think of, but the food tasted flat—it just didn't fill him up—and now he couldn't remember it.

There was no afterglow.

Perhaps because he was, at heart, a moral individual.

It was important to remember: There had been no choice in the matter.

He stared out at the smoggy skyline and muttered, "I did the right thing."

CHAPTER 32

Landry waited, then knocked on the cabin door again. No answer. The Hyundai Tucson was parked out front, so he knew they were there. He knocked again, harder—feeling helpless in this situation. This was an unusual feeling for him. He'd faced death many times, but this situation confounded him. What would he say? What would *she* say? Those two questions whirled around his head like moths around a night-light.

A raven landed on the bough of the ponderosa pine towering over the cabin. The sky's color was mirrored by its shiny wings. It made that cracking-knuckles sound, loud and ugly, and peered down at him through beady eyes.

"Get lost," Landry said.

The bird's gaze drilled harder. The thing was big, black, and ugly. Landry ignored him. "Cindi!" he called. "I know you're in there. We need to talk."

Thinking he sounded like a killer in a slasher movie.

There was a motion in the corner of his eye. The curtain again. He heard a scuffle, and then low voices. He stepped back, expecting one of them to open the door—and collided with the hummingbird feeder hanging from the rafters. Heard the angry buzz by his ear. The bee landed on his cheek and stung him and he swatted it away. It landed on the porch boards and crawled around in a circle.

The pain—it seemed much worse than just a bee sting. The raven made that cracked-knuckles sound again. He looked up into its black eyes, and it cocked its head quizzically. Landry looked down again. The dying bee toppled onto its back and was still.

He rapped on the door again. His knuckles sounded like the crack of a baseball bat. He heard Cindi's voice close to the door: "No! Don't do that!"

The door was flung open. Kristal held the knob. She wore skimpy shorts and a skimpier top; she'd changed out of her mourning clothes. Cindi was behind her, breathing hard, her hair pulled out of the barrette that held her ponytail, strands sticking out. It looked as if they had been struggling. Cindi yelled to their daughter, "Get back inside!" and grappled with her for the doorknob.

"No!" Kristal shouted. "He's my *dad*! I want to talk to him!"

Cindi glared at Landry, seething. Bright red points on both cheeks. Her mouth was a grim, angry line. "Cyril," she said. "I want you to leave *now*."

For a moment, Landry was speechless, even though he had been expecting this. He said, "We're still married."

"In name only. Whether or not you're dead or alive, I'm going to find a way to fix that."

She was beautiful. More beautiful than he remembered. Sure, she was older—early forties. But to him she was the most beautiful woman in the world. He'd never realized that before now.

He was aware that Kristal had slipped past her mother and was hugging him.

He closed his eyes and hugged her back, felt her warm tears bleed through his shirt. Her heart beating against his.

His baby.

"Kristal, get *into the house*!" Cindi screamed. She stood there, fists balled at her sides, the tendons of her neck straining as she jutted her chin up at him. He'd always teased her about being too short. Short and feisty.

Then she was on him, on Kristal, pulling Kristal away and back into the house. She tried to shut the door but he put his foot in the door and pushed his way in.

He'd never done that. Never used force—not with his family. Never so much as threw a coffee cup. Never spanked his daughter. Never touched either of them in anger.

Cindi had pulled Kristal back across the cabin. "I want you to leave, *now!*" she said.

"I just want to talk to you, Cin," he said.

He'd heard that line in a TV movie not long ago, where the husband was planning to kill his girlfriend. He'd seen it in more than one of those movies—probably twenty to thirty of them over his lifetime.

"We don't want to talk to *you.*"

He nodded toward Kristal. "Why not let her speak for herself?"

Cindi tightened her fingers on their daughter's arm. Her face was a mask. She'd smoothed it out so that she looked impassive. But her breath was coming in little gasps, and she was shaking.

Landry said, "If you want, we can get a divorce. But we have to talk in order to do that. We have to work this out."

Thinking to himself: *You sound so reasonable.*

Thinking, too, that he was also full of shit. A divorce wasn't in the cards. He wanted his family back. He wanted to talk her down, get her used to him being here in the cottage's little living room, get used to seeing him again—back to the way things used to be. All he needed to do was start the conversation—a way *in.*

He saw her fingers loosen on Kristal's arm. Her shoulders slumped.

I give up. He'd seen it before, a few times in their marriage. Cindi didn't like confrontation. Cindi didn't like drama.

Cindi liked the status quo. She liked the path of least resistance.

It had worked well for them. He was not overbearing; he was not pushy. Their marriage, he realized now, had always been about "live and let live."

And love—don't forget love.

But right now, love seemed like the other side of the world.

Cindi looked at him. There was a shine to her eyes. A "What do you want now?" kind of look.

"I just want to talk. I just want to see you. If you want this to be good-bye, at least let me say good-bye."

How smooth he sounded. Jesus! He'd talked his way out of life-threatening situations, he'd sat down with sheiks in Saudi Arabia and village elders in Afghanistan and soft-soaped spies who could kill him in an instant, and he'd learned to be a chameleon. To mirror people. To quell their objections and their fears. "Can we talk?" he asked.

Cindi nodded.

It would all fall into place now. He sat down on the chair across from them. They sat on the couch. Cindi had her arm around Kristal's shoulders—protective.

He said, "I couldn't let you know I was alive. It was for you, because I had to keep you safe. There were people after me, and I had to protect you. You have to understand that." He went on from there. Warmed to it. How he'd missed them, how he'd always thought about them, first thing, every day. He could hear himself saying the words, and they were true, but they sounded laughable, an "It's for your own good" kind of speech. He had to protect them, and the only way he could do that was keep up the pretense he was dead. It was what he believed in his soul, but as it rolled out of his mouth it came out canned. It sounded like dishonesty. He realized that and trailed off.

He took a breath, looked around the cottage—Todd's cottage. Cozy. The honey-colored pine paneling was rich and warm. Dust motes floated through the sunshine coming in through the windows. His gaze snagged a framed forest picture with a wooden frame—a photograph. There were several photographs on the wall, all with the same kind of wooden frame, all the same size. Some were of Big Bear Lake, and some were black-and-white photos of stars of old TV shows from the fifties and sixties. *Mr. Ed, Leave It to Beaver, Lucy.*

He looked at the kitchen. It was cute, but not to Cindi's taste. The oval braided rug on the floor wasn't to her taste either.

Maybe *because* it was Todd's cabin.

All the while he was looking around he kept talking. His lips moving, although he was so numb it was hard to know what he was saying. The usual, he thought—how he'd missed them. How he never planned for that to happen, but there was no choice. How he could understand why she would want to end their marriage, but he loved them and wanted to be part of his daughter's life.

Because, he realized, that was the truth. They had moved on, but he had moved on, too.

One moment, he desperately wanted them to be a family again. The next, he knew it would never work. Gary was right.

"I just want closure," he heard himself say.

Cindi snorted. "Closure? Jesus!" And looked away. She was the farthest away from him as she'd ever been, dwindling into a mirage before his eyes. But then he looked at Kristal.

Cindi's arm was around her. Kristal in her shorts and a top that left little to the imagination, a big girl now. A girl who made out with her boyfriend in the parking lot, who probably had birth-control pills in her dresser drawer.

He *hoped* she'd had birth-control pills in her dresser drawer.

There was more than one kind of protection. "You two have your guns?"

"Yes, Dad," Kristal said.

His wife glared at him, but nodded.

"Good."

Cindi looked away.

He had to say it. "I'm sorry about Luke, sweet pea."

Kristal stared at the floor. Mumbled something he couldn't hear.

"What's that, sweetheart?"

"Was it because of you, Daddy?"

"Me?"

Cindi said, "She wants to know if the man who shot up the school was there because of you. You know, what you in the trade call 'trying to draw you out.'"

The sarcasm in her voice.

He stared at them, his wife and daughter. The two of them perched on the couch, staring back at him, as if from a great distance. He said, "I don't know."

"You don't *know*? What kind of answer is that? Was that man—what do they call it in the trade—that *operator*—was that man trying to draw you out?"

"It's been three years, Cin. Why would anyone do that?"

"Why else would someone shoot up the school?" She glared at him. "Someone out there must have thought you were alive and—" She stopped, seemed to gather herself. "If you're the cause of this, if you're the cause of Luke's death . . ."

"He wouldn't!" Kristal said. "He wouldn't let that happen!" She looked at him, her eyes pleading. "You wouldn't let that happen, would you?"

He tried to make his face open, caring, but it felt like a stiff rubber mask.

"Daddy?"

He opened his mouth to speak, but couldn't. What could he say? That he was a couple of seconds too late?

"Daddy?"

Finally, he found his inner liar. "No, sweet pea. It had nothing to do with me."

"Oh, yeah. It was just a big *coincidence!*" Cindi stood. "I want you out of here. You owe us at least that much. Let us get on with our lives, okay? Just leave us alone!"

Again, he opened his mouth to argue. But no words came. He was the smoothest liar in the world, but this time he was tongue-tied.

Kristal stared at him. Her mouth opened like a fish seeking air. Finally her vocal cords gained purchase and she said, "Was it because of you? Daddy?"

Her voice was pleading; her eyes were pleading. She had always adored him, had always been Daddy's girl.

He heard a buzzing, saw that it was another bee, this time inside, crawling up the window screen. He touched his cheek. Could feel the venom there, twitching inside.

The room darkened as a cloud covered the sun. What could he tell her? Could he tell her the truth? He knew now that they would never be together as a family again. He knew that was impossible. Kristal had a new family now—her mother and Todd.

He felt his face stiffen. He might not be part of the family anymore, but he couldn't tell his daughter the truth. It would only hurt her. She still loved him, and he couldn't give up that love. It was the only thing he had left. "No, honey," he said. "The guy was there for another reason.

"He wasn't there for me."

- — -

As he climbed into his van, he saw that he'd left the flowers, candy, and card on the passenger seat. He took them out and set them on the little bench in front of the window.

The curtain twitched, then went still.

He'd given her one parting gift. A phone with his number pro-grammed into it—if she ever needed him. She'd accepted it—like someone reluctantly handling a snake—but she had accepted it.

He looked up at the pine. The raven was gone. He looked down at the porch floorboards. The bee was gone, too.

Gone, like his wife and his daughter.

He drove down the short dirt drive to Mill Creek Road.

A car went by on the road. It had to slow for the curve in the road before picking up speed and disappearing beyond the pines. The engine was loud, rumbling and sweet—

A new black Camaro.

Landry turned left instead of right. He followed the road but never caught up to the Camaro. The car was nowhere in sight.

He drove back the way he'd come, looking at the cabins on either side of the road. No black Camaro anywhere. He spent an hour and a half following every road and looking at every house, every parking lot, every business.

Maybe it was just a coincidence.

Too bad he didn't believe in coincidences.

CHAPTER 33

Landry sat in yet another hotel room, coming to grips with two facts. One: his marriage was over. And two: someone out there had ordered the hit—and they were still out there. The first situation, he could do nothing about. Cindi had fallen in love with another man, and as distasteful as it was, he couldn't change it.

Still, he would not stop seeing his daughter.

He needed to figure out a game plan. For all accounts and purposes, he was dead and he wanted to keep it that way. But he knew Cindi. She'd want a real marriage to Todd. She'd want a divorce, because in her mind it could never be a real marriage otherwise. Cindi was a stickler for things like that.

And Landry planned to see his daughter on a regular basis—try and stop him. He and Cindi would have to work it out—somehow.

But right now, there were more pressing issues.

On the good-news front, there had been no mention of a man named Cyril Landry on the news channels, on the Internet, or in the newspapers. The photo they'd flashed on television was long gone—just another grain of sand in the ever-moving flurry of television news.

Whoever had hired the hit on him thought he was dead. That was good. But he couldn't be sure they wouldn't find out the truth. He had no idea who had set the trap at Gordon C. Tuttle High School, but whoever it was hadn't cared if Kristal died. In fact, he'd gone out of his way to shoot at her. If Landry hadn't been there, Kristal would be dead. He couldn't take it for granted that the person who put the paper out on him would be satisfied with his death alone.

He might be out for revenge.

And if Landry could find his wife and daughter, other people could as well.

He doubted Todd would be much use in a firefight. Fortunately for his girls, they were well acquainted with weapons of all sorts, and both of them qualified as markswomen. If anyone was coming after them, he had no doubt that they would protect *Todd*.

But he needed to be there. He'd brought them into this, and it was his job to protect them now.

So the question was: Who put the paper out on him?

Landry knew it would be hard, if not impossible, to find out. The Toolshed didn't give up its secrets.

Landry went over in his mind what had happened so far. He had put himself out there in Austria. He had used good credentials—excellent credentials—for his alias, Jeffery Peterman.

Eric the Red, though, had no trouble recognizing him, so he could assume other operatives would be just as good on that score. Maybe that was the problem. Eric knew who Landry was just from what had been put up about him on the virtual bulletin board. Eric had seen right through Landry's deception.

Maybe someone else saw through it as well.

He glanced at the TV: some politician from Arizona talking about national security. Landry recognized him from his time in Iraq: the man in Kuwait City who had been in the process of loading a handcart full of money. This in itself wasn't all that unusual in Kuwait City. Landry had shuttled money into his own accounts that way.

The man hadn't been a senator back then, but he was a politician. He had been looking for a bodyguard.

There had been something iffy about him—not quite right. Landry tried to put his finger on it. The guy had seemed jumpy. Jumpy? No, more than that: cowed. Almost as if he was afraid of him. Landry knew he affected some people that way—something about his demeanor. His height, yes, but something else. People could tell he was former military—might as well carry a sign.

He switched off the TV, and tried to think: Could Eric be the man sent to kill him?

Of course Eric had had several chances to kill Landry. At the Gasthof. Meeting him twice in LA. *Any*time in Austria. Eric had been the one to tell him about the hit. Eric had helped him set it up, and it had gone off without a hitch. There was a dead kid—a killer—stashed in the canyon, hopefully never to be seen again.

All thanks to Eric.

But Landry also knew that what Eric had really done was gain Landry's trust. Eric knew that Landry would be careful, knew he would watch his back. Knew he would be constantly on the move, distrustful of pretty much any situation. Landry was good. Eric knew he was good because Eric, himself, was good.

Eric had proved himself trustworthy over and over. They had fought together side by side, and Landry always felt that they were the best of friends. He prided himself on knowing whom he could trust, and he could swear that he'd trust Eric with his life. *Had* trusted him up until now. But they were in the same game, and there was a lot of money to be made in assassination.

Landry had avoided that trap, so far. After Florida, he'd decided there would be no more killing for hire. He had standards. And not only that—he was no spring chicken. At forty-eight, he should be retired, sitting on some beach somewhere with an umbrella drink, enjoying the water with his wife and daughter.

But Eric was seven to nine years younger. And to look at him, Landry knew that Eric was hungry. Eric still had things to do.

Someone wanted him dead. For all intents and purposes they had their wish. He *was* dead. But if it was Eric . . .

Eric would know that Landry would relax. He wouldn't be able to help it. You couldn't keep up the paranoia all the time. You had to live your life. And when he was relaxed enough . . .

Landry realized he was going to have to find out. It was either that, or kill Eric.

As a friend, Landry needed to find out if Eric was part of this.

- — -

The hotel phone rang early the next morning—still dark. Landry glanced at the clock. Six a.m. He stared at the phone for a moment before deciding it was okay to answer. He lifted the receiver and was greeted by a loud dial tone. He replaced the handset.

Someone playing games. He reran the events of yesterday and landed on the Camaro driving around the cemetery and later at Big Bear Lake. He could see the car in his mind's eye, black, with a thin film of dust all over it from the dirt lane of the cemetery. Tinted windows, so Landry hadn't been able to see inside. The engine had been loud and sweet. Nothing sweeter than the sound of one of those muscle cars, unless you counted the sound of a P-38 or a B-24 flying overhead.

But in this case, the message was clear: the black Camaro had been following him.

He heard a bump at the bottom of the hotel door. Someone slipped what looked like a hotel key card under the door.

Paper thin.

Except, it buzzed.

Landry got up off the bed, padded over, and looked down. It was a cell phone. He picked it up off the carpet and placed it against his ear.

"Get your butt out of bed, asshole," Eric Blackburn said. "You think you're gonna sleep the day away?"

- — -

They went to another crowded restaurant. It wasn't difficult to find one—this was Sunday morning. Everyone and his brother was out for breakfast.

Three minutes in, Eric said above the cacophony, "You think I'm setting you up?"

Landry said, "Setting me up?"

Eric the Red sat back in the booth, legs sprawled. He looked like your average dad on a weekend: shorts, athletic shoes—no socks—and a horizontally striped T-shirt, XX large.

"Yeah, setting you up. If it was me I'd be wondering about *you* by now."

"Are you?"

Eric looked down at his big hands lying on the table. His expensive watch gleamed through the heavy dark hair on his sun-reddened arm. "If I was, bro, you'd be dead by now."

"You could still be planning how to do it."

"Why would I give you the info on the kid who was coming after you? He could've taken you out—no more problems."

"He *might* have taken me out, but it's doubtful."

"Your problem," Eric said, "is you play too much chess." He leaned forward. "Most of the time—in real life—people play checkers."

Landry nodded. "What made you think I had a problem?"

"Bro, we *always* have a problem. It's what we *do*, man. The nature of the beast."

Landry nodded again. Eric could be shining him on. But in reality, Blackburn had had plenty of chances to take him out, and plenty of ways to do it. Ricin, for instance. They'd been across the table from each other several times since they'd met in Austria, and it would have been easy. He could have taken him out at the Gasthof, or any other time in Austria. No problem there.

"No hard feelings, compadre," Eric said now. "I know you gotta be careful, so I thought I'd clear the air. Who do *you* think hired the hit on you?"

Landry thought about it. Maybe someone associated with Whitbread, but Whitbread had been out of business since Florida. Maybe someone from his time in Iraq. There were a lot of people he had gotten crosswise with in Iraq. Like when he was guarding the shrink-wrapped money, billions and billions of dollars, sitting on pallets out in the Green Zone.

He was working for Whitbread then. Those were the days— military and private security contractors were kings. He remembered the swagger of the time. Escorting the new viceroy and "cabinet" members and generals around in black SUVs. The guys refining their tans by the palace pool. Sex and rock 'n' roll, the feeling that they were in a conquered country and could do anything—as long as they were in the Green Zone and not, say, trying to make it to the airport. Black tees and camo pants, kicking back, cooler than cool, seeing the world through mirrored shades. It had been like Disneyland, if Disneyland stank of death, despair, victory, sex, and the underlying hatred of the conquered for the conqueror and vice versa. And the scams. Everyone scamming them. If there was one honest Iraqi within ten blocks of the Green Zone, Landry didn't know about him, although the majority of people in Iraq were like people anywhere—trying to survive and find some happiness in it. But in the Green Zone? They came like fleas to a corpse. He was younger then—had partaken of all the fun as well as the danger: Party Time in Baghdad.

Someone took the $6.6 billion in shrink-wrapped money. Landry was sure it wasn't on his watch, but he couldn't swear for the others in his company.

Eric leaned forward. "Anybody home?"

Landry had always been a believer in memory. That you remembered stuff you didn't think you took in. This memory concerned someone wanting him dead, and there were plenty of people like that. Whom you wanted to think about was someone who had a lot to lose, or a lot to win. Either someone who hated him (there were plenty of those), or someone who was afraid of him.

Someone who saw him here, stateside. Maybe not from Iraq. From a job. He'd done so many—it could be anyone.

Nothing recent, he thought . . .

Except for the guy with the bundles of money in Kuwait City. Except the same guy locking eyes with him at a checkpoint.

Except for the guy taking the walking tour of Whitbread Associates.

They say three times is the charm.

The guy had been nervous. He had refused to meet Landry's eyes. It was as if he'd tried to make himself smaller so Landry wouldn't notice him.

Mike Cardamone saying, "I want you to meet one of my best operatives."

The man looking, for just an instant, like a deer in the headlights. Smoothing it over with a practiced politician's smile. But it had been there. It was like a double image. The smooth, handsome, young politician in search of personal protection—and the soldier with the dirty, sweat-streaked face in a Humvee in Iraq.

Cam Mills, stacking bricks of money into a handcart outside the biggest bank in Kuwait City.

Landry did a quick calculation in his head. He'd guarded the pallets of shrink-wrapped money. He knew how much there was in each bundle. A hundred one-hundred-dollar bills per brick. Extrapolate that out to how much had been stacked on the hand truck, and it could be a billion right there. If Cam Mills had gone back out to his Humvee for more . . .

Landry said to Eric, "You know anything about the presidential candidates?"

Eric's expression blank from confusion.

"Who's running for president?"

"Shit, how do *I* know?"

"Come on, you must read the papers."

"Read the papers? WTF? Get out of the Stone Age, bud. Okay, I'll play. Republican? Or Democrat?"

"Both. We just had a two-term president."

Eric stared beyond Landry, thinking. "There's Raul Alacrán. Republican, right? And the vice president, Jack Klebold—whiny little bitch, you ask me. What're you thinking?"

"What about the senator with the funny name? Cam Mills. You know, like Rand Paul, Ted Cruz? Kind of memorable, two short names."

"Yeah, I've seen him on TV."

"What do you think?"

Eric shrugged. "I'm not into politics, but if you pressed me, I'd say he's just another Democrat asshole."

"Why?" Landry asked.

"Why what? He just is."

"No other reason?"

"He's a lightweight? He looks like a weasel? I dunno."

"I ran into him. Three times."

"You did?"

"Twice in Iraq, and once stateside."

"And?"

The waitress came and set down their plates. "Anything else I can do for you?" she asked.

"You got a phone number?" Eric quipped.

She poured more coffee for him, a lot of it ending up on the table, and whisked away.

"Guess she showed *me*," Eric said after she'd left.

Landry said, "She works hard for a living."

"Forgot for a minute you're Prince Galahad."

"Sir Galahad."

"What?"

"*Sir* Galahad. Or maybe you were thinking of Prince Charming."

"Jesus, you're fucking Wikipedia! It's not cool to be correcting people all the time."

Landry took a sip of his coffee. "How much money do you need for a presidential campaign?"

Eric said, "A whole helluva lot?"

Landry nodded. Aware of the snap of plastic plates and the buzz of conversation, even though where he really was, was back in the Green Zone, guarding pallets of shrink-wrapped hundred-dollar bills under the blazing Iraq sun. "Uh-huh."

"Uh-huh? You want to tell me what's going on in that fucking crazy head of yours?"

Landry grinned. "A whole helluva lot."

CHAPTER 34

It was easy to determine the whereabouts of presidential candidate Cameron Mills. Just Google him. He was in California, as a matter of fact, staying at the home of his friend and chief fund-raiser, Stefan Graybill. Stefan Graybill was the head of a group called the Rancho Santa Fe Democrats Association.

Landry had known a few horseracing people who lived in Rancho Santa Fe—it was very close to Del Mar and the racetrack there. All the people he knew were Republicans. Rancho Santa Fe was a conservative enclave, home to some of the wealthiest people in the country, many of whom were prominent racehorse owners. In fact, most of the residents of Rancho Santa Fe were horse people of one stripe or another.

But there were Democrats—retired movie and TV executives, Internet moguls, and the odd actor or two.

Landry had been to Rancho Santa Fe once, fifteen years ago, to assess a potential racing prospect for a friend. He had been impressed by the beauty of the area. The farm he'd gone to was built in the twenties. He remembered shady dirt lanes lined by white board fences, eucalyptus, and pepper trees. He remembered lush pastures and white-painted barns with red tile roofs. The barns echoed the main house—California mission style. Of course the house was much grander.

So he was surprised to discover that the rancho where the senator was staying was the same place he'd visited—a remarkable coincidence. He already knew the layout. He'd already seen inside the barns; he'd already been inside the main room of the house, as well as the kitchen. Of course, that was fifteen years ago, and the owner might have renovated the house since then. But as he glassed the house from a nearby hill, he didn't see any disturbance to the flora and fauna. The date-palm trees were still in the same place; it would have been impossible to build around them. The oblong pool looked the same, and the worn-brick terrace lapped right up to the glass doors leading to the solarium.

He'd looked at Stefan Graybill's rancho on Google Earth. He had even found a recent blueprint of the Rancho Santa Fe area in a small corner of the Internet. Although it was difficult to read, he could see the general layout of the house.

Rancho Santa Fe had been established as the Covenant of Rancho Santa Fe in 1932, built by a developer and his rich friends to preserve the beauty of the area and to keep the riffraff out. It must have worked. By 2006, Rancho Santa Fe was the second-most prosperous area in the country, with an average home costing over $2 million—$2,585,000, to be exact.

Landry had read up on both Senator Cameron Mills and Stefan Graybill. Graybill, a Silicon Valley billionaire who had made the Forbes 500 list for seventeen years in a row, was determined to turn the San Diego area blue—an impossibly uphill battle, in Landry's opinion. He was the primary mover and shaker behind Senator Mills's presidential campaign.

The official presidential campaign, he knew, wouldn't start for another year and a half. But anyone who wanted the job was running now, and that meant they were fund-raising.

In a way, none of it made sense, because if Landry was correct, Cam had plenty of money for his campaign. More than enough.

Landry needed to find out who had called the hit on him. It could have been Cam Mills, or it could have been someone who worked for Mills. Or, it could have been someone else entirely—someone and something completely out of left field. Landry couldn't think of anyone else who wanted him dead, but then again, it all depended on who knew he was alive. After his photo showed up on television, there would be a virtual army of people. But who had the most to lose?

Cameron Mills: the guy who made off with the $6.6 billion that had famously gone missing from Iraq.

Now he was running for president. If it ever came out that he had stolen the money, his presidential campaign would go up in flames.

A lot was left unsaid between a politician and his staff. The polite term for that unspoken transaction was "plausible deniability."

If Cam had mentioned Landry as a threat—even in passing—his body man would know. His security people would know. A few mentions, a few dropped hints, and his people would intuit what was expected of them without actual words ever crossing the politician's lips.

Landry could not rule out Cam's body man, Duncan Welty—the pale, ferret-faced man always by his side. Welty was former military himself. He could not rule out the head of Cam's security, either.

Landry had worked security for politicians in the past. He knew that a body man was a politician's closest ally and friend—his Man Friday. The body man even supplanted the politician's wife as chief cheerleader and confidant.

He needed to start with Welty.

- — -

Before he could eliminate a threat, he had to define it. The fund-raiser event at Graybill's farm was two days away. Landry had found a nice little spot on an oak-covered hill above the barns where he could watch the house. The parabolic mic he'd brought with him hadn't picked up anything more interesting than casual conversation and birdcalls—yet. There were comings and goings, mostly a train of black Chevrolet Suburbans with tinted glass. Landry noticed that Cam's body man drove the same Suburban on his trips away, which were surprisingly frequent. He went on all sorts of errands, bringing back dry cleaning and food. Apparently the Mills family loved the burger place in the village. Landry memorized the license plate.

It was time for a shopping trip. Landry had several items on his list. Everything he needed could be found in San Diego.

He bought a portable computer printer for his laptop, a laminate badge-holder with a clip, and a pack of manila envelopes. He drove up the street to a Walgreens (there was one on every corner, it seemed), and paid cash for a disposable phone with sixty prepaid minutes.

From the drugstore he drove to a sign shop he'd checked out earlier in the week, in a run-down section of San Diego proper. The street was crammed with auto-body shops, strip malls, and other small businesses catering to small industry.

Landry had a good ear and spoke two languages—German and French—fluently. (He also knew some Pashto.) He was good at accents. He stopped at a graphics shop that was actually pretty busy, and picked out the guy who seemed least motivated—a kid with slumped shoulders who smelled like he'd been smoking a joint out back. The kid was droopy eyed and barely paid attention. Landry addressed him in broken English—an Italian accent—and painstakingly described what he needed. He asked for two sets of wide striping, one blue, one red, and two sets of black letters, starting with *B* and ending with *T*. If you spread them out on the ground they would spell "Bellen Pohleet," a word he stressed a few times. It sounded vaguely Italian and the kid was no linguist. He did his job and provided the letters.

Fifteen minutes later Landry drove into a parking garage and found a dark corner with one vehicle on either side. There, he clamped the letters on to both sides of the van. Only this time they spelled "Bell Telephone."

He drove back to Rancho Santa Fe and parked beside a telephone pole, approximately three-quarters of a mile from the Graybill house. Using climbing spikes, he scaled the pole. From there he could observe the caterers and other vehicles—security, etc.—coming and going, and once again studied the layout beyond the gates. He reached into the satchel hanging from one shoulder and pulled out a camera with a telescopic zoom to check out the private security. They looked pretty good. He snapped pictures of the catering vehicles, security structure, and one very accommodating federal agent who faced out toward him. Landry got a good shot of the security ID on his jacket. He also photographed the catering van.

Landry now had an enlarged photo of the federal security badge. He would use the computer printer he'd bought at Staples to print up a reasonable facsimile of the federal ID, substituting his own passport photo for the agent's face. Then he'd slip it into the clip-on laminate sleeve, and voilà! He was official security.

One thing Landry kept in a bag in his shaving kit at all times: lapel pins from various agencies. They could be bought cheaply, and were essential to further the fiction that he was with a federal agency.

Surveillance done, Landry ditched the telephone-company lettering in the back of the van and drove back to another graphics shop down the street from the first one, this time with a roughly drawn sketch of the catering van's sign. He already had the address for his next stop—a men's clothing store. He decided on a handsome black suit. He bought two white button-down long-sleeved dress shirts and a dark tie—all in keeping with federal-agent apparel. Sitting in his van, Landry searched online for the nearest uniform shop. It was a drive, but worth it: he bought a white kitchen smock and apron.

With his purchases loaded into the back of the van, Landry returned to his place under the oaks. He had to walk from the road, but fortunately the area was hilly and there was plenty of cover. He stuck with the parabolic mic and watched the activity below.

The shadows were slanting across the hill, and the sun had turned the grass a lurid Day-Glo green, when a black Suburban drove out through the estate gates. Landry glassed the license plate. Sure enough, it was the Suburban Welty drove.

He waited until Welty made it to the main road, then discreetly followed. The Suburban stopped in the village. Welty got out and walked to the general store on the corner. The alarm beeped twice.

Welty had to turn the corner to reach the entrance. Landry figured he'd have plenty of time, but he would keep it to three minutes, tops.

Landry had programmed the phone and dropped it in a manila envelope. He scrawled "Duncan Welty" on the envelope, dropped a quick note inside, sealed it, and slipped the package under one of the windshield wipers.

Welty came outside about ten minutes later. Landry watched from a distance as he returned to the Suburban, and did a double take at the envelope. Landry snapped several shots from his phone: Welty pulling the envelope out from under the windshield wipers, peeking inside; Welty shaking the phone out into his hand. Welty turning this way and that, looking around. His face impassive— probably because he wore dark wraparound sunglasses.

He shoved the envelope under his arm, beeped the door lock, and climbed into the Suburban.

Sat there for a few minutes, staring down. Reading the note, no doubt. The note said: "Call this number if you value your job."

Looking around. His paranoia showing. Then he started the car.

The Suburban roared to life. Duncan Welty pulled out so fast the tires bounced off the curb. The tires chirped. Then he was out on the street.

Landry watched him drive a quarter mile, then come to an abrupt stop. He was parked under a cottonwood tree, the engine still running.

Landry's own throwaway phone buzzed. He thumbed it on but said nothing.

"Who are you?" Welty demanded.

Landry stayed silent.

"What are you trying to pull?"

Landry said nothing.

"This is bullshit! I'm hanging up right now."

Landry waited. He knew Welty wouldn't hang up.

"Who *are* you?"

"You know who this is."

"What? What are you talking about?"

"I'm calling to tell you your target is on to you."

"What? What are you *talking* about? Who *are* you?"

"I'm not telling you who this is. You need to be aware that your target is on to you. I suggest you look into it. Do it quickly."

"What are you *talking* about?"

Landry watched Welty gun the engine and drive away.

He thought: *Und now, ve vait.*

⌐ — ⌐

Landry watched the estate through the night-vision scope on his rifle. No one stirred. He'd half-expected Duncan to drive somewhere, but he didn't. It was a beautiful and warm California night, creaking with crickets. The lights were on in the house, throwing lozenges of light onto the terrace. The pool was lit from within, glowing turquoise, and Landry wished he could swim in it.

Mills's wife was swimming instead, her long body cleaving the water. A beautiful woman. Mills, his host, and his body man sat at a table under an umbrella.

Using the parabolic mic, Landry managed to get bits and pieces of conversation—a breeze picked up their voices. They talked about raising money, mostly. (Landry thought this was rich, considering how much Cam must have stashed away.) They discussed Cam's most likely opposition—the brash young senator from Michigan who was popular with the left wing of the party.

Duncan seemed content to sit there and not say a word. But to Landry's eye, Cameron Mills looked a little . . . off. Preoccupied, maybe? Hard to tell.

The jury was still out.

- — -

The next morning was all bustle. Early in the day the florist showed up. Then came the bakery van for the workers. White wooden collapsible tables and chairs were unloaded from a box truck and set up on the lawn.

There was much more security today than the day before. When guarding a high-profile subject at a large gathering, it was necessary to keep all threats out of the security perimeter. Usually that meant three rings of security: outer, inner, and at ground zero. It was most often the case, though, security loosened as the rings of security were penetrated. The most energy and resources went to holding the outer perimeter. The second perimeter was a little more lax, and inside—that's where everybody let their guard down.

That was almost always the case.

Almost always.

But Landry would not let *his* guard down, no matter where he was.

Landry had studied video clips of Cameron Mills from television and the Internet. He had read op-eds written by Mills and op-eds written about him, seen him speaking from the well of the Senate. He'd made a study of Cameron Mills, his wife, his daughter, and his body man. In his opinion, Cameron Mills had all the earmarks of a pompous ass. He did not appear to be any different this morning. If something bothered him, you'd never know it. He enjoyed an outdoor breakfast on the terrace with his family and his host's family. The conversation was desultory, the mood relaxed.

Cam's clothing was country-club-Republican casual, a wise choice on a day when the outside temperature might flirt with eighty degrees. He wore a dark blazer, fawn trousers, and a pale but crisp open-collared dress shirt. Years ago Landry had noticed that most candidates wore the exact same shade of blue. His former boss Michael Cardamone once told him the hue was called "Sincere Blue." The color was head and shoulders above any other when it came to creating the impression of honesty and trustworthiness. This was true for a candidate or for a defendant in court. "Sincere Blue" projected reliability, and God only knew how desperately Cameron Mills needed that.

Still, if Mills was worried about Duncan's mysterious caller, he did not let on. Landry noticed that the body man did not breakfast with them.

He glassed the SUVs in the parking area. (You knew someone was rich when they had a large "parking area.") Duncan's Suburban was there along with the rest.

Then the door opened and Welty emerged. It was hard to tell his expression from here, but he greeted everyone heartily.

Landry could pick up a few words and phrases, and one of them was Duncan apologizing for "sleeping in."

"Must be the air," Cam said.

Hard to decipher these two.

Did Welty tell him about the call? Landry had no idea. The body man's face was an impassive mask behind the dark glasses. After breakfast, he launched into his duties, directing the florists, the caterers, the sound people—all the while keeping his eye on the Big Dog.

But he also seemed nervous. He dropped a flower arrangement, but fortunately for him, the glass vase bounced on the springy lawn.

Was Duncan waiting for the other shoe to drop?

Landry thought he'd have to push him some more. Push *them*. On to plan B.

CHAPTER 35

Landry drove his recently transformed Del Rey Bakery van up to the gates of the estate. An agent standing by the gate holding a clipboard held up his hand: just a moment.

Landry waited.

The agent consulted his list, then motioned to two vans parked in the holding area. "How many cupcakes do they *need* for this thing?"

"Danny forgot the coffee and doughnuts for the staff."

"Can't have that." The agent motioned him through.

Landry parked and withdrew the pink boxes of doughnuts from the back of the van, placing the cardboard coffee caddy on top. There was another person with a clipboard closer to the staging area—a large swath of mowed grass now holding approximately sixty white folding chairs and tables.

He ran the gauntlet—one more agent outside and another inside the kitchen. The third agent said, "You just come in through the gate?"

He nodded. "More doughnuts and there's fresh coffee, too."

The agent sniffed appreciatively. "Any extras?"

"We'll see, sir. Let me get them to the kitchen and see what the boss says."

"Our little secret, okay?"

Landry obligingly opened the box. "You bet."

The agent took a jelly doughnut and Landry proceeded on. He had to hold the top box—the caddy containing the coffee—with his chin. The pink boxes rested on the tightly folded suit jacket. Wrapped inside the suit-jacket folds was a manila folder, identical to the one he'd left for Duncan Welty the day before.

Nobody questioned him. In fact, nobody even noticed him as he strode purposefully across the lawn in the cook whites. Underneath the smock, he wore a white dress shirt and suit trousers. A dark conservative tie was stuffed into the pocket. People only looked at his upper body—the boxes of doughnuts—not at his shoes. His shoes were black lace-ups of good quality. They wouldn't be unusual even for a bakery employee—this was a special occasion.

Landry made his way into the kitchen and nodded to the caterer, who was busy and shorthanded. "More coffee and doughnuts for the staff," he told her. The woman glanced at him from the large pot of soup she was stirring and said, "Put them on the counter."

He did so, dropping his hands to his sides, the suit still crumpled up in one hand, hidden slightly behind his hip. "May I use the bathroom?"

She didn't even look at him, just motioned with her chin. "That way."

He went down a short hallway to the bathroom, removed the baker's apron, and donned the neatly pressed suit jacket and clipped on the federal ID badge he'd printed up. Add shades, the conservative tie, and an earpiece that led to nowhere—and he was a Fed.

He followed the hallway down to another door to the outside, and worked his way back around to the front, where he spent his time standing around and looking alert. At one point he fell into step with Cam Mills and his people crossing the lawn toward the bunting-draped dais, where Cam checked the height of the microphone and couldn't resist his own sound check: "Testing, testing . . . As future nominee of our party . . ." He grinned boyishly at the smattering of applause, and strode off the stage. He joined a knot of people standing nearby. Landry stood at the edge, paying no attention to Cam but looking outward as a good agent would, scanning the grounds for threats and assessing the area. Cam told a humorous story about his time in Iraq—not the story Landry would have *liked* to have heard—and everyone laughed. It had been Landry's observation that powerful men were the soul of wit—even when they weren't.

The time wasn't quite right. He wanted to catch Cam walking.

And sure enough, soon Cam was walking, headed toward the koi pond, everyone else falling in line. Landry had joined a group strolling toward him from another direction. Cam was talking and Landry came close by and held out the envelope. "This just came for you, sir."

Cam glanced at it, midconversation, still on the move. "Thanks," he said, and went back to talking. Landry worked his way around the growing knots of people, back to the bathroom, and *presto change-o!* He was in cook whites again. He walked out to the van and drove out with a nod to the guard.

Landry followed the road over a couple of hills and, sure that no one could see him, dropped a lit match into some brush. He then changed the signs on the van back to Bell Telephone, drove to the telephone pole three-quarters of a mile away from Graybill's house, and climbed up.

He watched the gathering crowd through the scope of his sniper rifle, Betsy. More and more cars were directed into a cleared area to the right of the small show ring, and people began flooding the grounds as time drew closer for the fund-raising event to begin.

Landry kept his eye on the ball, but even so, he almost missed it. He caught Cam in his sights, walking briskly back to the house, the manila envelope clutched in his hand. He clearly had something on his mind, and it wasn't good. He disappeared inside.

Landry's burner phone chirped.

Landry checked his watch. This would be a three-minute conversation and no longer.

"Who are you?" Cam demanded. "Is this some kind of shakedown? Because if it is—"

"Don't waste my time," Landry said. "I need to make you aware that your target is on to you. You're going to act, I suggest you do it quickly."

"*What?* What is this?"

Landry smiled. It was the same response Cam's body man Duncan Welty had used.

He could see Cam—who had stiffened ramrod straight. He'd pushed his sunglasses up on his head, the phone jammed hard to his ear. "Who *is* this?" he demanded, with all the high expectations of an answer that a pampered and handled candidate could muster.

Landry could see the tension in every line of the man's body. The way he held the phone in a death grip. The almost skeletal rictus of his face.

Duncan—the body man—frozen beside him. Listening but not listening. Close, but trying to appear unaware.

"I'm an acquaintance of yours, and normally I wouldn't take up your time at an important event like this. But here's the deal. The safety of my family is threatened by the guy standing at your right elbow."

Cam stiffened, and looked over at Duncan.

"Whoever he's working with knows I'm watching him."

"What?" Cam lowered his voice. "What is this?"

"What this is: I don't appreciate someone attempting to kill me or my family. Look to your direct right."

Cam stared at Duncan. His lips moving.

"If I can see you, I can hurt you. Your body man can't help you. If you are not involved in this, I won't hold you responsible, but if you ignore what I'm telling you, you will deal with me. I guarantee you won't like the way it turns out."

Can stared at Duncan. Duncan looked like he'd wet his pants.

Landry smelled smoke, and glanced in the direction of the brushfire, which was already licking the top of the hill. "Raise your hand if you understand me. If you don't address this problem, then I will."

"Look, I wouldn't—"

"Fix the problem. If you tell anyone, if you involve the Secret Service, there will be no second warning."

He disconnected. Down below, Landry could see people shading their eyes and looking in the direction of the fire. One of them pointing. People gathering, putting phones to their ears.

Landry drew the champagne glass on the table at Cam's elbow into Betsy's crosshairs. Took his time, allowed for the breeze, which was not enough to discourage him from the shot.

He squeezed the trigger.

The champagne glass shattered where it stood. Cam stepped back, his face white with shock. No one else had reacted—they hadn't seen the glass break. He covered his eyes and scanned the horizon, then looked at the broken shards of glass in horror.

Landry said, "It's that easy."

He had no doubt that this time, Cam got the message.

CHAPTER 36

At breakfast the next morning, Landry paged through the *LA Times*. He was most interested in two headlines. The larger headline was slightly hysterical in nature: "Senator Unhurt in Assassination Attempt."

The article recounted Cam Mills's close brush with death, and the brushfire that burned twenty acres. Fortunately, the wind direction kept it from destroying any homes or other structures, and it was put out quickly.

The other headline was much smaller. It concerned the suspicious death of a man in an alley in a run-down part of San Diego. He had been burned beyond recognition and it would be a while before he was identified—if ever.

Two days later Cam Mills gave a speech in LA. Landry was in the audience. Afterward, he was able to get down to the underground garage and watch him leave.

Duncan Welty was not with him.

Landry kept tabs on Mills. It didn't take him long to figure out that Duncan Welty was gone.

Perhaps permanently.

CHAPTER 37

Special Agent Andrew Keller used his own time when he surveilled Cindi Landry's townhome. He was sure Cyril Landry was alive, but so far he'd seen no sign of him. Granted, he had very little time to keep up the surveillance, since it was off the books. But he was sure that at some point Cyril Landry would contact his wife.

For a day or two Landry's photo was everywhere in the media— TV, Internet, newspaper. No one had come forward. Maybe there were people who knew him and were afraid of him. Or he had been like the virtual tree falling in the forest—nobody seemed to know who the mystery man was.

He'd interviewed the wife and daughter, and they had seemed mystified. They had presented a consolidated front. Neither had seen or heard from him, and were as shocked as he was that Cindi's husband and Kristal's father was still alive.

Landry had trained them well.

So he decided on surveillance. It could be true that they did not "give a rat's ass" about him, as Cindi indelicately put it, or it could be that they were hiding him. So he made it a practice to watch the house as often as he could, especially at night.

Just an average townhome, no different from any other on the street, the car all locked up in the garage at night. Cindi would drive home from work and her daughter would drive in at different times in her little yellow car.

Sometimes he'd see the boyfriend. Cindi's boyfriend, Todd Barclay, who seemed solid enough. Or, more likely, *stolid* enough. No excitement there. After being married to a Navy SEAL and black-ops specialist, it must have been soothing to be with a comptroller.

It was late afternoon and Cindi had just driven home. She parked out front. He'd already seen her daughter come home. The garage door had rolled up and she'd driven her little yellow car inside and closed the garage door behind her, entering the house that way. But her mother parked outside.

It was Friday, the beginning of the weekend. Agent Keller had seen this pattern before—last week, in fact. He'd followed them a ways last time, but had been called back in to work on another matter.

The thing was, they had overnight bags last weekend.

He waited on the short rise overlooking their subdivision—thank heaven for the fact that this area was mostly hills. He glassed the place, waiting to see if they would go somewhere *this* weekend as well. He thought the chances were pretty good, since Cindi had left her Hyundai Tucson out front.

Sure enough, they emerged from the house, loaded down with grocery bags and a suitcase for Kristal and a duffle for Mama.

This time he was ready to follow them.

He'd planted a tracking device inside the wheel well of the Hyundai.

All he had to do was track the signal.

— — —

On television, Cameron Mills appeared distraught. A body found in San Diego had been identified as an employee of his named Duncan Welty.

A reporter caught him in a sound bite—one that Landry had no doubt he'd rehearsed. Duncan had been his right-hand man, and he had been surprised and devastated to learn that he had been involved with drugs. "Prescription drugs are such a problem," Cam said. "And it's one of many issues I want to deal with. This is just untenable. Duncan leaves behind a wife and a beautiful daughter . . ."

He choked up, couldn't continue.

Landry turned the TV off. Sitting, once again, on a bed that was too short for him in another hotel room.

He didn't know if Cameron had put the hit on him. It could have been all Duncan Welty. But Mills had made the problem go away. It was a message to Landry, either way. Cam Mills was saying there would be no further attempts on Landry's life. Not now, not ever.

But Landry decided he would keep in touch with Cam.

Just to keep him on the straight and narrow.

By disposing of Duncan, Cam was saying, "We understand each other."

Landry hoped Cam was telling the truth. He probably was. Landry was too much trouble. He was now way too dangerous to mess with.

Could have been Duncan guarding his main man, or it could have been Cam running the show.

Either way, Landry thought it was over—

—but he wouldn't let his guard down.

- — -

Special Agent Andrew Keller had found a good place to watch the comings and goings at Todd Barclay's cabin. He was higher up, on a hill across from the cabin, and he had time—it was the weekend.

It seemed like the worst of long shots, but he was pretty sure that at some point Landry would visit his wife and daughter. Landry didn't strike him as the kind of man who would give up on his family. It might not pan out, but if it did . . .

He was next in line for special agent in charge.

And he had a unique relationship with Landry. He had talked to him for a long period of time on the phone.

Too bad that Landry had only given him bullshit. The brother with the lodge in Montana. The school shooting that never was. The escapee—

Lies, all of it.

He'd been played for a fool.

Nobody does that to me.

So he would watch and wait. He couldn't be here all the time, but he figured it was worth doing—if he hit with Landry, he'd hit big.

Darkness was closing in. As far as he could tell, everyone was home.

It was quiet at dusk. The lights came on in the cabin, warm and inviting. Gingham curtains. Keller had always been the cabin-in-the-woods kind of guy, and this reminded him of how he'd bought Landry's story—hook, line, and sinker (pun not intended). All the man had to do was Google him and play to his bliss.

Maybe Landry didn't care about his wife and daughter anymore. But it was a lead worth following. There wasn't any other way to hunt down Landry that he could see. And the upside would be incredible.

The night sounds started up. Rustling animals, insects buzzing and crickets chirping. He looked out at the dark lake through the trunks of the trees, lights from several homes glowing on the water. Settled in. But he was ready to go.

Time passed and nothing happened. Which was typical of surveillance. Around ten p.m. the side door opened and Todd Barclay came out. He walked around to the back of the house, where his boat was kept under a blue cover. He was carrying a trouble light, plugged it in, and worked on his boat.

More time went by. Keller couldn't see Barclay, but he could hear him using a drill.

The area was quiet. Occasionally a car drove by, but none turned into the short lane that ran uphill to the cabin. While the road wasn't far from Big Bear Lake, this was an isolated patch of woods, thanks to the configuration of the mountain.

Inside, through the sheerness of the gingham curtains (he thought them precious, and wondered if that was Cindi Landry's taste), he could see the blue flicker of the television.

The drilling stopped, then started up again.

Added to that was the sound of a generator, a loud fuzzy hum.

Another car drove by, headlights casting beams on the small curve where it bottomed out. It continued on. He heard the engine cut, and a door open and close, farther up the road. Had to be another cabin in that direction, although he couldn't see any lights.

He glanced at his watch: ten thirty p.m. It would be a long, boring night. Another car drove by. He watched the taillights disappear around the bend, and reappear farther along the mountain—not many cabins in this area, and fewer out that way.

He shifted position. What was the man doing behind the house? He decided to get closer. His leg was beginning to fall asleep anyway. He pushed himself to his feet and walked toward the house.

As he reached the yard, a harsh light turned right on him, blinding him.

Like those guys who headlight deer.

It was his last thought.

- — -

Landry was surprised when his phone buzzed—and it wasn't the one he was using at the time. No, it was the other one. The phone he had given his wife.

He answered.

He expected to hear Cindi's voice. Or Kristal's.

But the voice was male. Male and scared: Todd Barclay. "I—Cindi told me I should call you, something's happened—"

Landry gripped the phone hard against his ear. "Kristal?"

"No, no, but it's . . . Oh God, oh God." His voice trailed off in a wail.

Disconcerting, hearing even a wuss like Barclay cry like that. "What's wrong?" he asked.

"Oh God, oh God, it just happened, I thought it was a . . . I don't know." The man seemed to suck it up then. "I . . . shot someone."

"You *shot* someone?"

"I heard something outside the cabin—there have been break-ins around here—and so I . . . I . . ."

"What happened?"

"I shot him."

"Him?"

"I shot this man. I think, I think . . . I think he's dead."

"You don't know?"

"No! He was dressed all in black. He might be alive. Kristal!" he shouted. "Don't go outside! There might be more."

"Why'd you call me?"

"Because . . . I thought you'd . . . You were a spy. You'd know what to do."

Landry had been many things, but he was never a spy. His wife's fiancé needed him now. Or rather, he needed the kind of person Landry was. Landry knew what he meant. Someone who killed people. Someone who made people disappear. Someone who did the dirty work. *Someone dumb enough to fight for his country in a foreign land.*

"What do you want?"

"What do I want you to do? I want you take *care* of it!" The last four words were part terror and part command.

Landry thought: *He thinks I'm a cleaner. Like he's seen in the movies.*

His heart felt like a stone. A cold stone. "I'm sure you can figure it out yourself," he said.

He was greeted by silence.

Then: *"Please."*

Landry had been working on forgiveness. He had been working on accepting the fact that Cindi loved this milquetoast asshole, that she had moved on, and because he loved her and knew how badly she had suffered during and after their marriage, he would *accept*.

Fuck acceptance.

"Looks like you've got some work to do," Landry said before hanging up.

CHAPTER 38

A few minutes later, Eric shoved a phone under his hotel room door and then knocked.

Landry called Eric back.

"Meet me in the lobby?"

"Yeah."

Landry was ready to go. He shouldered his duffle and met Eric by the potted palm.

"Car's outside," Eric said.

The drive to Big Bear Lake seemed to go on forever, even though Eric was making good time.

"What made you change your mind?"

"My wife and daughter."

"Yeah. What I thought. You don't want them mixed up in that."

Landry nodded. He leaned against the window on the passenger side, watching the headlights stream toward them as they headed up into the pass. Todd Barclay could go to prison for life for all he cared, but he had to think about Cindi and Kristal.

He had always protected his girls and he always would.

Maybe these days a man wasn't supposed to call his wife and daughter—let alone a soon-to-be *ex*-wife and daughter—"his girls," but that was the way he'd always seen them. They belonged to him. It went both ways: he belonged to them, too.

So now Toddy Boy had gotten himself into a mess, and it wouldn't just be a mess for him, but for Cindi and Kristal. There had already been news vans parked out in front of her house. *Now* what would that look like? He could see the story, the insinuation that she was a married woman (now that he was alive), that she was shacking up at Big Bear Lake. That she was having too much fun for a woman whose daughter's boyfriend had been shot to death.

Maybe none of that would happen, but Todd Barclay had been right about one thing: he *was* the expert.

And so he had called Barclay back. "Don't touch anything," he'd instructed a very grateful Todd.

"Have to figure out how to get rid of this guy," Landry said now.

"Yeah," Eric said. "His vehicle, too."

At Big Bear, they parked by an empty cottage up the road, checked their weapons, and shouldered their duffles and hiked in. They split up—Eric melting into the forest.

Unspoken between them: if Eric found a body in the forest, he would take measures to hide him. Didn't have to talk about it, either. It was SOP—standard operating procedure.

Barclay was standing on the porch of his cabin, his face fright-wig white.

"Where is he?" Landry called up. Wishing he didn't even have to talk to the creep.

He pointed behind Landry. "Down that hill, down near the creek. I can go with you, if you want me to."

"No thanks," Landry said. "First I'd like to see Cindi and Kristal."

Todd backed up inside the door, held it open. "Sure. Thanks for doing this, Cyril."

Cyril said, "You can call me Mr. Landry."

Todd had the grace to look chastened. "I'm going to head back over there. Maybe there's something I can do."

"If you wait I can go with you."

"No, that's okay, maybe I was wrong and he's not dead."

"Don't touch anything."

"I won't. Maybe he's okay, though. I should probably stay with him. If you call out, I can signal you with my flashlight."

Don't strain yourself.

Landry went inside.

His wife and daughter were sitting on the couch, both of them leaning forward. Cindi propping her chin on her hand, Kristal's hands slid down between her knees and clasped. She wore perhaps the shortest skirt ever known to man—but she didn't look the least flirtatious. Her mascara had run.

His baby wore mascara. Of course he knew that. But she looked even more vulnerable with the dark stains under her eyes. When she saw him she launched off the couch and into his arms.

He closed his eyes and breathed her in. Felt the warmth of her against him rise up into his chest. He felt contentment. She was pressed against him; she called him "Daddy." "He could have killed us, Daddy."

"The man?" Landry asked.

"I didn't see him, but you're here now."

You're here now.

Warmth spread through him. He was here now, with his girls.

For now, for a little while, they were still his girls.

First thing to do was secure the cabin, make sure they were safe, just in case the man Todd shot had a friend. "You know the drill. Stick together, stay away from windows, and stay down."

"Bathroom?" Cindi said.

"Better safe than sorry. Lock yourselves in. Cindi, you have your Glock, right?"

Cindi nodded.

"Remember to—"

"Shoot to kill. I know. Center mass."

"What about the garage? Is the rolldown door the only opening?"

Cindi nodded.

"Where's the door opener? In case we have to make a quick getaway?"

Cindi went to a kitchen drawer and produced it.

Her fingertips touched his, and for a moment he lost his place in the world. She pulled back, faced away from him.

"Okay," he said. "I'm going to check out the garage and the rest of the house. Stay down and away from the wind—"

"—windows. We know, Dad," Kristal said.

Just hearing her say "Dad" nearly undid him. He drew his weapon and headed into the short hallway. Checked the bathroom. The window was too small to crawl through—either in or out—so that was neither a help nor a hindrance.

He took the door from the little kitchen into the garage.

It was dark.

He flicked on the light, and donned latex gloves.

It was a two-car garage, spacious. Almost as big as the cabin it was attached to—it had clearly been an add-on.

Framed photographs hung on the walls at intervals—all of them of one plane or another. A Cessna Stationair, some kind of commuter plane he did not recognize, and helicopters. One of them, a Chinook in Iraq. Landry was pretty sure it was Iraq. Looked like it.

It seemed like an eclectic collection.

A Chinook in Iraq.

Cindi's SUV was closest to him.

He checked the door switch to see how it raised. Raised it about two feet and then lowered it.

Walked around the SUV, his shoes gritting on the pavement.

The other car was under a cover.

Interesting—why cover it inside a garage? He knew guys who did that. Guys who prized their cars, treated them like newly laid eggs.

He registered the shape under the car cover. Distinctive. A muscle car. He was pretty sure he knew what kind of car it was.

He reached down and pulled up the side of the cover over the front wheel well.

Felt it in his stomach, that feeling. Like something had crawled up in there. Excitement and just a thrill of recognition.

Pulled the cover back farther.

You'd think he would be surprised. But he wasn't, not surprised at all, to be looking at a 2014 black Camaro SS—

At that moment, from inside the house, he heard Cindi scream.

CHAPTER 39

Rifle in hand, Landry stepped out of the short hallway to the living area.

Todd Barclay stood in the center of the room. Kristal was locked into a half nelson. He pressed a SIG Sauer nine-millimeter hard into her cheek. "Stay back!" he shouted. "Or I'll blow her brains all over the ceiling."

Landry lowered the rifle slowly.

"Set it on the floor and push it my way," Todd said.

Landry shoved it with the toe of his boot.

"Do you know who I am?" Todd said.

"No."

"You really don't, do you? Well—I'm your worst nightmare."

It was hard to respect someone who used a line like that.

But he needed to take Barclay seriously. He'd put the man in a little box—passed him off as a mild-mannered accountant.

Todd was talking. "You sure you don't know who I am? Don't see a family resemblance maybe?"

Landry was mystified. Then he thought of the photographs of the planes, the helicopter.

The Chinook. Barclay was former military. Landry needed to keep talking. *Keep him engaged.* "We've met?"

The guy looked incredulous. His incredulity quickly turned to anger. "You don't remember what happened in Florida?"

"You're going to have to clue me in." He kept calm. The man was agitated, seething. Angry men made mistakes.

Barclay jerked hard on Kristal's throat, crushing the flesh under her chin. Landry looked at her, trying to convey calm. He looked at Cindi, too. She had both hands around her weapon, but it was pointed down. Uncertain what to do, with her daughter held at gunpoint. Barclay saw the gun and bellowed, "Drop it, Cindi! I'm on a hair trigger here!"

Landry caught her eyes and nodded.

She dropped it.

"Kick it away."

She did.

"Get around me so I can see you. Go sit on the couch." Added with true loathing— *"Honey."* Looked back at Landry. "You don't know who I am, okay, that's fair. We were only introduced once, and we were all busy that day. I was just another helo pilot to you. How many helo pilots have you spoken to over the years? Ten? Twenty? Thirty? All those missions in Iraq and Afghanistan?"

Landry said, "Want to get to the point?"

"Oh, yeah. The *point.* Fuck you, asshole. Here's the point. Ever heard of Peters, Jackson, Davis, and Green? That ring any kind of bell?"

Landry remembered his former team members well. He had killed them in a well-planned ambush at the safe house in Port Saint Joe, Florida. "Which one?"

"Guess."

Guess? *Seriously?* "If whoever it was meant something to you, don't you think we should stop with the games?"

"Oh, yeah, your family. That's what's important. Your *daughter.* Wish my guy had shot her when he had the chance."

Landry heard his wife gasp. He looked past Barclay to Cindi, and shook his head.

"You understand now? I hired the guy who shot up the school. Cindi!" Barclay yelled. "Get around here so I can see you better!"

She did.

"Who do you think took your wife and daughter?"

Landry said nothing. He looked at his wife, trying to tell her with his eyes: *Don't react. Don't give anything away. I'm here.*

I'm here.

She nodded. It was so small you'd miss it, normally. She kept her eyes on him. Kristal kept her eyes on him, too.

Landry knew from having a gun pressed to his own temple—on three separate occasions—that fear was not a maintainable emotion. At first you were terrified. The fear would spread through you like wildfire, blotting out all thought. You were going to die. You were at the edge of the darkness, and you were going to die.

But the longer the gun was pressed to your head, the more stray thoughts wandered in. Thoughts like: *I'm still here.* Thoughts like: *How can I get out of this?* And the adrenaline backed off a little, the blood moved back out to the extremities, the heartbeat slowed. The human body was mostly hopeful. *Still alive, still alive, as long as I'm here there has to be a way out.*

Landry had known this feeling often enough to recognize it in his wife and daughter. And in himself.

He knew the man wanted to talk. He wanted to gloat, he wanted to tell his side of the story, because he'd never had the chance before.

So if the guy wanted to vent, to tell him the story, to tell him how he had been screwed over by one Cyril Landry, what was the harm? It would buy them time. Barclay—if that was his name—wanted to share the injustice of it. He wanted to kill Landry, yes, but *first*, he wanted to tell him why.

"I am afraid I don't remember," Landry said softly. "Maybe you could remind me?"

"God damn you to hell!" Barclay screamed. "I should shoot you right now."

Landry held his hands up slightly, in the universal gesture of surrender. He felt as if he were in a TV western, might as well go through the motions. "Maybe you can tell me," he said.

"Peters, Davis, Jackson, and *Green*!" Barclay yelled. "What you did to them!"

Green.

Now he remembered. It wasn't his best moment. In fact, it had been one of his worst. He had planned to dispatch the blond kid with an icepick to the base of his skull. Death would be instantaneous—he would have felt no pain.

But it hadn't worked out that way. The icepick had slipped. The kid had fought him. It was ugly. He had died badly.

Landry said nothing.

"He suffered!" Barclay shouted. "He suffered like *she's* going to suffer!" He pushed harder at Kristal's cheek, pinching the skin with the sight of his handgun.

Landry said, "So this was the plan? To get to know my wife and daughter, hoping that they would lead you to me?"

The man was shaking. His anger getting the better of him. That was good for Landry. But it was bad for Kristal because angry people did stupid things.

Landry needed to give the man what he wanted. If confession was good for the soul, then airing grievances was even better. And taking credit for something clever was even better than that. Landry said, "How did you know I was alive?"

"I didn't. Not for sure."

"But you guessed."

"Oh, it was more than a guess. Let's call it an educated guess."

Good, if all went well, the man would launch into an explanation. If that happened, he would concentrate more on telling his story, airing that grievance, boasting about his smarts, than on holding the gun to Landry's daughter's head. Landry could see that the muzzle wasn't pressed so hard against her cheek.

"How'd you know?" Landry asked. He tried to sound puzzled, incredulous, and dismayed all at once.

"Simple. I saw you."

"You saw me? Where?"

"That day off Cape San Blas. I saw you swimming."

"You couldn't have. You couldn't have flown in that weather."

"But I did. You must have noticed. That sound of rotors you heard right above you? Come on, don't lie to me."

"Nobody could fly through that," Landry said.

"I could. I had to get out of there, sure, it was a cat-2 storm—but I spotted you swimming. I knew you'd survive to live another day."

"You couldn't be sure. I swam all night."

"You know the old saying. 'Never assume a SEAL is dead until you see his body.' No, I didn't know for *sure* you were alive, but it was worth a try. When you lose everything, when you lose your little brother to an animal like you? I figured it was worth a damn *try*."

"You hired someone to shoot the school up just to get me?"

"Damn right I did." He smiled serenely. He thought he held all the cards. "And look what happened."

Landry became aware that the crickets had stopped chirping. Out of the corner of his eye he could see the side window. It was dark—black almost—but there was something darker there. The side window was out of Barclay's line of sight, because Barclay was concentrating on *him*.

The dark object was there and then it wasn't. "I can't believe you'd go through so much just to get to me." *Show weakness*. "Can't we talk about this?"

"You have to admit, it worked. I drew you out. You're standing here right in front of me, the *dead Cyril Landry*. I might have been playing out in left field, but I threw you out at home."

Landry almost smiled at the man's self-congratulatory tone. "What happened to the man you said was trying to break in? Did you shoot him?"

"The guy hanging around my house? Turns out he is—was?—a special agent with the FBI. Guess he was looking for you."

"Is he dead?"

"Beats me. Probably."

"How'd you manage that?"

"I'm sorry? Manage what?"

"Getting the drop on an FBI agent?" Landry said.

"He was careless. What can I say? He underestimated me, like pretty much everyone else does—did."

Pride creeping in.

He thinks it's all over. Done.

Suddenly the front window exploded—shards of glass flying through the room like missiles.

In an instant, Eric the Red was crouched on the kitchen counter, his rifle trained on Barclay. Landry crashed into Barclay and shoved his daughter to the floor.

One spit from the rifle, and Barclay's head snapped backward. The hole in his forehead bubbled, then drizzled blood, and with a liquid plop Todd Barclay hit the floor face-first.

Kristal had to scramble to get out of the way, and fell into her father's arms.

Eric jumped down, twisted the sound suppressor off his rifle.

Landry held his daughter close and smiled through his tears. "It's okay now, sweetie. I've got you."

CHAPTER 40

There was a lot to do—and Landry needed to get it right. The first thing: get his wife and daughter out of the house and on the road.

"Pack up whatever you keep here—toilet articles or extra clothes or books. Throw it into the Hyundai Tucson and go. If you miss something, we'll take care of it. Go the long way around. When you get home keep the car in the garage and don't answer the door."

"What are you going to do?"

"Make like a cleaner."

"What about the rifle shot?"

"Eric used a silencer."

"No—the other rifle shot—when Todd shot . . . killed the man outside. He was FBI, right?"

"Don't worry about it. You didn't see the sheriff drive by, did you?"

"No. No one drove by."

"If they haven't come by now, we're good." He put his hands on her shoulders. He wanted to hold her to him, but he could feel her resistance. Even at this moment, when all their lives were on the line. "One rifle shot in the forest—and we're on forest land—nobody's going to react to that. Not out here. It could be anybody."

"But—"

"Trust me. If law enforcement didn't show up by now, they won't."

He knew she understood—that he didn't have to explain to her that even in a city or the suburbs, your average citizen would be reluctant to call in about one gunshot. Most people waited to hear if there was anything else going on. They either didn't want to get involved, or they feared retribution, or they just didn't want the hassle.

"So what are you going to do?" Cindi asked.

"Clean up this mess. Where are the keys to the Camaro?"

"On the hook by the door. What about the agent?"

That was a problem. Especially since Special Agent Keller had been focused on Landry. "We're going to have to dispose of him and his car."

Cindi stared at him, emotions flitting across her face: horror, fear, anger, and, finally, acceptance. "They'll look for him."

"That's why his car is going to crash and burn."

She looked away.

It came home to him that if he'd ever held out hope that they could be a family again, this was the end.

She stared off into the trees. "I thought I loved Todd." She hugged her arms to her body, and Landry thought there were tears in her eyes. "I feel like a . . . a goddamn fool and the worst mother in the world."

He opened his mouth to reply, but she gave him a look.

"If he was still alive, I swear to God I would kill him *again*!"

Then she turned on her heel and went inside to start the cleanup.

"So this is what we're gonna do?" Eric said. "Burn the van with him in it? You think it's gonna work?"

"Work?" Abruptly, Landry felt a coldness in his core.

"Hey, earth to Cyril."

Landry saw it, a movie in his head. Two choices: Burying Todd somewhere and parking his car in a place where it was sure to be

315

stolen. Putting Agent Keller's body into his vehicle, torching it, then sending it into a ravine.

"It's not going to work," he said.

"What I was thinking," Eric said. "For one thing, this is the FBI we're dealing with—one of their own. This isn't some Podunk cop shop we're talking about. If he isn't completely burned—hell, even if he is—they might still be able to ID him. Forensics, these days."

Landry said, "The VIN number."

"Yeah. There's that. So what do we do?"

Landry thought about it. There were other problems as well. What if he left the Camaro out for someone to steal—another loose end to tie up—and no one took it? The whole idea was problematic. Where was Todd when his car was being stolen? Something like that could turn into another investigation.

More than one crime would lead a good investigator to question the whole scenario, so he might see that the stolen Camaro and the missing special agent were too much of a coincidence—especially if the FBI knew that SA Keller was surveilling Cindi and Kristal Landry.

And Landry was sure in his bones that Special Agent Keller had watched his wife and daughter, that he had followed them to Big Bear Lake.

Two many elements. Too many coincidences. Too many . . . vectors. All of those vectors could converge on one target: Cyril Landry. He would be at the center of it all.

"Here's what we do," he said.

CHAPTER 41

Landry stepped inside the cabin. His girls—he would always think of them as that—were a dervish of activity. They'd pulled out a box of jumbo trash bags from under the sink and were stuffing items inside them—clothing from the drawers in the bedroom, jackets and blouses still on their hangers from the closet, toilet articles. Working as fast as they could.

"Cindi," Landry said. "There's been a change of plans."

She stopped—poised above the trash bag, mid-shove—two pairs of athletic shoes—and glared at him. Anger seemed to roll off her in waves. He knew it was mostly humiliation and betrayal, but the look she gave him made him think she could cheerfully roast him on a spit.

Which didn't make sense, since it was Todd Barclay who had made a fool of them all. He put that out of his mind as unconstructive. "Let's sit down and go over the plan," he said.

They sat down, Landry on a kitchen chair, his girls on the couch. Eric remained standing. Cindi and Krystal sat there, arms crossed, looking anywhere but at him. The room felt like the preface to a bad thunderstorm—dark, heavy, and foreboding. He could feel the electricity in the air.

It didn't help that the iron stink of blood pervaded the cabin.

Landry wondered which way Cindi would focus her anger. He resigned himself to the fact that he would get his share. He'd dragged her into this—or rather his past did.

"This is what we're going to do," he said. "I can't do this without your full cooperation. If we don't do it this way, then I can tell you for sure: we're all going down. Cindi? Do you hear what I'm saying?"

She glared at him. Finally, she nodded.

"Kristal?"

She nodded as well. Her face was pale—she seemed to be in shock.

"First, you have to put everything back where it was."

Without a word, they complied. The shoes and clothes went back into the closet of the bedroom. The suitcases were set under the window. The roll of paper towels, the vinegar and baking soda from under the sink, all to sop up the blood from the hardwood floor of the cottage—back in the cupboard.

Fortunately, Landry and Eric had not gotten around to moving the body. Barclay lay where he'd fallen, forehead smacked into the floorboards, the exit wound out the back of his head turned sticky.

Time to rehearse what they would say.

Landry stressed that they had to keep the story simple—and true.

Cindi would call the local police and tell them that her fiancé had been shot by an intruder. He was shot through the window of the cabin. The details would stay exactly the same: the man had shot his rifle through the window and killed Todd instantly.

The same assailant had encountered someone else outside the cabin—that man would turn out to be Special Agent Andrew Keller, of the FBI.

Why the special agent was spying on her cabin, Cindi didn't know. She'd had no idea he was out there.

But she recognized the man who had shot into the cabin. She'd met him once or twice at parties—he was a friend of her late husband, Cyril Landry. They had been Navy SEALs together. But she didn't remember his name.

Cindi said, "How about 'Mark' something?"

"That's fine. You only met him once or twice."

"Got it."

They went over their story several times. There had been some kind of ruckus outside the house. Todd started toward the kitchen and that was when he was shot through the window. Cindi saw a man's face briefly, and then he was gone.

"And the man was?"

"A friend of my husband, but I can't remember his name—except for 'Mark.' He worked with my husband—they were on the same SEAL team."

"Do you have any theories why he would do such a thing?"

"He shouted something . . . It was right after he shot Todd."

"What did he say?"

"He said, 'I've repaid my debt.'"

"Do you have any idea what that means?"

"I have no idea."

"No idea?"

"Maybe . . . maybe he didn't like the idea that Todd took my husband's place."

There was the other man, SA Andrew Keller. "Did you know that Agent Keller was watching you?"

"He came and interviewed me about Cyril, once. He thought he was alive."

"Is he alive?"

"No. I'd know if he was."

"And then this guy Keller, he showed up here?"

"I had no idea he was watching the house."

"Think back. Did the friend of your husband—Mark—say anything about the man?"

"He said: 'I got them both.'"

"What did he mean by that? Got them both?"

"He said I didn't have to worry anymore—he did it for his buddy. In his memory."

"Why would Keller think your husband was alive?"

"I have no idea."

"You're sure your husband is dead?"

"I'd know if he was alive."

- — -

It was the best they could do. Landry thought it would work. Eric wasn't so sure.

They had gone over Cindi's story several times. It was time to go. Landry looked at his wife and daughter. "I would practice it a few times," he said.

"Just get out of here," Cindi said. She held on to her daughter and, when Landry reached out, put Kristal behind her. "You wrecked our lives. You're the reason Luke is dead. Just do us both a favor and *leave.*"

Landry felt as if the earth had opened up and swallowed him. Burying him in sand, filling his throat, choking him. He realized it wasn't sand filling his throat, but tears.

"Cindi—"

She covered her ears with her hands. "*Please!* Just go!"

It registered with him at last. The desperation in her voice. As if she had been torn apart—and he was the cause. He had been the cause of everything, including Luke Brodsky's death.

Landry knew he needed to go, that he needed to leave them to their lives. It was the only good thing left that he could do.

A breeze blew through, lifting the ponderosa pine needles. A branch creaked against the house. The windows threw squares of light onto the porch.

"Okay," he said at last. "I'll go."

He walked out with Eric to the car, neither of them speaking. Aware of his wife's gaze on the back of his neck, his daughter's.

He turned and looked at his wife. "I want to be there," he said. "For you. For Kristal. She *is* my daughter."

Cindi gave him a short nod.

"Not now, maybe, but . . ."

"I understand," Cindi said, her voice neutral. His daughter staring at him, part in shock, but part, he thought, with love.

"I wish . . ." He stopped.

There was that small chance. An opening, but not now.

The sky had lightened. Landry looked out to the lake through the trees and saw the first streaks of pink on the water—the hint of a beautiful day.

He did not look back.

ACKNOWLEDGMENTS

Many thanks to the experts who helped make this book a reality. First and foremost, thanks to John Peters, CEO of Pro-Tect International Operations and Lightning Force Training, whose expertise in weaponry, military tactics, spy-craft, war, intelligence, and all manner of nefarious arts introduced me to places I never knew existed. Places you won't find on any map. This book would not be the book it is without his encyclopedic and practical knowledge, and his willingness to share that knowledge with me. John, you always think on your feet and you have been an absolute joy to work with.

Thanks also to my friend Mohur Sarah Sidhwa, who sat me down one sunny Tucson morning and walked me through the day in the life of a presidential candidate on the campaign trail. I am fascinated by the process, and it left me appreciating politicians for their dedication. They actually *do* work hard. Who knew?

And thanks again to my good friend William Simon, who writes under the name Will Graham. I don't know how many panic attacks I've had over lost electronic manuscripts or the need for that special something to fix a plot problem, but you've always been there for me. Cheers to the big brother I never had. Thanks to my dear friend Pam Stack, who blitzed the radio waves relentlessly to help gain me listeners and fans. I am so grateful to you, Pam, and happy for our kinship.

It takes a village to raise a book, and I am grateful to every one of the Thomas & Mercer team. Thanks to Anh Schluep, my editor, who shepherded me through the always-enjoyable publishing process at Thomas & Mercer, and to Kevin Smith, whose remarkable editing skills made *Hard Return* a much better book. Kevin, you haven't just made a difference in my manuscripts, you've made a difference in my writing, and I will always be grateful for that. Many thanks to the wonderful Thomas & Mercer Author Team: Jacque Ben-Zekry, Marketing; Tiffany Pokorny, Author Relations; Paul Morrissey, Production; and Justine Fowler, Merchandising.

As ever, I owe a great debt of gratitude to Deborah Schneider and to all the folks at Gelfman Schneider who have supported me every step of the way. I feel so lucky to have found safe harbor at last.

And last, but not least, my love and gratitude to my mother, Mary Falk, and my husband, Glenn McCreedy. Glenn, you're the best partner imaginable, and I am one damn lucky person to have you in my corner and in my heart.